The Duet

R.S. Grey

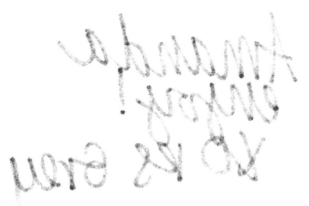

The Duet
Copyright © 2014 R.S. Grey

Published: R.S. Grey 2014
authorrsgrey@gmail.com
Editing: Taylor K's Editing Service
Proofreading: Grammar Inspection Task Force
Cover Design: R.S. Grey
Stock Photos courtesy of Shutterstock ®
ISBN: 978-1502898814
ISBN-13: 1502898810

For you. I hope this book makes you smile.

Chapter One

"Mama is gonna get laid tonight!" I sang out while shimmying my shoulders from side to side. I puckered my lips in front of my bedroom mirror and attempted to apply another coat of bright red lipstick, which was impossible in the dress I'd chosen for the night. *I couldn't actually move in it- per se.* I had to bend my neck down at an awkward angle and contort my arm to get the lipstick tube in contact with my mouth. To be honest, the dress was most likely made for a petite doll— as in, Barbie's little sister. *Damn you, Skipper.* I was neither petite, nor a doll, but the night called for extreme measures.

"Ew. God, stop. You can't call yourself 'mama' if you aren't actually a mother. And as your sister, I'd like to pretend that you don't have a sex life at all," Cameron said, holding her hands over her ears as she chastised me from across the room.

I laughed and dropped the tube of MAC lipstick back into my acrylic make-up tray. When I spun around to face her, she was still holding her hands up in warning.

1

"Cammie, my sweet, innocent little sister," I said, walking toward her on my four inch Jimmy Choos. "When you're twenty-seven, if you've gone a whole year without having sex, I will personally take an ad out in the newspaper for you and it will say: Cammie Heart will put out for nearly anyone. Age not important. Job unnecessary—"

I didn't get the chance to continue my joke because Cammie reached forward and covered my mouth with her hand.

"No need, sissaroo, because I had sex *just last month.*"

She was full on gloating. What a dirty hooker. You don't gloat about having sex to someone during her dry spell. *Had I taught her nothing?*

I peeled her hand away from my mouth so I could respond. "What?! With who?"

She shrugged as if it wasn't that big of a deal. Who knows, maybe it wasn't. "It was just this kid in one of my architecture classes. We were studying together and I wanted to blow off some steam."

I laughed as the wheels started spinning in my mind. "Oh I bet you blew off some stream, all right." That joke may have been accompanied by a crude hand gesture near, or around, my mouth. *Depending on how delicate your sensibilities are.*

"Brooklyn! You perv!" Cammie said, pinching my arm before I could step out of her reach. She was a couple of inches shorter than me, and five years younger, but she was scarily scrappy.

A knock on my condo door distracted me just before I could retaliate.

"Ms. Heart, are you girls ready? I've just pulled the car around," Jerry, my driver, called through the door.

"Yes! Thank you, Jer-Bear. We'll just be another second!" I yelled back, widening my eyes at Cammie so that she'd know to hurry up.

Cammie scrambled toward my closet, no doubt in search of a pair of shoes that she'd "borrow" for the night and then conveniently forget to ever give back to me. I once thought I'd had a Chanel bag stolen from me in France, and then three years later Cammie waltzed into my apartment with it on her arm. We'd settled it with an old-fashioned duel. (i.e., I sat on her until she begged for mercy).

"Can I wear these white Manolo Blahniks you got from that magazine shoot?" she asked as I spun in a circle to inspect my miniscule dress one last time. Seriously, I feared that the seams might pop at any moment, but I wasn't going to take any chances. If I didn't get laid that night, I'd no longer be held accountable for my actions. *I can only go so long living the life of a nun.* Abstinence is *not* always the way. It makes you moody, and I swear my road rage had really kicked up a notch over the last few months.

But it's not as easy as you'd think. It's not like I could just zip-off to the club and have a one-night stand whenever I wanted. The paparazzi would be all over my ass and the story would end up on every newsstand by the following morning. So, to ensure that my PR team didn't rip my head off, I tried to play it cool. I dated off and on and I kept my distance from the standard Hollywood crowd. *Who needs booze and blow? No thanks. All I wanted was a good ol' fashioned, wake the neighbors, scratch marks down his back orgasm.*

3

"Did you just say 'all I want is an orgasm'?" Cammie asked, coming out of the closet looking like a million-bucks in my high-heels. I already knew I'd let her keep them. They looked better on her anyway. The white suede material set off her tan and complemented the royal blue dress she'd also pulled out of my closet earlier. Her brown hair was styled in loose waves and she had this jeweled headband across her forehead— a look that a cool twenty-two year old could pull off flawlessly, whereas I would have just looked like a weird gypsy.

I decided to be honest with Cammie. "Yeah, I'm giving myself a pep talk before we leave."

Cammie laughed and walked over to me, setting her hands on top of my shoulders and staring me straight in the eye.

"Brooklyn Heart, you are one sexy motherfucker."

"Cammie, watch your fucking mouth!"

She rolled her eyes. "Your hair looks flawless. They did a good job with the blonde at the salon this time," she said, fingering a long strand. "Your make-up— très magnifique, and that dress, damnnnnnn."

I started laughing as she eyed me up and down. Only Cammie could go from a French accent to a downtown Compton accent in zero seconds flat.

"Enough, you weirdo, let's go. My orgasm is waiting."

• • •

Cammie had one night left of spring break before her semester started back up. She was a senior, finishing up her strenuous architecture program that allowed her to complete both a bachelor's and master's degree in architecture in just five years. Just saying that sentence made me want to gag a little bit. I'd rather stab my eyes out than take an architecture course. She definitely got the math and engineering genes, whereas I'd been graced with the singing and dancing genes.

"So, Smarty McSmarterpants, where should we start our night?" I asked as we climbed into the limousine waiting outside my downtown LA condo.

"Let's go to M Lounge and then we can head somewhere else if the prospects aren't looking great. I'm sure it won't be crazy packed since it's Sunday, but we can still try."

I nodded. "Sounds good."

The M Lounge was the hippest and most discreet club in LA. If there was any hope of me locking down a one-night stand, M Lounge was the place to go.

"I can't drink much tonight because I have that meeting with my record label in the morning," I warned as we passed through the back entrance to the club and headed up a set of stairs that were used exclusively for the VIP level. *Fun fact: one time I was going up those stairs when P. Diddy was coming down, and he totally touched my ass. Allegedly.*

"Just to clarify: if you're begging me for tequila shots at midnight, threatening to kill my first born if I don't give them to you, I should still tell you no?" Cammie asked, just to ensure the boundaries were set. Better safe than sorry.

"That was *one time* and it was in Cabo," I protested. "What else are you supposed to do in Cabo other than challenge a mariachi band to a tequila shot contest until the lead singer passes out beside a donkey?"

Cammie held up her hands and started listing off items. "I dunno— enjoy the beach, check out the museums and the culture—"

"That was a rhetorical question," I interrupted as we made it to the top of the stairs.

As if by magic, the black curtain in front of us swept to the side, opening up an entire room of drunken debauchery before us. In one corner, a celebrity who shall remain nameless (we'll call her Nennifer Janiston) was sucking face with a sexy man, and across the room two of the funniest women in comedy were doing body shots off of a waiter from the club.

"Welcome to the behind the scenes of Hollywood," I whispered to Cammie. She giggled as we moved toward the circular bar in the center of the room. I waved to everyone that we passed, none of them were really my friends, but snubbing a celebrity in the clubs was a sure-fire way to end a career. Even if I didn't love everyone, it was my job to make it look like I did. The last thing I needed was for a horde of Justin Bieber fans to take over my Twitter feed with death threats. (I'd learned that the hard way.)

"Hey ladies, what can I get for you?" the beefy bartender asked us as Cammie and I approached. There were a few other VIPs in line ahead of us, but he didn't seem to care.

I shrugged, staring down at Cammie for a second before we both simultaneously asked for Lemon Drops. Our laughter was cut short though.

"Hah. *Cute*," a nameless socialite spat, eyeing us as if we were last year's Berkin bag. "Are you guys like twins or something?"

Her question seemed innocent, but her posture and tone hinted at how dirty she was actually playing.

I'd been drilled by my PR team to stay calm in situations like this. I didn't need to read headlines in the morning of "Popstar Brooklyn Heart Knocks Out LA Socialite." (And yes, *of course* I'd knock her out. She weighed like 85 pounds.)

But unfortunately, Cammie didn't have to worry about her public image as much as I did. Before I could stop her, she took a step toward the girl.

"I'm sorry, is there a problem?" she asked. I couldn't help but laugh at Cammie's honey-dipped tone.

The girl batted her overly mascaraed eyelashes at us. "Uh, *yeah*. We've been waiting here for ten minutes and you guys just cut the line."

"Ladies, ladies. Cool it. I was the one who let them cut the line. Here you go, Brooklyn," the bartender said, cutting the tension and holding out two martini glasses garnished with lemon peel and dipped in sugar. *Yum*.

We took the drinks, and I dragged Cammie toward a table in the corner before a brawl broke out. Cammie had much less patience with entitled yuppies than I did.

The lighting was dim inside the club, especially near the perimeter where separate tables were tucked away into little alcoves. Instead of chairs, there were miniature couches covered in rich brown velvet—a bit tacky for my taste— but they were so soft so who cares.

"You're making me regret not bringing along Hank tonight. I didn't think we'd need security if we were in the VIP section," I said as we took our seats across from each other.

Cammie shrugged innocently before holding her glass out toward me. "Sometimes I just can't stand the people in these clubs. I feel like we'd have more fun downstairs with people who don't have poles up their asses."

I laughed. "Well, to be fair, most of these people want those poles in their asses."

That little comment pulled Cammie out of her funk. She threw her head back and laughed before sitting up and locking eyes with me.

"To sisters," Cammie said, clinking her glass with mine.

"To sisters!" I yelled back.

• • •

Although that certainly wasn't the last cheers of the night, it was definitely the last one I remembered. Our little hunky bartender had put so much vodka in that first drink that I was buzzed within minutes.

I didn't remember the Brazilian underwear model introducing himself at our table and I somehow missed his name altogether. It was either Hector or Jorge. I tried to get Cammie to introduce herself so she could get his name, but she wasn't playing along because she thought it was funnier if I didn't know. *The little cow.*

As the night wore on, I was too embarrassed to bring it up again, but whatever, I just needed some sex; I didn't need to know the guy's name. I was on birth control and I had condoms. Not to mention, I recognized his face from billboards around town, so if he murdered me, Cammie could definitely avenge my death.

Around midnight, Cammie told me she was going to have my driver drop her back at the dorms. I didn't want her to leave because I was having so much fun, but I really needed some alone time with Mr. HectorJorge considering he was attached to my neck. *No really, he was like one of those suckerfish.* I knew I'd be undoubtedly sporting a sloppy hickey the next day.

Cammie left after I'd given her a dozen hugs, and the second she was safe at home (I had her send me a selfie from her dorm), I turned to the model and laid out the plan.

He was pretty to look at up-close, like a Snickers bar. I looked at him and just knew I'd have one naughty night with him, enjoying all of his chocolaty-goodness, except *without* the guilt and the early-morning workout the next day.

"I need you to come home with me," I declared, staring into his eyes, but not really seeing anything. *How many drinks had I consumed? I thought I told Cammie to cut me off early?*

"Okay. Let's go," he said, standing up and taking me with him. Blood rushed to my head as I stood and I had to squeeze my eyes closed for a moment or I knew I was going to throw up all over his pointy loafers.

"You have to go out by yourself first," I told him as we walked down the stairs out of the club. Usually, paparazzi weren't allowed in the back alley, but some of their cameras had crazy zoom abilities and I wanted to play it safe. "I'll come out a few minutes later. Just wait for me in the limousine."

"Whatever you want," he said, running a hand through his gelled hair and pushing open the back door. A blast of fresh air hit me, sobering me up enough that, for a second, the idea of having a meaningless one-night-stand didn't sound so appealing anymore.

I shoved that dumb thought aside. Thoughts like that were how I'd landed in this mess in the first place. One

9

year without sex had been long enough. I was not about to test out the *"If you don't use it, you lose it"* theory. Nope. My vagina was not going to disappear on my watch.

After an appropriate amount of time had passed, I held my jacket up to shield any stray camera flashes and darted for the limousine. Mr. Brazilian model was waiting for me inside, checking out the champagne and taking it upon himself to open every compartment.

"Want something to drink?" he asked as he popped the cork. I watched it ricochet throughout the interior, smacking the window and then bouncing back so quickly that he had to duck out of the way. Sheesh. The last thing I needed was for Mr. Model to lose his eye in the back of my limousine.

He held the bottle out for me, but I shook my head. If I had any more alcohol, I'd be in a coma for three days.

The ride back to my condo was not exactly what you would call *romantic*. Brazilian model was taking shots of champagne (what kind of man does that?) and I was checking my email to see if there were any updates about my meeting scheduled for the following morning.

A ping from my phone alerted me to two new messages. One was from my agent and the other was from my assistant, Summer.

Summer Neilson (BrooklynHeartAssist@gmail.com) 7:00 P.M.

Whattup Boss? Just an update about the meeting tomorrow with Global Records. It's still at 8:00 A.M. at their downtown offices, but now Jason Monroe will be there as well. They haven't briefed me about what they'll be discussing with you guys, but I thought I'd give you a heads up in case you wanted to forget to wear a bra or something. I've attached a photo of him, just as a reminder of how seriously hot he is. (You're welcome.)

Your badass assistant,
Summer

I laughed and rolled my eyes. Some people might argue that my relationship with my thirty-year-old assistant crossed boundaries. Summer had bright purple hair and usually sported black on black for all occasions. I don't think I could have reined her in even if I tried. Not to mention, she got shit done *and* made me laugh while she did it, so I didn't see any problems.

"Oh, no way. You have a meeting with Jason Monroe tomorrow? That guy can seriously rock," the Brazilian model said over my shoulder. I hadn't even realized he'd slid over to my bench while I'd been reading my email. *Creepy.*

I turned my phone away quickly, hoping he hadn't had enough time to read the rest of the email, where Summer had attached a shirtless photo of Jason. If so, I was going to have to find the guys from Men in Black so that I could use that pen thing to erase his memory.

"Oh, um, yeah, we're under the same music label," I answered nonchalantly, trying to read his features for any tell of whether he read the bra-less comment.

"That guy has *soul.* Have you seen his acoustic performances?" he asked, seemingly more interested in the idea of Jason Monroe than the idea of having sex with me. Something was wrong with this picture. "He headlined ACL and Coachella last year."

I rolled my eyes and dropped my phone back into my purse. It's not like I had anything against Jason Monroe; we just had *very* different styles. The songs I wrote usually skewed toward a younger, mainstream crowd, whereas Jason Monroe was more of a gritty, folk singer. He'd come out of the woodwork after Mumford and Sons blew up, but his songs had a little more rock and a little less banjo, and the crowd loved him for it.

Before he'd come along, I was the number one performer at Global Records, the largest music label in the world. In the last two years, our label had constantly reminded me that he and I were neck and neck for the top-selling status. We'd never met before, as our schedules kept us busy, but I loved his music and was a fan myself, so I was happy for his success. I doubted that respect went both ways. Most people brushed my songs off as pop ballads, but I wrote every word and there was a reason that teenage girls everywhere could relate to them.

They were *good* songs.

The rest of the ride to my condo, and even as we rode the elevator up to my floor, I wondered what the record label had up their sleeves concerning me and the seriously sexy Jason Monroe. (Yes, of course, I went back to look at the photo Summer had sent me in the email. Here's a hint: he was on stage at a music festival with his guitar. His eyes were closed, sweat was dripping down his neck, his brown hair was disheveled, and he was singing a song with every bit of soul he had in him. I couldn't look away until the Brazilian model literally pried the phone out of my hand.)

Chapter Two

Beep. Beep. Beep.

"Turn it off," I groaned, rolling over to shove my pillow over my head so that the incessant beeping would disappear.

Beep. Beep. Beep.

"Seriously. I will *end* you if you don't turn that off," I said again, this time coming out of my sleepy haze enough to realize that I'd just threatened to kill someone.

"Um, that's not my alarm and it's been going off for the past hour."

That voice. That was a male's voice in my bed.

I shot up out of my covers and turned to see Mr. Brazilian Model laying in a suggestive pose on top of my duvet. As in, his hand was on his hip with his legs spread apart suggestively. *Seriously*? Did he just lounge around in his underwear waiting for someone to snap a picture of him? *So odd.*

"Oh, jeez. You should get out of my condo," I said slowly, trying to comprehend the scene before me. It sounded like I was relearning the English language, but his package was a *little* bit distracting. I mean, I hadn't seen one in the light of day in over a year.

His dark brows tugged together as he pushed up off the bed. "I thought we could have another go this morning?" he said, his pouty lips trying to entice me back in. When I thought back to how fuck-tastically terrible the sex had been the night before, it wasn't hard to shake my head.

"I'd love that, really, but I am now—" I glanced at my clock and my eyes bulged out of my head. "Ten minutes late to a meeting with my label!"

I didn't even bother waiting for his reply. Once I saw the time on my bedside clock, I flew into action. I am *not* a late person. I am responsible and polite. I show up on time to everything from doctor's appointments to Bat Mitzvahs – you name it and I'm there five minutes early smiling and proud of my timeliness. (Side note, I'm not Jewish, but I get invited to a strangely large number of Bat Mitzvahs.)

My massive closet presented me with every clothing option under the sun, but I tossed on a pair of skinny jeans and grabbed the first shirt I saw hanging up. I shoved my makeup bag in my purse, gripped my brown leather flats under my armpit, and then grabbed a banana from the counter.

All the while, Model Man just posed in my bedroom doorway like he was in the middle of a Fruit of the Loom photoshoot. Before, it'd been a tinsy bit cute, now it was just creepy.

"Dude, you have to leave," I said, walking toward the door and hoping he'd follow suit.

"I think you should stay with me and we can make love in this bed for hours and hours," he said with his thick

Brazilian accent. I could imagine that fifty-percent of the female population would consider him a wet dream come to life, but seriously, he needed to get out of my condo so I could lock up.

"Yeahhhh, no. I'm sorry, but I have to go, so you can hangout here or you can—" I glanced around my spacious condo, trying to figure out what to say to this guy to get him to leave. Was he just going to live here full-time? I'd come home from work and he'd be on the sofa with his feet propped up on the coffee table? I was *not* prepared to give up my condo just because this guy had an accent and a cute butt.

Instead of thinking of something to say, I just turned and left. If Model Man wanted my condo for the morning, then so be it. I knew my driver would be waiting for me downstairs. I'd have ten minutes to brush my hair and make myself presentable in the backseat on the way to my meeting. *My meeting with Jason Monroe.* Dammit, I couldn't believe I was already ten minutes late. I glanced down at my watch. *Make that twenty minutes late.*

I flew down the stairs while slipping on my flats, too impatient to wait for the elevator, and then shouted out to the concierge as I passed by in a full-run. "Could you make sure that the person in my condo leaves? I'd like it to be discreet so have him leave through the back entrance. And maybe give him some kind of parting gift or something!"

The concierge eyed me suspiciously, but I didn't have time to explain any further. Whatever. I couldn't worry about my new roommate; I had to start focusing on the meeting.

My driver, Jerry, was standing in the private garage with a frown pulled tight over his mouth. It was hard to see it beneath his bushy, brown mustache, but I knew it was there.

"I tried to call you, Ms. Heart, but you never answered. I was about to go up and knock on your door," he said, pulling the back door open for me.

Poor Jerry, he always did his best to look out for me.

"I'm so sorry. My alarm didn't wake me up. We have to be downtown at Global Records as quickly as possible," I said, patting him on arm and sliding into the back seat.

Jerry ran around the front of the car and in two seconds flat we pulled out into Monday morning traffic. Most of the time Jerry drove at the precise speed limit, offering a smooth and comfortable ride. But that morning he was a speed demon and I almost poked my eye out with my mascara like four times. After I'd spun my hair into a low bun and applied what I hoped was enough make-up to cover up last night's hangover, I realized that I'd forgotten the most important parts: I hadn't brushed my teeth *or* put on deodorant.

Awesome. Great. I tried out the standard blow-into-the-palm-of-your-hand to test my breath and yes, on a scale of one to ten, I could kill a small puppy with that wretchedness.

"Jerry, you don't have a breath mint, do you?" I asked, leaning forward toward the front seat.

"No ma'am. Would you like me to stop and pick some up?"

I glanced toward the car's clock and flinched. "No. We don't have time, but thank you."

I sat back and glanced down at my lap, trying to find inspiration to cure my hygiene woes. I had a make-up bag and my purse. My make-up bag was out unless I wanted to coat my tongue in foundation and hope that would mask the stench. I turned to my purse, and thanked the holy lord, because stuck at the very bottom was a half opened piece of gum. Sure, some of it was coated in an unidentified, pink glitter substance, but I was desperate.

Next to it, I found a small sample-sized vial of perfume. I sprayed it directly on my armpits and smiled. Sure, I smelled like a retirement home, but I didn't care. *I was actually going to pull this off.* I'd walk in and apologize profusely for being late and then they'd smile and offer me coffee and a chocolate croissant. *This day was going to turn out okay, I knew it.*

We pulled up outside of Global Records and I took in the glossy building. Two iron statues, in the form of lions, guarded the front entrance and people, donned in power suits, walked in and out of the sleek front doors. They probably weren't even talking to anyone through their Bluetooth headsets, but it was all about the image.

"Good luck, Ms. Heart," Jerry said as he pulled open my back door. I bolted from the car and thanked him as I darted past, but he called out for me.

"Wait! Would you like my jacket?" he called out.

The paparazzi were lined up along the street already snapping away, and I cringed at how terrible I probably looked after last night. I didn't want to stay out there for another second.

"No, thank you, Jerry!" I answered, pushing through the front doors and heading straight to the elevator. The lobby staff hadn't asked me check-in for years, but the woman behind the front desk gave me a strange look as I passed. *Maybe I hadn't put as much make-up on as I should have.*

It wasn't until the doors to the elevators were closed, and I was well on my way to the thirty-fifth floor, that I thought back to Jerry's question. *Why would he offer me his jacket?* I frowned and then glanced down at my shirt.

Oh dear god. No. No. This was not happening to me.

The t-shirt I'd pulled out of my closet earlier was not just a plain white t-shirt like I'd assumed. Nope. Instead, "FUCK DA POLICE" was printed in big, black letters across my chest.

For ten seconds, I just stood there, trying to grasp how I could have possibly been so stupid. I contemplated the idea that I'd woken up in an alternate universe, or that maybe I was in an episode of the Twilight Zone, but no. This was my life.

And if you're wondering why I even owned a shirt like that, Cammie and I had gone as rappers for Halloween the year before and we'd purchased the shirts as a joke. I respect all law enforcement personnel, so don't get your panties in a wad. *I mean, who doesn't love a man in uniform?*

Dammit. I still had the shirt on.

I dropped my purse on the elevator floor and then reached for the hem of the shirt so that I could turn it inside out. It'd look completely ridiculous, but it was better than walking into the meeting with the offensive phrase on display for everyone.

I'd just pulled the shirt up over my bra when the elevator chimed and the doors slid open. I froze. There, directly in front of me, was the conference room I was supposed to have been in thirty minutes earlier. I'd always thought the room was spectacular. It had floor to ceiling glass so that everyone could easily see inside and out. Unfortunately, on that morning, I hated the see-through glass with every fiber of my being because as the doors slid open, my eyes locked directly with Jason Monroe. Like a slow-motion movie he glanced up to see me standing there in my bra, with my shirt half over my head.

"Fucking hell," I hissed under my breath, tugging my shirt back down to cover myself. It was time for Plan B: Try to force a heart attack to get out of the meeting.

As I stepped out of the elevator, Jason Monroe's eyes slid over the letters on my shirt and then he dropped his gaze to the desk and shook his head as if he couldn't believe my nerve.

Oh yeah, great. Join the club, bucko.

With a deep breath, I pushed open the glass door to the conference room and all five heads swiveled around to face me. These were five people that had the power to drastically change my career, and they were all reading the words on my t-shirt. My brain yelled at me to say something, anything, so I just blurted out whatever I could think of.

"This is not my shirt and I have no clue how I put it on this morning," I said, moving toward the empty chair next to Jason's. "I am, and always have been, a staunch advocate of the Los Angeles Police Department, and first responders everywhere."

Awesome, I sounded like a loony-tune.

"Do you think this is some kind of joke, Brooklyn?" Mr. Daniels asked. Mr. Daniels was the head of the record label and he was arguably the most important person in the music industry. Oh, and he did *not* find my shirt funny at all.

"Absolutely not. This is not my type of humor. It's not funny at all. I was running late this morning, as you all know," I rambled on, making eye contact with everyone but Jason. The guy had seen my bra, so I wasn't quite ready to meet his gaze. I could feel him staring at me though, judging me silently. "I'm very sorry about being late and this shirt is just— I can't — Is there water in here?"

Suddenly I felt like my throat was closing up and I feared that I was going to die in the middle of that conference room, with a dumb graphic tee on. There'd be a group of old dudes, and one seriously hot Jason Monroe, just standing over me as I slowly stopped breathing.

I was so enamored by the disturbing fantasy that I didn't realize Jason was pouring me a cup of water until he'd slid it over in front of me. I swallowed my breath and then reached for the glass, glancing toward him quickly to see if his appearance had loosened up yet. No. *God, he was really good looking.* His cheekbones could have cut glass and his jaw was defined and strong.

I could have written a song about his appearance, it was *that* fascinating. The song would be titled *Black*. Black hair, black eyes, black five o'clock shadow. He was wrapped in darkness, but it was so mysterious and appealing that you couldn't help but want to lean in a little closer and see if he'd turn those dark eyes back on you.

"If you're properly hydrated, we'd like to begin the meeting now," Mr. Daniels said with a stern tone. I gulped down another sip of water and took a seat, turning away from Jason. I couldn't turn back time and re-do the entire morning, so I just wanted to get the meeting over with as quickly as possible.

"You might be wondering why we called both of you in this morning," he began. "You two are our top performers here at Global Records. You have different fan bases, both equally strong, but you bring different talents to the table."

I started to breathe easier as Mr. Daniels talked about my talents. At least it didn't sound like he was going to be dropping me from the label anytime soon.

"The Grammys are coming up in a little over a month and originally you were both slotted for individual performances."

I nodded. I already knew all of this. The Academy of Recording Arts had sent out nominations a few weeks earlier, and directly after that my agent notified me that they'd asked me to perform a solo song during the award show. I'd already been practicing my song for the night with my voice coach and choreographer.

"But that's changed now," Mr. Daniels continued.

If there were a DJ set up in the room, he would have scratched the vinyl to make that declaration even more dramatic.

"We've decided to try something new, to bridge the gap between both of your individual fan bases."

Jason leaned forward and I slid my gaze to him, taking in his features as inconspicuously as possible. The guy was sexy with a capital S-E-X-Y. Yes, that's right, all of his letters deserved to be capitalized.

"I'm sorry. Are you saying that we're going to perform *together*?" he asked, with a gruff voice. It was the first time he'd spoken since I'd arrived and I let his voice wash over me for a moment before I realized what he'd actually said. *Wow.* He was really not keen on the idea. I fidgeted in my seat and kept my mouth shut as Mr. Daniels addressed Jason.

"That's correct. We've discussed it already and we'd like the two of you to write and perform a duet at the award show."

"No," Jason answered. One word spoken with enough confidence to send a shiver down my spine. *Alright then, meeting adjourned.*

"Excuse me?" Mr. Daniels asked, sitting up an inch taller so that even more of his charcoal-grey designer suit was on display. His sharp jaw clicked back and forth as he stared at Jason with enough heat to start a fire.

Oy. If I could have, I would have warned Jason to back down. I'd been with Global Records for five years and I couldn't remember *ever* talking back to Mr. Daniels. I don't think anyone in the music industry ever had.

"I'm a solo artist. I've never performed on stage with another singer before. If I'm going to start now, it's not going to be with *Brooklyn Heart.*"

Whoa.

"Excuse me?" I asked, leaning forward to meet his eye. "What's that supposed to mean?" I was furious. In the matter of five minutes, this man had created not one, but two enemies. Maybe I wasn't as intimidating as Mr. Daniels, but I had pepper spray in my purse and killer aim from this distance.

Jason gave me a once over, his lip curling into a condescending sneer.

"No offense, princess. But you and I are like apples and oranges. We'd never be able to collaborate on a song together."

I scoffed. "You don't even know me."

He grunted and sat back in his chair, clasping his hands together over his stomach. "I've witnessed a pretty telling first impression."

I let myself take one deep, calming breath before I turned toward Mr. Daniels. With a sugarcoated smile and a twinkle in my eye, I gave him my response.

"I'd be *happy* to collaborate with Jason. Just let me know when and where I need to be to get the job done." I paused and looked right at Jason as I nailed home the last sentence. "Some of us are *professionals*."

Chapter Three

Oh my god, if I hadn't been wearing that ridiculous shirt and chewing on glitter gum, that exit would have been so badass. Like, James Bond explosion badass. I hadn't turned around as I exited the glass conference room, even though I was only 50% sure the meeting was over. They could have had other stuff to talk to us about, but I just went with it. They could email me about the details later. Sometimes, you gotta work the moment for what it is.

"Wow. I think you're making the whole thing sound much cooler than it actually was," Cammie said over the phone. I'd called her from the car the instant I'd left Global Records.

"No, seriously. I could hear slow motion applause as I was waiting for the elevator," I told her as Jerry headed toward a downtown coffee shop. Last week I'd made plans to have coffee with an old friend from college, so even though I wanted to crawl back into bed and nurse my hangover, I didn't want to cancel.

"So they applauded you as you stood waiting for the elevator? Why? That's not even that cool."

"Whatever. Let's go back to the shirt issue and the fact that you can't buy me gag gifts and then hang them up in my closet and expect me not to wear them to important meetings on accident," I said, not truly that angry with her. If the situation had been reversed I would have been rolling in laughter over the entire thing.

"It was part of a costume! You should have thrown it away after you got home. Also, I figured that the text would have been large enough for your brain to inform you not to wear it to an important meeting with your bosses. Just saying."

"Oh, Cameron, you are just so funny at 10:00 A.M. in the morning, but I have to go. I need to confirm that Grayson is meeting me for coffee in like fifteen minutes."

There was a pregnant pause across the phone line before Cammie responded. "Grayson Cole?"

I laughed, "Is there any other Grayson that I'm friends with?"

She grunted, "I don't know, there could be."

I stared out the window as the streets flashed by. Luckily, Jerry no longer had to drive like a maniac since I was right on time for coffee. "Do you want me to come pick you up? Do you have a free period?"

"No!"

I pulled my phone away from my face to glance at the screen, wondering why her reaction was so strong.

"Why not? Do you have class?" I asked.

"Yes, I have my Advanced Design class in an hour."

"Okay, well, I still think it'd be a good idea for you to meet up with Grayson soon and go over career opportunities. It'd be silly not to use him. I mean he owns his own architecture firm."

I heard random street sounds on the other end of the phone line - cars rushing past and then the sound of a metal door opening and closing. Finally, Cammie replied, "I know. I just don't think Grayson likes me very much and maybe I want to make it in this world on my own without relying on my big sister's friend to get me a job."

She had a point, even though I didn't necessarily agree.

"Okay, well, I'll bring it up to him during coffee and I'll see what he says."

"Oh, whatever. I have to go; I'm going to the studio before my class. I'm behind on this final project."

"Love you," I said.

"Love you, too."

I looked down at my phone, thinking of Cammie in her college classes. Sometimes when she talked about her finals and her course work, I felt a pang of envy. I never went to college. It was never really an option for me. After our parents died when we were young, they'd left Cammie and me a small fortune. Most of it was tucked away in a trust, but after high school, I'd used some of it for voice lessons as well as a slew of dance classes. I'd worked my ass off, knowing I only had a few years to really make a name for myself before a newer, hotter singer would be vying for my same spot.

The hard work had paid off when an executive at Global Records had seen a video of me singing one of my original songs. My fate was sealed and college was pushed aside for good. I jumped straight into recording my first EP. I wrote every song and helped create most of the music to accompany the lyrics. I was so proud of that first album, mostly because I'd done it on my own. With the money I made from that record, plus all of my subsequent ones, I'd never needed to touch the money in my parent's trust again. It was all there, waiting for Cammie to use it to follow her dream, just as I'd used it to follow mine.

When the car pulled up outside of the coffee shop, Grayson Cole was standing near the door, eyes focused on his phone in hand. I smiled, realizing some things never changed. He was a workaholic, always had been. His dark navy suit was tailored to perfection and his dark hair was styled well. He wasn't the type to go out with a single hair out of place. The guy was a control freak to the max. Which probably had something to do with why he'd started his own architecture firm as soon as he'd become certified at twenty-six, turning it into a global firm by the time he celebrated his twenty-ninth birthday.

I thanked Jerry for the ride and gave him instructions to be back in about an hour. I doubted Grayson had any more time than that to spare for coffee on a workday.

"Excuse me, is that the oh-so-important Grayson Cole, of Cole Designs?" I joked as I stepped out of the car, pretending to be amazed at my friend.

He smirked and slid his phone back into his pocket. The light caught his brown hair, highlighting his sharp features that were too good-looking not to notice. "Good to know you haven't let the fame take away your humor," he said.

I laughed as he held the door open for me. "Cammie makes sure of that," I said.

He narrowed his eyes ever so gently as he turned his attention to the chalkboard menu hanging on the wall over our heads. That reaction, on top of Cammie's emphatic "no" to my invitation earlier, piqued my curiosity about the two of them.

"Hey, you've never had a problem with my sister, right?" I asked, trying to sound casual. The patrons in front of us stepped up to the counter and I heard the woman order what sounded like a Cinnamon Roll Mocha. *Um, yes please. I'll take a dozen of those.*

"No. Of course not. Why do you ask?" he asked, continuing to peruse the chalkboard. He was using his business tone. He never used his business tone with me.

"Oh, it's just that she graduates from college soon and it seems like it would make perfect sense for her to get her feet wet working for you, but neither one of you seems very keen on the idea."

His dark brows tugged together and I studied the way his blue eyes purposely focused on the wall behind my head.

"I have no problem with it. I'm just not sure if she could meet the standards that I hold my employees accountable to."

Oh god, why did he sound like a more polished version of Jason Monroe? *What was it with guys underestimating my sister and me?*

"She's won like a billion architecture awards in her program. I don't know what any of them mean, but she assures me that she's one of the top students in her program," I declared. My sister was smart and I knew she could hold her own at any firm in the city.

Grayson rubbed his clean jaw and I noticed the scent of a clean after-shave for the first time since joining him. I knew most of the women in the shop were purposely glancing in his direction while trying to be inconspicuous about it. *The Grayson Cole curse.*

28

"That might be true that she's one of the top students. However, I usually hire *the* top student."

I groaned and rolled my eyes. "Give me a break, Grayson. She's brilliant and if you took two seconds to look at her designs you'd know that."

"I've seen all of her designs," he answered in a clipped tone before gently pushing me toward the front of the line so we could order.

A hippie barista with dreadlocks asked for our order before I was able to expand on that very interesting point. *Did he always take an interest in architecture student work?* By the time we'd moved down to the end of the bar and I'd taken pictures with two very sweet fans, I was too distracted to ask.

We found a booth in the far corner so that we'd have some semblance of privacy. At first, I used to care that paparazzi constantly thought that Grayson and I were dating. In the beginning they'd photograph us together anytime we stepped out in public, but now they'd come to understand that we were just friends, that we'd *always* just been friends. I didn't see Grayson like that, even though every other warm-blooded female did.

"So how is work going?" Grayson asked, taking a sip of his coffee. I watched him unbutton his suit jacket to get situated, revealing a crisp, white button-down shirt.

"It's going well. I have that tour coming up later this year, but just this morning my record label dropped a little bomb on me."

His brow quirked up in interest, but he didn't feel the need to ask me for details. He knew I'd offer him *more* than enough information on the subject.

"Have you heard of Jason Monroe?" I asked, secretly praying that he hadn't.

With a little smirk, he replied, "Of course. Everyone has."

I rolled my eyes. *Not everyone.* Everyone has heard of the Beatles and Elvis. Jason Monroe was not Elvis. "Well, *yours truly* will be forced to write a duet with him to perform at The Grammys next month."

His smirk fell slightly. "Very interesting. What did Monroe think of this?"

"Monroe?" I laughed, choosing to push his buttons. "What, are you on a nickname basis with him?"

Grayson's blue eyes narrowed on me and I was reminded for the one-thousandth time that he was not someone who liked to be teased. Even when we were younger, he was the serious, brooding type. Oh, hmm, maybe he and Monroe would be best friends after all. They could sit in a circle and moan about the woes of manhood. Then they could give each other massages and... wait, that didn't sound so bad. *Maybe I'd like to watch that actually.*

"Sounds like it'll be a good challenge for you," Grayson suggested, pulling me out of my daydream of him rubbing baby oil on Jason Monroe. *Yeah, I know I said I didn't see Grayson like that, but he probably knew his way around a bottle of massage oil as well as the next guy.*

"He was a little hesitant about the set-up," I replied, not wanting to admit the truth. He'd essentially scoffed at the idea of working with me. *Let's get real.*

"We'll see, I guess."

He took another long sip of his coffee before setting it back on the table and fidgeting with the lid. His gaze focused on his hands as if he were performing heart surgery.

"So has your sister had any interviews with firms for post-grad?" he asked, not meeting my eyes.

I smirked at the fact that Grayson seemed to care about my sister even if he tried hard not to. The two of them were going to get along one day if it was the last thing I did. No, wait, if there was ever going to be "the last thing I did" I would want it to be something a little juicer, like sex with Jason Monroe. *Whoa. What?* I snapped my gaze up to Grayson to see if he'd somehow heard my internal ramblings.

"So has she?" he asked again, reminding me of his question.

"Not that I know of," I answered him just as his phone started vibrating under the table.

He cursed under his breath when he saw who was calling. With an apologetic nod, he answered the call and replied in clipped, sharp sentences.

"We've gone over the Jenson Project budget ten times and if they want marble in the master bath, they're delusional at this point. No. Tell Jon to give me a call. No. If we go over, it'll be coming out of your pocket. Jenson approved the cheaper stone two weeks ago."

I took the opportunity to study him in parts: his sharp cheekbones, his straight nose that led down to his strong jaw. His dark hair reminded me of Jason's, but that's where the similarities between them ended. Grayson Cole was a businessman with enough confidence to make the President shake in his boots, while Jason was a rough-around-the-edges musician with a killer smile and forgotten facial hair.

If I ever had a type, it was Jason Monroe.

Clearly, Jason had obviously taken root in my head. I just needed to replace him with something else. Maybe that Brazilian model was still camped out in my condo, eating my food and watching my TV. *Only problem: he hadn't given me an orgasm.* No. That wouldn't do. I definitely needed a good ol' orgasm so that I could push Jason out of my head.

Grayson ended his call and shoved his phone into his suit pocket. I could tell by the remorseful glance he was aiming at me that he was going to have to cut our hangout short.

"I'm sorry to do this, but I have to go check on a project."

I waved my hand and smiled. "No worries. I've gotta run anyway."

"It was good seeing you, Brook," he said, wrapping me in a quick side hug before taking a step back. As if wrestling with himself, he stood staring toward the door for a moment before turning back to me. "And have Cameron call me. I might have something for her."

Cameron.

Grayson was all business. No one called my sister by her full name, and the way he said it made it sound as if it pained him to offer. *Was it seriously so much to ask him to help her out?* If he had a brother that wanted to be a pop star, I wouldn't have hesitated to help. Although the image of a man like Grayson trying to slip into one of my spandex costumes was too hilarious to imagine.

"I'll tell her," I said as he slipped on a pair of aviators and stepped out into the bright LA sun.

I watched him head to his fancy-pants sports car and then I went back to our booth so I could text Jerry to come pick me up early. When I pulled my phone out of my purse I saw I had a voice mail waiting for me from a blocked number. *Interesting.*

I pressed play and held the phone up to my ear just as Jason's deep voice crooned over the airwaves. He wasn't even singing and still the guy sounded like he was trying to serenade me.

That is, until I actually listened to what he was saying.

That *motherfucker*.

Chapter Four

"Brooklyn, this is Jason Monroe. We obviously have some things to discuss, so I'll leave you the number for my assistant and you can coordinate it all with her. After you stormed out of the meeting, I spoke with Mr. Daniels about a potential Plan B. There is no plan B. We'll have to work together, so give Sandy a call at 555-9010."

The line cut off after that. No goodbye, no sorry about our rough start. Also, he'd blocked his number so that I couldn't even call him back to tell him how rude he'd been. I was left with Sandy, his assistant.

After I'd shot a quick text to Jerry, I dialed Sandy's number and told myself that whatever anger I felt toward Jason should not be taken out on her. If she had to work with him all day every day, she probably hated him as much as I did. Maybe I'd offer her a new job.

"Hello, this is Sandy speaking."

"Oh, hi, Sandy. This is Brooklyn Heart."

"Shut the fuck up," she screeched so loudly that I had to hold the phone away from my ear for fear that she was going to rupture my ear drums.

An awkward, "umm," and a laugh were the only things I could muster in reply.

"Oh god, I'm sorry about that. You'd think I'd get used to talking to celebrities, but you're Brooklyn Heart. Wow. This is insane."

I smiled at her excitement. At least Jason Monroe's *assistant* liked me.

"Alright," she said, taking an audible breath. "I'm fine now." Two more deep breaths and then she finally continued. "I assume you're calling to coordinate things with Jason concerning the duet."

I was about to reply when I saw Jerry and the town car pull up out front of the coffee shop.

"Yes, actually," I said to Sandy as I exited the coffee shop with my head down, pulling my bun out so that I could use my curtain of blonde hair to shield me from the lurking cameras. There was a rustling of paper through the phone line and then Sandy spoke up again.

"Okay, well you'll leave here in a week's time. You'll be at the ranch for a few weeks, or however long it takes you two to finalize the song—"

I cut her off. "I'm sorry, what are you talking about? What ranch?"

Sandy cleared her throat. "Oh," she paused, clearly confused about why we weren't on the same page. "I thought Jason discussed this with you. Didn't you guys speak after the meeting?" When I stayed silent, she continued. "Jason doesn't write in LA. Whenever he's creating new projects, he goes home to his ranch in Montana."

"Ohhkaayy," I dragged out, trying to clear things up in my head. "Sandy, could you give me Jason's number please? I think it's better if I speak with him about all of this first."

She hesitated for a few seconds before answering, "Well, usually he doesn't like me giving out his number to anyone."

Of course. I wondered if Jason even put his own pants on in the morning.

"Well, Sandy, this can be the one exception," I said with a sweet tone. I knew I was putting her in a bad position, but her boss kind of sucked-ass anyway.

It took a bit more sweet-talking, and tickets to my next concert, but eventually she gave me the number. I would have called Jason right away, but I had a meeting with a perfume company to customize my signature scent and then directly after that I had a dress fitting with Givenchy. Finally around 6:00 P.M., I headed back to my condo so that I could make the call to Jason in the privacy of my four walls.

When I walked into my building, the sweet concierge from that morning waved me over with a small gesture. She was a young girl, no more than twenty-five, with a simple, tight bun pulled back at the base of her neck. When she spoke, her eyes darted around the room as if she wanted to ensure that we weren't being overheard.

"Ms. Heart, the situation from earlier was taken care of," she said with a whisper. "The *gentleman* left shortly after you and we gifted him a fruit basket on his way out."

Oh good, apparently when you have sex with Brooklyn Heart, you leave with a fruit basket. What a lovely experience.

"Thank you so much," I said, trying hard not to cringe at how embarrassing the entire situation was before heading toward the elevator. This is why I don't have sex. It's not worth the trouble. *I've never had to buy my vibrator a fruit basket.*

As soon as I arrived inside my condo, I pressed my back to the door and scanned my living room. It was gorgeous, all whites and creams with plush furniture and bright light-blue wallpaper. I knew I wouldn't be in that condo forever, but it'd been home for the past three years and in a world that was constantly bustling around me, it felt good to have my little sanctuary.

"Whattup, sis," Cammie called from the kitchen, slamming the refrigerator door.

Well *kind* of a sanctuary.

"What are you doing here? I thought you had that design class?" I asked, dropping my purse on the front-entry table and kicking my shoes off.

When I got closer, I realized Cammie had a plate piled high with hummus, pita chips, carrots, and celery. It was enough food to feed five people.

"Yeah, that was like four hours ago," she answered.

Oh, right.

Cammie lived in the dorms on campus, but whenever she could get away, she stayed at my condo— which lately had been more often than not. I knew she was feeling the pressure of transitioning from student to full-time employee in the coming months. She probably wanted to be somewhere that felt constant whenever she could. *Also, she really enjoyed stealing my food.*

"Bring that over here," I said, falling back on the couch. "I haven't had food all day."

"Because you were boning the model and slept in?" Cammie said, dipping a carrot into the hummus and popping it into her mouth.

"Yes," I admitted sheepishly.

"Poor Jorge," she said with a wicked smile.

I laughed. "Don't you worry about ol' Jorge. He got enough fruit to last him a year."

"What does that mean? Is fruit slang for anal or something?"

I spit out the pita chip I'd just put in my mouth and it landed with a thud on my pristine carpet.

"Cammie! Jeez."

That only made her laugh even more. I think she lived to give me a heart attack.

"Relax," Cammie said. "I know that you and underwear boy didn't go *that* far. I just wish he was a little better in the sack."

"It's just... have you ever had sex with a Brazilian underwear model and thought, 'Seriously, I thought this would be better'?"

"Can't say that I have."

I laughed at her dry retort. "Okay, well, it was terrible. No tingles, no fireworks, and definitely no happy ending."

"Are you serious?"

"Dead serious." I shrugged. "I'm over it. From now on, I'm just going to think of other things to do with my vagina."

"Yeah, you could probably store your receipts in there," Cammie joked.

I held my hand up to stop her from expanding on that subject. I'd like to keep my morning coffee in my stomach, thank you very much.

"If I make a phone call will you stay silent or should I lock you in the bathroom again?"

She shrugged. "I don't see what the big deal is. You called Channing Tatum, and I made sex noises in the background. Seriously, how was I supposed to resist?"

I shot her a blank stare and she held up her hands in defense.

"Look, I'll go grab my laptop and do some work while you make your oh-so-important phone call." *Yes, she put air quotes around oh-so-important.*

"Good," I said, taking a deep breath and reaching for my phone on the coffee table. The sooner I called Jason, the sooner we could move on and get started on this dumb project.

My fingers shook in the most annoying way as I scrolled through my contact list trying to find the M's, but I did my best to ignore it. Coffee always made me jittery anyway.

Jason Monroe.

There he was.

I had a sudden urge to program the devil to appear whenever he called me, but then I remembered that he'd never call me so it'd be a waste of time.

"Are you going to make a call or just stare at your screen like a weirdo?" Cammie said, plopping down next to me with her MacBook.

"Oh, I was just trying to make sure I knew what I wanted to discuss before I pressed send," I replied, defending my awkwardness.

She replied with a "mmhhmm" that only sassy grandmas could truly get away with. I hit send and then held the phone to my ear. One… two… three rings passed before the call clicked on.

"Jason."

That's how he answered. *What was I supposed to do with that? Just say my name back too?*

"Uh, Jason, this is Brooklyn."

"Brooklyn who?"

Oh, c'mon. *How many people did he know named after a borough in New York?*

"Heart," I replied with a sharp tone.

"How did you get this number?"

Cammie scoffed next to me, and that's when I realized that the little snitch had her ear pressed to the phone on the other side of me. *Oh well, it'd save me the trouble of telling her how rude he'd been as soon as I hung up.*

"Does it matter? We need to talk about how we're going to figure out this duet."

He sighed. "It's been decided. We're going out to my ranch in Montana to write and record the song. If you can't go, I'll write the song myself and you can just learn it before the award show. I'm sure you're perfectly capable of doing that."

What in-all-that-is-holy was shoved up this guy's butt?

"Wow. You are probably the assholiest person I've ever met."

He chuckled at that. The bastard actually laughed. "Assholiest isn't a word, and if you're going to suggest words like that for our song, I'd rather not have you show up in Montana."

Cammie pinched my leg and I knew she was just as angry as I was over the way he was talking to me.

"Listen up, Mr. God's Gift to Music, we're going to do this duet together, and it's going to be an amazing song.

We'll perform it on stage and then we're never going to talk to each other again. Sound good?"

"I can't wait," he said, dragging out the word wait in a way that shouldn't have made my stomach dip, but it did anyway, because apparently my libido was still attracted to jerks even if my brain wasn't.

I hung up before he could say anything else and then Cammie and I stared at each other in silence for what felt like two hours.

Finally, her blank expression twisted into a little smile.

"Well, I guess you're going to Montana."

Chapter Five

Leaving to go to Montana for a few weeks actually didn't sound so bad. My life in LA was not a cakewalk (as much as it seemed to be from the way the media spun it). *Oh, poor celebrity has to have designer dress fittings and nail appointments*. The truth is my days were regimented and scheduled down to a "T".

Five days a week I woke up at 6:00 A.M. and had a two-hour workout session with my trainer. Then I had thirty minutes to shower and get across town for my voice lessons. Those seeped into my piano and guitar lessons. Then I usually had an afternoon appointment with my choreographer so that I could practice for any upcoming performances and start memorizing routines for future tours.

On top of all of that, if I was working on an album, I'd head into the studio and spend hours writing and rewriting lyrics until they were exactly the way I wanted them.

It was a lot to handle on a good day.

I wouldn't trade any of it for the world, but the prospect of getting away from it all for a few weeks sounded really nice. *Even if I would have to spend that time away with someone who hated my guts. For no reason.* Seriously, we'd spent all of five minutes together and the guy thought I was Medusa come to life.

After my phone call with Jason, Cammie and I spent an hour dissecting his actions, and coming up with all sorts of theories about why he acted the way he did:

1. His parents were part of a traveling circus so he had to grow up around crazy carnies.

2. He was born without a frontal lobe so he couldn't process human emotions properly.

And our personal favorite:

3. He was a Russian robot spy, sent to the US under strict orders to infiltrate our pop culture and slowly drive singers, like myself, insane.

We hadn't worked out all the details of his assignment yet, but we were pretty convinced that we were on the right track.

• • •

Later that week, I was sitting across from my assistant, Summer, inside of a small LA deli. A turkey sandwich with all the fixings sat in front of me while Summer filled me in on all the details I'd need to know before departing for Montana in a few days.

"Are you sure you want to do this? You know Montana is in the middle of nowhere, right?"

I rolled my eyes. "That's exactly why I want to go." The quiet, calm atmosphere was calling to me.

Summer sneered. "Sounds like a snooze fest. At least you can hangout with Jason. Maybe he'll teach you how to ride bareback."

"Yeah, right before he kills me and hides my body where no one can find me."

"Ew. Not cute," she said, before taking a bite of her Greek salad. Her purple hair was a shade darker than it'd been the last time I'd seen her and she'd styled her eyeliner into a dramatic cat-eye effect.

"So, I've been coordinating with Sandy, Jason's assistant," she began. "She's super nice. I feel bad that she has to work for that shmuck."

"Agreed," I said.

"Anyway, she gave me the details on the ranch in Montana. Apparently 'ranch' is a relative term. She said it's a really gorgeous house in the woods. You'll have your own room and bathroom, secluded away from Jason's."

"Wow, I'm surprised he's letting me stay in the house at all. I figured I'd be exiled to the barn."

Summer coughed and stared down at her salad. "Well, actually at first you were staying in a cheap hotel in town. But Sandy and I convinced Jason that that setup would be a bit ridiculous."

I grunted. "Of course. Okay, go on."

She nodded, running her finger down the itinerary on her iPhone. "You'll fly out of LAX in three days and you'll be in Montana for however long it takes to finalize the song. I postponed most of your commitments until after The Grammys. For the ones that I couldn't move, I've either coordinated with them to have a meeting over Skype or the company will fly someone to Montana to meet with you."

"Sounds good."

"So you just need to start thinking of what you'd like to take with you and I'll help you pack. You don't have much time to wrap things up here before you leave."

I shrugged. "I don't have much to wrap up honestly. I'll have to break the news to Cammie. She knew I was leaving soon, but I'm pretty sure she thought we'd have a bit more time."

Summer arched a brow. "You aren't leaving LA forever. It's like a month."

I pursed my lips. No one understood my relationship with Cammie. For the last fifteen years, Cammie and I were all each other had. Our relationship wasn't normal or healthy, but we were each other's best friends and we'd never been apart for a whole month before.

Summer must have read the distress on my features. "If it makes you feel better, I can coordinate a weekend where she can come visit you."

I sat up straighter, already planning our weekend in my mind. *Does Montana have nightclubs?* "That's perfect. I'm sure she'll need a break from her projects anyway."

She nodded and started typing away on her phone. "Don't forget her graduation is the weekend before the award show. I'll schedule your flight home to ensure that you can be there."

"Perfect."

Summer sat back in her chair and crossed her arms, eyeing me curiously.

"So now we just need to figure out what the hell people wear in Montana."

"Brokeback-chic?" I offered.

• • •

I was opening a bottle of wine in my kitchen later that evening when I realized that I should probably attempt to contact Jason again. I knew our assistants had been in constant communication, but it would be he and I staying together in Montana and it felt strange to know nothing about the man. I could have googled him, but I refused to get any information about someone from the Internet. *If everyone trusted what they read on the Internet, then I was apparently a transvestite alien with four illegitimate children and a drinking problem.*

So instead, I scrolled through my phone, past all of the contacts, to find Jason Monroe lurking where I'd programmed him in the other day.

I thought back to our two previous interactions and honestly, I didn't think our first and second impressions of each other could be more off. I don't know how he perceived me after seeing me in my bra on the elevator, but I definitely thought he erred on the arrogant asshole side of things, so maybe it was time to straighten that out.

Before I could stop myself, I hit dial and held the phone up to ear while I poured myself a big ol' glass of Chardonnay. Liquid courage at its finest.

The phone rang five times and I was about to hang up, sure it was about to kick over to his voicemail, when he finally answered.

"Do you have any idea what time it is?" he said when the call clicked on.

My eyes flew to the kitchen clock. 12:03 A.M. *Damn.* Cammie had come over and we'd watched a marathon of Real Housewives.

"Oh my god, I'm so sorry to wake you."

Although, seriously, what rock star goes to bed early anyway? Shouldn't he be snorting crack off hookers or picking between which Playboy Bunnies he wanted to take to bed?

He didn't respond to my apology so I was left with dead air hanging on the phone.

"I'll let you go," I said.

Still nothing.

I moved the phone away from my ear to hang up, but just before my thumb hit the red button, I heard him growl, literally growl, through the line.

"What is it?" he said.

Even though my first instinct was to tell him off for being so rude, I forced myself to remember why I'd called him in the first place. I was trying to make amends. He and I were about to be secluded in the woods together so it was time to start singing Kumbaya.

"I just wanted to let you know that I'm leaving for Montana in a few days."

"So you called me to tell me something that my assistant already confirmed with me days ago?"

Wow. If I could have reached through the phone and stomped on his foot, I would have. I'd never done that to anyone and you know, I usually didn't condone violence, but this guy pushed every one of my buttons.

"Do you have any friends?" I blurted, genuinely curious if there was anyone on earth that enjoyed this man's presence.

"Plenty. Do you want to know why I'm friends with them?" he responded.

"Yes." I was so interested in this man's personal life. I was even tempted to break my Internet rule, just to learn more about him.

"They don't call and wake me up at 3:00 A.M."

I rolled my eyes and took a long sip of wine. Now he was being dramatic. It wasn't even close to 3:00 A.M. My eyes flew open when it hit me—he wasn't in LA. Summer had told me he was in New York for some press thing and that's why we were flying to Montana individually.

Wow. I could not win with this guy.

"Oh my god, seriously. I'm sorry," I said this with an awkward laugh I was helpless to contain. But it was either that or tears, and I had a feeling Jason would respond even worse if I started to cry.

"You've already said that," he replied and for the first time I could hear the exhaustion in his voice.

"Well, I really mean it."

He grunted. "I'll be sure to tell my trainer that when he comes knocking on my door in two hours."

I couldn't stand it anymore. I laughed. I know I shouldn't have, but I'd never had anyone in life literally see my bad side from every angle. No wonder he hated me so much. *I would have hated me, too.*

"Good night, Jason."

"Please don't call me again at night. Or better yet, just don't call me. I'll see you in Montana in a few days."

He hung up and I leaned forward onto my kitchen island, letting my forehead rest against the cold marble. It's not that I was someone that had to have the admiration of everyone around me. I just knew that I wasn't a half-bad human being. I mean, sure, sometimes I stole soda at restaurants when I told them I was only getting water. And occasionally, I lied to my dentist about flossing. *Sue me.*

But I held doors open for people behind me and always let cars in when lanes were merging. So, I needed

Jason to know that. I needed him to know I was a door-holding Good Samaritan.

I needed to win over Jason Monroe, but I had no clue where to start.

Chapter Six

"What if they have Ebola in Montana?"

I put down my magazine and glanced up at Cammie. Her dark brown eyes were wide with worry and for a second, I think she *actually* thought I'd get the Ebola virus.

"They don't."

That didn't calm her nerves. She started pacing through my living room, back and forth. Back and forth.

"What if you get a tape worm from eating something bad and then you have to have surgery to get it out of you because it's like the size of a snake?"

"Do they really get that big?" I asked, genuinely concerned about why I hadn't heard about this sooner.

"In Montana? Probably," she said, throwing her hands into the air for emphasis.

I started laughing at her dramatic flair. It was time to rein her in before she got too carried away. I tossed my magazine onto my coffee table and stood up to give her a hug.

"All right, psycho. I'll be okay. I won't be getting any tape worms or random viruses," I said, reassuringly rubbing her long brown hair. It felt good to console her; it kept me from thinking about the loneliness that would surely sink in as soon as I stepped onto the plane.

"And you're sure you want to leave me for a month? Just abandon me in LA to fend for myself? Who will clutch me in their bosom when you're gone?" I glanced down to see that she wasn't even kidding, I did have her face pretty much smashed into my boobs. Whoops.

"Oh! That reminds me. I had coffee the other day with Grayson, remember? And I talked to him about you."

Her eyes flew up to mine, as she pulled out of my arms. "What, why?"

"Uh, because you're both architects. Well, you're *about* to be one. I wanted him to give you some advice."

She stared up at the ceiling as if I was the biggest nag in the world. "No. I don't need his help."

I was seriously over her "I can do everything on my own" rant. It wouldn't kill her to get some advice. "Well he owns one of the biggest firms in LA, and he told me to tell you to call him," I explained, pulling out a piece of paper from my kitchen junk drawer so I could write his number down for her.

"He did?" she asked with a note of curiosity.

"Yes, so here is his number. You don't have to go work for him, but don't you think he'd have a few pointers for you since he's gone through everything you're going through?"

She shrugged but she still took the piece of paper when I handed it out to her.

"Are you going to call him?" I asked, when she continued to stare at the number without saying a word.

She shook her head slightly and blinked as if pulling herself out of a deep thought.

"Yeah. I'm not sure when, but I guess I will."

When she and Grayson had first met, Cammie was a senior in high school and Grayson, who was two years older than me, was already two years out from completing his master's degree at MIT. I can't recall them ever getting into a fight or anything. I think if anything, their age difference was just too much. Maybe Cammie looked at him like an old, stiff loser and he just thought she was still a young, naive girl.

I watched her tuck his number into her wallet and then she glanced up at me with a pitiful smile.

"Is that honestly what you're wearing to Montana?" she asked, eyeing my ensemble.

I glanced down and smiled. I was wearing my favorite skinny jeans with my gray cashmere sweater. I was sporting my Louis Vuitton sling-backs and I had just enough make-up on to make it look like I was wearing none at all. I didn't see the problem.

"I always try to travel in style or I feel gross when I land," I explained, smoothing down the cashmere.

"Do I even want to know what else you packed in your suitcase?" she asked.

I went through a mental checklist: designer jeans, high heels, a slew of nice sweaters and blouses. Summer and I had spent the day before packing anything and everything that I may have needed. The closest shopping mall was over two hours away from Jason's house in Montana. Summer had literally shuddered at that fact when we'd Google mapped it.

"Don't you worry about me. I'll be fine. We're just writing music, we aren't traipsing through the woods."

Cammie nodded and jutted out her bottom lip like she used to do when she was little.

"We better get going if you're going to catch your flight on time," she said, reaching to grab my carry on bag for me. "I can't believe you're flying commercial."

I rolled my eyes. "There's no reason to take a private plane to Montana. There's no one coming with me."

She nodded and frowned even deeper. "I wish I was coming with you."

"You're coming in two weeks. Summer already has your ticket and everything."

I reached forward and grabbed her arms so I could shake her silly. "Snap out of it. We'll be fine. Give Grayson a call and focus on school. The two weeks will fly by."

"Alright. Alright, let's go. I'll drop you off at LAX before my morning seminar."

• • •

It wasn't until I caught my connecting flight from Salt Lake City, Utah to Bozeman, Montana that my trip started to sink in. For the last ten years, I'd stitched together a close-knit team of people to surround me: my publicist, assistant, managers, and trainers. Sure, they were all being paid, but other than Cammie, they were the only real family I had. So why was I ditching them and heading eighteen hours away from Los Angeles, to stay with a man who hated me? No, really. If he had a list of people he never wanted to see again, it would read like this:

1. Brooklyn Heart
2. Hitler

Because of my ranking on that list, I'd done a little bit of recon with the help of Summer and Sandy, and as a result my carry-on was full of house-warming gifts (aka Brook-warming gifts) for Jason. There were cookies from Milk Jar and some of this expensive shaving cream from a boutique downtown. I had no clue if he'd even accept the gifts, but I wanted to make an effort so that I wouldn't have to worry about him murdering me in my sleep.

I'd just settled into my seat during the flight to Bozeman when a whisper caught my attention.

"Psst."

I jerked my eyes open.

"Hey… PSSSSTTTTT. Lady!"

I glanced over to see a little boy next to me, leaning over the arm rest and nearly climbing onto my lap. (Which was actually harder than it sounded considering how spacious the seating arrangement was in first class.)

"You smell like cookies," he said, sniffing the air around me like a puppy.

I glanced around to try and find his parents, but the only other adult on our aisle was passed out with a facemask and a pair of giant noise-canceling headphones. From her snoring level, I guessed that she wouldn't be waking up anytime soon even if the plane suddenly started falling from the sky.

The boy's sniffing caught my attention again, and then he poked my shoulder, annoyed that I wasn't paying him enough attention.

"Oh, yeah. I have cookies in my bag for the friend I'm meeting in Montana."

He pursed his lips. "Oh. I'm going to Montana to ride my ponies. My parents send me away for a month every summer with my nana," he said, pointing to the sleeping woman. "I get to do whatever I want and she doesn't even care. It's awesome."

I nodded, wondering how I could extricate myself from the conversation as quickly as possible.

"I'll probably play video games until my eyes pop out. Hey, wait, are you a singer or something? You look like this person that my sister has a poster of in her room. Uggh, I hate her. My sister turns her music up so loud and she dances around her room and I can't hear my video games anymore."

I had one dangerous thought about whether or not he'd fit in an overhead compartment. He'd think it was a "fun adventure" and I'd get some peace and quiet. Instead of attempting that and getting tackled by an air marshal, I decided to give myself a little space.

"I'm going to go to the bathroom really quick," I said, holding my finger up to silence him. Luckily, there was no one in the lavatory, so I closed the door and took a deep breath, taking in my appearance in the bathroom mirror. My mascara was smudged from the nap I'd taken on my earlier flight and my cashmere sweater now sported a bright red ketchup stain from the burger I'd scarfed down during our lay-over. *So much for traveling in style.*

I gave myself the maximum amount of time to hang out in the bathroom before people would start to get suspicious of what I was doing in there. Apparently five minutes was too long.

"C'mon lady, hurry up!" someone yelled before they pounded on the other side of the door. I groaned and pushed off the wall, sliding the lock open just as two bodies pushed open the door and fell into the bathroom. A man and a woman going at it like rabid dogs.

"Jesus!" I said, trying to shove past them while simultaneously trying to figure out if they were fighting or having sex.

"Oh, my god. Yes, take me. Take me right now," the woman said, pulling up her dress.

They didn't even care that I was technically still in the tiny stall with them or that the door was wide open. The guy started working on his belt and I practically tackled them to get out. I shoved the door closed with all of my strength and then sighed.

What the hell? Is that just a normal thing now? Damn you, Fifty Shades of Grey for turning everyone into crazed horn dogs.

Fortunately, by the time I returned to my seat, the young boy was enamored with what I could only identify as a space-age Gameboy. The rest of the flight he left me alone and I even got another short nap in before our plane touched down in Bozeman, Montana at 4:00 P.M. I still had an hour drive before we arrived at Jason's ranch out of Big Timber, Montana, but that would be in the comfort of a quiet car.

The second our plane landed and I got my first view of Montana, I was amazed by the landscape. The sheer number of mountains in every direction was not something I was used to seeing in LA. The grass and trees were blooming green in late spring, but there were still patches of brown from the cold winter.

I pushed through the airport doors, enjoying the first moment of anonymity I'd felt in years. There wasn't a single paparazzi waiting for me outside, and the few people that gave me second glances didn't bother coming up to talk to me. They probably thought exactly what I was thinking, "What would Brooklyn Heart be doing in the middle of Montana?" *No freaking clue*.

A blast of wind swept my hair back as I realized the temperature was definitely chillier than it'd been in southern California. As I pulled out a scarf, I tried to wrack my brain for details of my departure from the Montana airport. Usually when I traveled, there was a limousine waiting for me outside on the private landing strip. In Montana, I was completely on my own and I felt like I was in everyone's way as I stood in the middle of the path, looking around for a sign with my name on it.

At a loss for what to do, I pulled my bags over to the side and sat down on the edge of the flower bed so I could pull my phone out of the front pocket of my purse. A part of me was hoping that there would be a missed call from Jason, or that maybe he'd be at the airport to pick me up, but obviously that was just wishful thinking.

I attempted to call Summer, but she didn't answer. (*What did I pay her for?!*). After that, I contemplated calling Jason. Hah. That was a fleeting thought. I'd rather walk to his ranch in the middle of nowhere than bother him. God forbid he was taking an afternoon nap or something. Nope. No, thank you.

"Brooklyn?"

I heard my name and glanced up to see a cowboy, like a *real* cowboy, standing in front of me. He had on tight jeans, a white t-shirt that was adorably dirty and even a low-slung hat. He looked like a stripper I'd hired for Cammie's twenty-first birthday party. Fun fact: Cammie hates strippers and wouldn't let him take his pants off, so we just played Would You Rather with him for like an hour and then I paid him the thousand dollars I owed him before he left. *And that's how I played the most expensive game of Would You Rather ever.*

"Brooklyn?" he asked again. Oh right, there was a hunky cowboy waiting for me to respond.

"Yes. Hi, that's me," I said with a dopey smile.

He grinned, a wide grin full of confidence and sex appeal, and then I noticed that he had twinkling blue eyes. Oh, good grief. *I guess they knew how to make 'em in Montana.*

He reached his hand out for mine. "I'm Derek — a ranch hand over at Jason's. I was the only one free, so I offered to come pick you up and drive you back."

For some reason, I hadn't considered the idea that there would be other people at the house besides just Jason and me.

Derek reached for my bags. "How many people stay at the ranch?"

He mulled over my question as he walked toward a beat-up red truck sitting idle on the curb. Without a second thought, he tossed my bags into the cab and I heard an audible clink as my bathroom items crashed against the metal. *Strike one, cowboy.*

"It changes all the time, but usually it's just me and LuAnne. She manages the house for Jason. Y'know, makes sure everything is running well while he's gone."

Ah, so there was a lady. *LuAnne.*

"Are you guys together?" I asked as he held the passenger door open for me.

That question earned me a barking laugh. "Lu turned 55 this year and she has no time for my nonsense."

"Huh, I like her already," I joked, throwing in a little wink.

Derek appreciated the wink; his smile widened even further as he helped me close my door.

So maybe Montana wouldn't be all that bad. If Jason hated me, I'd just hang out with Derek and LuAnne.

As Derek pulled out onto the open country road, I grabbed my phone and shot off texts to Summer and Cammie so they'd know I arrived in Montana safely. It took three tries to get the texts to send; the signal bars on my phone were sitting at a one out of five. Lovely. I rolled down the truck's window and held my phone out in hopes that that would help.

"What are you doing?" Derek asked, peering over at me for a second before looking back at the road.

"Trying to get these text messages to send."

"By holding your phone out of the car? Is that an LA thing?" he asked with a rich, deep laugh.

My cheeks stained red. "No, it's, well I'm holding it closer to the satellite." Right? Is that why people held their phones up when they were struggling to get signal?

"The satellite in outer space? You realize we just have a few cell towers between Bozeman and Big Timber. I doubt your iPhone has the power to transmit signals into outer space."

All right, yes when you put it like that, I feel very dumb. *Brooklyn: 0. Cowboy: 1.*

Just then my phone pinged in my hand and I glanced down to read the text.

Cammie: FINALLY. We've been out of contact for like 5 hours. Have you picked up any Montana hookers yet?

I laughed, holding my hand over my mouth to block the sound.

"Did it send?" Derek asked.

"Yes and my crazy sister already replied."

His eyes widened. "There are *two* of you?"

I laughed. "She's younger and has brown hair and brown eyes, but other than that we could be twins."

"You have blue eyes, right?" he asked, squinting at me.

I nodded as I glanced back down at my phone.

Brooklyn: Had one in the airport bathroom and now I'm riding a cowboy.

Cammie: WHAT?!

Brooklyn: Sorry, I'm riding *with* a cowboy... to the ranch. Hehe

"You and your sister close?" Derek asked from the driver's seat.

I purposely positioned my phone so that he couldn't read what I was saying about him over text.

"Very close. She's the only family I have."

Before he could ask for more details, I continued with a question I was wondering about. "How long have you worked for Jason Monroe?"

He tapped his thumbs on the steering wheel as he thought of the answer. "At least seven years, maybe more. I was jobless after high school and Jason needed help on the ranch so it worked out."

So Cowboy Derek was younger than me.

"He seems like a private person."

Derek stripped his cowboy hat off his head and set it on the center console so that he could brush back his dirty blonde hair. Not that it was dark blonde, just actually dirty from work. Hopefully they had showers at the ranch.

"Nah, he's probably private to you LA people, but Jason grew up in town and I knew him from high school. He's four years older than me, but he was friends with my older brother."

Interesting. I wanted to pick Derek's brain about Jason forever.

"Do you like working for him?" I asked, leaning over.

Derek slid me a sideways glance. "Of course. I wouldn't be here if I didn't."

"So he's a nice boss?"

His brow quirked and I knew he was starting to get suspicious of my inquisition.

"Aren't you guys friends? Isn't that why you're collaborating on this song?" he asked, effectively bursting my balloon. I sat back in my seat and crossed my arms over my chest.

Luckily, I wasn't forced to answer his question because his phone rang and he had to take the call about lumber or something equally country-ish. Our turn off the highway came up on the right and Derek pulled off onto a thin gravel road. The gravel was uneven and the truck's suspension was put to the test as we journeyed farther from the highway.

I had a sudden realization that I hadn't checked Derek's credentials or questioned him at all. What if he was just driving me to some random location in the backwoods of Montana so he could kill me? *Oh, dear god, I just got into a car with a stranger*.

When I peered over at him from under my lashes, I didn't get the sense that he was a serial killer. He was still talking on the phone so I quickly texted Cammie from mine.

Brooklyn: If I hypothetically get kidnapped soon, I love you.

Cammie: You are so weird. Should I call the cops?

Brooklyn: Not yet.

Cammie: Should I call Hannah Montana?

Brooklyn: You've been sitting on that one since I told you I was coming here, haven't you?

Cammie: Yes.....But, seriously, I'm never letting you go to Montana by yourself again. Please don't die.

I couldn't respond to her because my signal cut out for good.

Oh, well. Time to welcome death. *I wonder who they'll get to play me in the movie adaption of my life. Hopefully Jennifer Lawrence even though we look nothing alike. With my luck, it'd be Miley.*

When I glanced up, I saw a clearing in the woods a few miles ahead of us. Even though Derek had finished up on the phone, we sat in silence as he rounded the curve on the county road. Light seeped through the trees ahead of us, but I couldn't see anything until he crested the top of a hill.

As soon as the cabin came into view, I held my breath. It was beautiful; a secluded oasis in the middle of the Montana woods. There were mountains spanning the backdrop behind the house, but trees sprouted up everywhere, blocking out the first floor of the cabin completely.

The sun was still up, but it was nearing the top of the mountain ridge, painting the sky with colorful pink and orange hues. It was breathtaking, but that wasn't where I focused. I was completely enamored by the top story of the cabin that was bathed in a warm glow. When I thought of a cabin in the woods, I thought of a one story, one bedroom house. This was a cabin on steroids, and as we drove closer I could see even more details.

Stone bricks made up the base of the cabin, but the top floor was open, with large windows bordered by massive logs. A wraparound porch opened up the house even more, and at the very top, on what looked like the third level, there was a small balcony completely secluded away from everything else.

Martha Stewart would have coveted this place and I was more excited than ever to have Cammie come for a visit so she'd get to see how amazing it was. No wonder Jason wrote his songs here. I'm surprised he ever left.

Derek pulled up into the gravel driveway behind a black Jeep Wrangler and cut the engine.

"You made it," he said, glancing over.

I smiled. "Thanks so much for the ride." *And also for not being a murderer*.

"Why don't you go on up and I'll bring your bags."

I hopped out of the truck and stretched out my limbs. Every part of my body was sore from a day of travel.

Once Derek grabbed my bags, I turned to the cabin in time to see Jason step out onto the small balcony on the third floor. He was barefoot, wearing a worn t-shirt and jeans. His hair was mussed up and from where I stood, it looked like he hadn't shaved in the last few days.

When our eyes met, he didn't smile or nod. We just stared at each other for a moment in silence and I felt a shiver of something run down my spine. That was probably my body's physical reaction to the hate signals he was trying to send my way.

Then I realized that I was in the middle of some bizarro Romeo and Juliet balcony scene where Romeo was standing on the balcony instead of Juliet.

"O Romeo, Romeo! Wherefore art thou Romeo?"
And all he said in reply was: "Begone, wench!"

Chapter Seven

"You must be Brooklyn! You're such a looker!"

I smiled at the plump woman who'd answered the cabin's front door for us. She was wearing a crisp white shirt that matched her curly white hair. She had bright blue eyes, painted red lips, and a warm complexion. Mostly, she reminded me of a Montana version of Paula Dean. And from the smell permeating from the kitchen, I figured she probably wasn't far off.

"Yes, hi. Are you LuAnne?" I asked, holding out a tentative hand for her to shake. She promptly ignored it and pulled me forward into a long hug. And when I say long, I meant long enough for Jason to make his way down the stairs and take us in as he stood with his arms crossed wearing a permanent scowl.

When she finally released me from the hug, she held onto my shoulders and kept inspecting me.

"Really, you are the prettiest thing we've had here in a while," LuAnne said, scanning me from head to toe. I winced at the reminder of my stained and wrinkled clothes.

I'd even added a coffee stain on top of the ketchup. *Apparently you shouldn't take a sip of coffee while the plane is taking off.*

"Jasper would take offense to that," Jason said from behind her. I hadn't heard his voice in a few days, but it was just as deep and melodic as I remembered it being on the phone.

LuAnne turned toward Jason and waved him off. "Oh, please."

I smiled, glancing back and forth between them. "Who's Jasper?"

"Our newest Arabian gelding," LuAnne replied.

I didn't know anything about horses, but that sounded like a pretty breed.

"Jason, would you stop being such a brute and welcome our guest? Look at Derek, helping with her bags and picking her up from the airport. What a gentleman."

We turned to watch Derek drop my bags near the doorway and tip his hat down in appreciation of LuAnn's praise.

"It was nothin' much. I've got a few last things to wrap up in the barn. Do you need anything else before I go, Ms. Heart?"

He looked so eager to please, but he'd done enough and I had faith that I'd be able to help myself if something came up. "No. Thanks again, Derek."

We watched him leave through the front door and then LuAnne clapped her hands.

"Well, I'm just finishing dinner. Why don't you freshen up and then the food will be ready," she suggested as she started backing up out of the main corridor, heading toward what I assumed to be the kitchen.

I didn't think to protest before she was gone, and soon it was just me and Jason, who was still standing with his arms crossed by the stairs. I did my best to take in the house around me. The foyer and the living room just off of the front door were both decorated in rich, modern interiors. Bright walls contrasted with dark, stained wood furniture. It was a beautiful house, but I couldn't just stand there craning my neck around all day, so I bit the bullet and slid my gaze to him.

His brown eyes, rimmed with even darker lashes, were locked on me. "You have the room upstairs on the left."

"You know most people usually greet their guests with a hello," I said with a little smile so that he'd know I was teasing.

He shrugged. "Most guests are invited, not thrust upon the host for forced collaboration."

Alrighty then. I was at a loss for words, but then I remembered the gifts I'd brought him from LA.

"Oh, I have something for you!" I said, confident that I'd done the right thing in bringing him a few of his favorite things. Derek had set my carry-on bag next to the door, on top of my giant suitcase. The box of cookies and the shaving cream were sitting at the very top, so I grabbed them and turned to him with a giant smile plastered on my face.

His gaze slid down to the boxes in my hands as I stepped toward him.

"Cookies?" he asked, taking the box reluctantly.

I smiled wider. "Your favorite. I wanted to bring a peace offering."

He flipped open the lid to the cookie box and frowned. *What? Why the frown? Did I get the wrong flavor or something?*

I leaned forward to inspect the contents and my smile froze. The box was completely empty save for a few crumbs and one half-eaten cookie.

"You ate my cookies on the way here?" he asked, less than impressed with my gift.

I slapped my hand over my eyes. "That asshole kid!"

"What?"

My hand stayed planted over my eyes as I explained to him what happened. "There was a kid sitting next to me on the plane and he must have eaten the cookies while I went to the bathroom."

Jason laughed, an actual laugh that made me peel my hand away from my face and glance back up at him.

There was still a hint of smile on his face when he said, "That's a shame. Those are good cookies."

I frowned. "I know. I asked your assistant what your favorite bakery in LA was."

He kept his gaze locked with mine and I saw a hint of lightness trying its best to seep through. "Oh, well."

No matter what I did, I could not win with Jason Monroe. The universe was intent on making us mortal enemies. Except, I didn't approve of enemies that were as good-looking as he was. Now that we were standing closer, I could smell the faint hints of his cologne and each of his features that were breathtaking from a distance, his lips especially, were only better up close. They were clearer, sharper, more interesting to behold.

But I just gave him an empty box of cookies, so what did it matter.

"I've got some stuff to finish up before dinner," he said, turning toward the stairs with the cookie box still in his hand. As I watched him ascend the staircase and turn out of my sight, I assessed our first encounter. It could have gone a lot better. With a sigh, I went to retrieve my bags so I could carry them upstairs. I still had his shaving cream clutched in my hand, but I'd find another time to give it to him.

"Leave your bags," Jason called from the second floor. "I'll get them in a minute."

A door closed a second later, so I assumed that he couldn't hear me even if I wanted to protest.

Since I wasn't left with much of a choice, I grabbed my purse, left my bags, and decided to try to find my room on my own. LuAnne probably thought that Jason would give me a tour or at least lead me to where I was staying, but she obviously didn't know him the way I did. Or maybe he was only an asshole to me.

When I arrived on the second-floor landing, I peered down the hall. There were six doors flanking the hallway on each side, and then at the end, there was another set of stairs that I assumed led to the room on the third floor. Every one of the six doors in the hallway was closed except for one. I headed in that direction and smiled when I realized I'd guessed right.

It was a guest room and it was fit for a queen. The bed in the center of the room was topped with fluffy white linens and overstuffed pillows. The table next to the bed had a bouquet of pink peonies on it with a card that said my name on the front.

I took a step inside and spun in a circle. There was a flat-screen TV over the armoire across from the bed. A medium-sized bathroom connected to the side of the room and there was already a terry-cloth robe and all the bathroom essentials waiting for me inside.

The only problem was the closet. It was a the smallest thing I'd ever seen, with just one hanging bar behind a thin door, and I doubted I could fit even one-fourth of the clothes I'd brought with me for the trip inside of it.

"Brooklyn, dinner is ready!" LuAnne called from the first floor. Since there wasn't much I could do about the closet situation, I went into the bathroom and washed my hands. I even dabbed some water on my face to get the layer of airport off my skin.

After I'd patted my face dry, I made my way back down the stairs, taking in the smell of roasted chicken as I hit the landing. *Oh, hell yes.* The last time I'd had a home cooked meal, Cammie had attempted to make sushi but had only succeeded in making my condo smell like fish for two weeks.

LuAnne's cooking smelled divine. Garlic and spices mingled in the air and I let the smell lead me toward the kitchen. When I made it to the doorway, I paused to take it all in. Each part of the house seemed to be even better than the last. The kitchen was a dream with dark stained wood cabinets and speckled granite countertops. A massive window hung over the sink and I realized that many of the walls in the cabin had been sliced up to include as many windows as possible. It wasn't a mystery as to why they'd done it. In every direction there was a spectacular view waiting to be seen: mountains, forests, barns, and stables. It was mesmerizing to take everything in and I hardly noticed that LuAnne was watching me from the island.

"I bet they don't have houses like this in LA," she said with a warm smile.

I laughed, "Definitely not. I mean there are some amazing houses, but this is just different. You can't compare them," I explained.

She nodded thoughtfully.

I offered to help her prep the rest of dinner, but she shooed me off and told me to wait at the table. Most everything was already laid out: two plates, two glasses with chilled wine waiting to be poured into them, and mounds upon mounds of food.

"Will it just be the two of us at dinner?" I asked, purposely keeping any notes of disappointment hidden beneath my smile.

I suppose she sensed it anyway. "Afraid so. Jason seems to be working hard upstairs and Derek is still out working in the barn."

"That's okay. I don't think Jason would want to eat with me anyway," I said, surprised at my loose lips. LuAnne just had that way about her, she gave off a grandmotherly vibe, like if you stared into her blue eyes, you knew you could tell her all your secrets and she'd pat your shoulder and tell you how to fix your life, all while shoving food in front of you.

"Nonsense, why would you think that? Did he help you find your room and get situated?"

I knew that LuAnne technically worked for Jason, but I had a feeling that if I told her the truth he'd be in major trouble with her later.

I shrugged it off. "I found it really easily. The room is awesome. Do I have you to thank for those flowers?"

"Oh! I'm glad you liked them. Normally the guys hate it if I leave flowers in their room."

We laughed as she came to sit across from me. Over a plate of garlic mashed potatoes, green beans, and roasted chicken, I got to learn a bit more about LuAnne. She told me that she'd lived in Montana her whole life. She'd married young but never had any children of her own, and ten years ago her husband had cheated on her with "a skank from outta town" and they'd divorced soon after. Since then, she's worked for Jason.

"Do you ever get bored out here on your own when Jason travels for work?"

She studied the stem of her wine glass, smiled, and then shook her head. "I think other people might get lonely, but the country life is for me. I'm old-fashioned in a lot of ways and I appreciate the quiet. I have my hobbies and I go into town when I need some social interaction. We have a little book club in town and those girls give me more than enough drama to keep me going."

I laughed and nodded. "I don't have too many friends, but my younger sister and I have always been close."

She smiled, "What about a boyfriend?"

I puffed my lips out so that they made a puttering sound. LuAnne cracked up and poured us each a bit more wine.

"My job doesn't make it very easy to date. I had a seriously pitiful hook-up before leaving LA and I fear that might be the only action I'll get for quite a while."

"Well, let's hope you have a good vibrator."

My eyes shot to her. "LuAnne!"

She shrugged innocently. "What? Are we not close enough to talk about that yet?"

I thought about it for a second. "You just look very prim and proper."

She grinned. "Don't let my ironed button-down fool you. I was quite the wild child in my day."

"Good to know," I laughed.

"So what do you think about Derek?"

I glanced around the open kitchen, wondering if we could talk privately in here without being overheard.

"He's still out working and Jason locked himself up in that room, so you're free to speak your mind," she said, reassuring me of our privacy.

"He's a little young," I answered honestly.

"And Jason?"

I choked on the sip of wine I'd taken a second before. LuAnne had to come around and pat my back for fear that I was going to keel over on her kitchen table.

"That bad, huh?" she asked, taking her seat across from me once she was assured I was okay.

I laughed and coughed out the remaining wine. "You have no idea."

What did she think I wanted? Jason's heart? I was there to write music and then be on my merry way.

She narrowed her eyes, studying my features before speaking again. "Jason is a rough around the edges kind of guy. I won't pretend to understand the intricacies of that man, but he's had an interesting last few years. Lots of ups and lots of downs. After everything that happened with Kim and Lacy, I think he keeps his heart well-protected."

Interesting.

"Who's Kim?" I asked, trying to sound like I wasn't aching to know more details of his life.

She stilled. "Oh, no one. Let's not talk about that boring stuff," she said, trying to brush her slip of tongue under the rug.

I tried to think of something else to talk about, but Jason was still clouding my thoughts so we sat in comfortable silence for a beat.

"Why don't you go head up and get some sleep. I'm sure Jason has plans for you tomorrow."

The dishes that were piled in the sink caught my gaze.

"Don't even think about it. I can handle all of those. It's my job and I'm pretty picky about how my kitchen is cleaned."

I laughed and stood up to leave, but before I could, LuAnne stood to give me a hug.

"I'm really glad you're visiting us, Brooklyn. It's about time we had some roses up here to balance out the thorns."

Maybe it was the smell of butter in her hair or the wine floating in my veins. Either way, that hug felt like a million bucks, and I softened into her so that she could hug me even tighter. It'd been over eight years since my parents had passed away and even though that ache in my heart had lessened slightly over the years, it still felt really good to be hugged by LuAnne.

"See you in the morning," I said as she released me.

I made my way upstairs. The house seemed even quieter since the sun had set, and each one of my high-heeled steps on the hardwood floor echoed through the house. There were no signs of Jason in the hallway, but I could see a soft glow from the third floor as I made my way to my room.

When I got to the doorway, I stopped in my tracks. I hadn't even noticed the absence of my bags in the foyer on my way upstairs, but they were up in my room now, and not only that, but there was an empty metal garment rack pushed up against the wall next to them. I guess when Jason had carried my bags, he'd realized that the closet wouldn't be big enough.

I couldn't process the sweet gesture, so I closed the door and stripped into some comfortable pajamas so I could try to call Cammie. California's time zone was an hour behind Montana, so I knew she wasn't asleep yet.

When she answered on the second ring, a giant smile broke out across my face.

"Hey, I can't talk for long. I'm still in the studio."

"Are you serious? It's so late," I complained, grabbing my watch from the nightstand to check the time. 8:00 P.M. California time.

"Yeah, and I'll be here through the night probably. I have a presentation later this week on a design project."

I felt bad for leaving when she was so busy. "I'm sorry, Cammie. If I were there I could have brought you dinner or something."

"No worries, I'm subsisting on caffeine and granola bars. Food is for weak babies and invalids."

Something clanked to the ground on her end of the phone line and then she cursed under her breath.

"Are you okay?" I asked.

"Yes, sorry. I'm trying to finish this damn model and a few parts don't want to stay glued together."

"I'll let you go so you can finish working."

"Okay, love you."

"Love you, too," I laughed.

Immediately after I hung up, I dialed Cammie's favorite Thai restaurant and ordered a few dishes to be delivered to her studio's address. There was probably a group of ravenous grad students ready to consume anything that smelled remotely like food.

After that, my phone's service started cutting in and out so I couldn't call Summer and get an update about how things were going in LA. I didn't mind. I was exhausted from traveling and the longer I lounged on the bed in my cotton nightshirt, the better sleep sounded.

The pile of pillows and the soft duvet cover called my name and when I laid down I realized they were just as good as they'd looked. I was nearly asleep when my eyes flew open at the sound of a knock at my door. I laid completely still, wondering if I'd imagined it before another soft knock followed a moment later. I pushed off the bed and crept toward the door before turning the handle and checking to see who was on the other side.

Jason.

He was standing at the threshold of my bedroom, rubbing the stubble on his chin with his right hand. He looked significantly more tired than he had a few hours earlier and I wondered if he ever took breaks from working.

"Oh, you were asleep," he said, taking in my blinking eyes and nightshirt.

I tugged the hem down my legs instinctively and shook my head.

"Just dozed off for a second. What's up?"

He cleared his throat as his gaze hit mine. "I just wanted you to know that I've set aside some time tomorrow morning to work with you if you have the time."

Of course I had the time. My schedule had literally been cleared off so I could come to Montana. I had a Skype meeting with a clothing line in the afternoon, but even that could be moved around.

"That sounds good," I said with a warm smile.

He knocked twice on the door frame and then stepped back.

"We're even now," he said.

I scrunched my brows. "About what?"

The right side of his sensual lips turned up. "You woke me up the other night and I just woke you up."

"Ah."

He turned to head back toward the third story and I was left standing there with the image of his little smirk hanging in my mind. We were so far from even. I'd woken him up with a brief phone call, but the idea of Jason Monroe was going to keep me up the entire night.

When I crawled back into bed later after I'd washed my makeup off, I found a text from Cammie waiting for me.

Cammie: Thanks for the food. We were all about to turn into zombies.

Brooklyn: I hope you got enough.

Cammie: Yeah — two of my classmates fought for the spring rolls though.

Brooklyn: You guys need to eat more. That's not right.

Cammie: It's like a rite of passage to be a starving grad student.

Brooklyn: Oh whatever. If you lose any more weight, I'm hooking an IV up to your dumb workstation.

Cammie: Awesome. Let's put chicken noodle soup in it and we can hook a straw up to my mouth.

Brooklyn: You.Are.So.Weird. PS. I have a writing date tomorrow morning with Jason.

Cammie: What is a "writing date"?

Brooklyn: Oh, I just meant we're going to try to write together tomorrow morning.

Cammie (1): Oh okay. So not a date at all, you liar......He's so hot. I don't even know how you're going to sit by him for that long. Those lips. That voice. Sometimes he takes his shirt off on stage

Cammie (2): because he's hot and it's just too much to wear a shirt. Poor guy, wouldn't want him to get overheated. Will you take a close up picture of his eyes so I can see what they look like?

Cammie (3): I think they're like a rich dark brown but it's hard to tell.

Brooklyn: OMG. Stop. You're blowing up my phone with texts about his dumb eyes.

Cammie: fine. Night. Let me know when to expect my chicken noodle soup IV. PS. Wiki says his eyes are brown. Mmm like Belgian chocolate.

Chapter Eight

I woke up the next morning to a text message from Cammie that included a Photoshopped picture of me and Jason. The little devil didn't have time to go get dinner, but she apparently had all the time in the world to whip up prank photos. I glanced down at the photo in its full-color HD glory. There was Jason performing on stage without his shirt on, just like Cammie told me he was wont to do, except she'd cropped me into the photo in a compromising pose. I was bent forward, licking Jason's sweaty chest while he kept right on singing. I had no clue where she'd found that picture of me, but I suspected it was from one of our nights where we stayed in and had one too many bottles of wine. After much deliberation, I decided to keep the photo saved to my phone just for research purposes. *Of course.*

I didn't bother texting Cammie back because the message would have just been filled with random curse words and a suggestion of where she could shove a pineapple. Instead, I stretched out in my comfy bed and then I pushed out from beneath my warm blankets to start the day. I knew it was going to be chilly, so after my shower, I wrapped myself in another sweater and paired it with jeans and heeled ankle boots.

When I journeyed downstairs after getting ready, I found the house deserted, save for the delicious aroma of fresh coffee. That smell was like my crack and it pulled me toward the kitchen where I found a note from LuAnne propped up on the counter.

Made you some breakfast. Help yourself, love Lu. PS. There's a bottle of Bailey's in the fridge…in case that's how you roll.

I laughed and placed the note back where I'd found it. The universe would have loved for me to get drunk on my morning cup of coffee. It would have given Jason one more reason to hate me. He'd be trying to write a song and I'd be throwing up on his carpet. *Classy.*

In the fridge I found a bowl of fresh fruit and on the counter under a tiny heat lamp, there was a plate piled high with bacon and sausage. I loved meat as much as the next girl, but if I started each day off with bacon while in Montana, I'd be heading back to LA in a pair of Derek's XL sweat pants.

After I'd gathered all the essentials, I sat down at the table where LuAnne and I had eaten dinner the night before. In the morning light, the view from the kitchen windows was even better. As I ate my breakfast, I peered through the glass and tried to spot different entrances to walking paths. It looked like I could get a decent hike in after lunch if I wanted to. There were distinct paths that led from the base of the house up into the forest.

Maybe I'd find a wilderness man chopping down wood topless and he'd need water. I'd, of course, give him a sip of mine and we'd strike up a conversation about how we're both dog lovers, but our lifestyles never allowed us to get one of our own. We'd fall down into the brush of the forest and we'd make love to—

"Morning, Brooklyn."

Oh god, I nearly choked on the piece of fruit I'd been chewing while fantasizing. But I recovered nicely, and by the time I turned around to see Derek piling his plate with food, I knew my face wasn't as bright red as it'd been a moment before.

"Hi Derek," I said with a welcoming smile.

He plopped down across from me with enough food on his plate to feed a small group of starving grad students. He probably worked it all off on the ranch each day. I mean, I knew he did because the cowboy was *fit*.

"Did you sleep well?" he asked, trying to make polite conversation.

"Oh, yeah. That bed in the guest room is really comfortable."

He nodded, "That's good. It didn't used to be a guest room, but Jason had it done up before you arrived. I think he used to store guitars or something in that room."

"Oh, really?" I asked.

That seemed like a thoughtful thing to do. I could have just taken the couch or something. I'm sure it would have been comfortable enough.

"Yeah, said something about 'a pop princess' and 'beauty sleep'," he answered with a little smile.

I groaned. Thoughtfulness *ruined*.

Derek must have picked up on my annoyance because he changed the subject. "Do you have some time after breakfast to come out and see the barn and stable? I can show you our new horse and the other animals."

"Oh, yeah. Okay," I smiled. I already had plans to inspect the grounds by myself later, but his option seemed better. I didn't think Jason was even awake yet, and we hadn't set up a time to start writing, so I figured it wouldn't hurt to peek outside with Derek.

After I'd finished my granola and yogurt, and Derek had wolfed down his food (which probably equated to three small pigs), we headed outside. I was expecting to be greeted by a brisk chill, but the blast of wind that hit me as I walked down the front path had me wrapping my arms around my chest. My damn sweater had too many holes to actually keep me warm, but it was too cute to get rid of.

Derek led the way around the side of the house, following a loose gravel path. The sounds of the animals could already be heard and I wondered if they would reach my room if I opened my windows in the morning. I could wake up to the sounds of horses and chickens. *Wait, who am I kidding, I'm not that 'one with nature'.*

"So the barn is up there on the right. We have a few pigs and chickens in there," he said, pointing to the first wooden structure. "And just beyond that is the horse stable."

"Oh! Can we go inside the stable?" I asked, anxious to see the horses. I'd ridden once or twice as a girl, but never as an adult. It was definitely on my bucket list though. Well, riding bareback with a sexy man... then after we were done, we'd saddle up and actually go horseback riding. Hah.

"Sure. Let's go," he said, resting his hand on the small of my back to steer me toward the building.

The stable itself was nearly twice the size of the barn. A massive wooden door was already pushed to the side. Just beyond the entrance, the gravel path turned into a cobblestone floor. On each side there were rows of stalls, maybe eight in all. They were spacious and open on the top with black metal bars that let us peek inside to see the horses. The stable was impeccably clean, but that aroma of horses was impossible to ignore. I loved it.

"I've already fed them this morning, but I've got some sugar cubes in the office. I'll be right back," he said, turning and heading toward a door near the entrance, which led to what I assumed to be the office. I turned back toward the stables and crept forward hoping to get a good look at the horses. The first stall on the right was occupied by a small white horse who was sticking its nose out on top of the black bars, anxious to see who'd just entered the stable. I stepped forward tentatively and held my hand out to see if the horse would scare. It pushed its body against the door even more, trying to get to my hand. I laughed and stroked its cheek. Its mane was brushed free of tangles and it felt so soft to pet that I stood there for a few minutes rubbing back and forth before Derek came back out of the door.

"Sorry about that, I couldn't find any. I'll have to grab some at the store when I run into town later."

I smiled, keeping my hand on the horse. "No worries, I think this one likes me even without the sugar cubes."

He laughed, "That's Dotty. She'll love anyone who will give her a bit of attention. Don't expect the same from Jason Jr. though."

"Aw man," I said, suddenly feeling much less special. For a second I thought I'd been a horse whisperer.

Derek took me down the aisle of horses, introducing each one to me until we finished up at the end where there was a black horse sticking close to the back wall. I knew right away that the horse was Jasper, the Arabian gelding that Jason had told me about the night before. (Aka Jason

Jr.) His coat was a deep, shiny black and his mane was just as dark and glossy. He held his head high, but didn't make a move to greet us.

"This is our newest one. We got him a couple months ago and I still haven't quite figured him out yet," Derek said, propping his elbows up on the stall.

"He's gorgeous."

"Yeah, he is," a voice said from across the stable. I whipped my head around to see Jason standing near the door with his hands shoved in the front pockets of his dark jeans. The morning light silhouetted him from behind and I stood motionless for a moment, unsure of what to do. *Oh, jeez. Was I not allowed to look at his precious horse?*

"Mornin' Jason," Derek said, pushing off of Jasper's stall and nodding toward his boss.

Jason dipped his head in greeting but didn't offer anything more as he strolled toward us. He was wearing a white long-sleeved Henley shirt. He'd tugged the sleeves up to his elbows and his dark expression was aimed straight at me. I swallowed hard as I waited for whatever he clearly wanted to yell at me about. That morning it could have been nearly anything. Maybe I'd snored in my sleep and woken him up. Maybe I was just breathing wrong and it was pissing him off.

"I've been looking for you," he said, stopping a few feet in front of me.

I frowned. "I came out here after breakfast. Derek wanted to show me the place," I explained, looking to Derek for back-up. He was eyeing Jason with a curious brow, but didn't offer any backup. *Gee, thanks.*

"Did you forget about our plan to write this morning?" he asked, his brows furrowed in annoyance.

"No," I said, meeting his attitude head on. "I was just about to head back inside."

He nodded once, glaring at Derek, and then he moved past me toward Jasper's stall. He clicked his tongue twice and the horse shook out its mane and walked slowly toward the front of the stall. Jason reached his hand out and Jasper gently rubbed his head against in, emitting a low rumble through his nostrils that made Jason smile.

Derek and I just stood there, watching him. It was a side of Jason I wasn't used to seeing. *What was it about the horse that Jason was drawn to and vice versa? Were they just both brooding types that called to one another?* Maybe that's why Jason hated me. I wasn't exactly quiet or contemplative.

After another minute, Jason stepped away from Jasper's stall and started heading toward the door of the stable.

"Coming?" he asked over his shoulder.

Derek and I exchanged an amused glance and then I trotted to catch up to him, my high-heeled boots clacking against the cobblestone floor. Just as I was about to catch up, the heel on my left shoe got caught in-between two cobblestones and I fell forward, smack dab into Jason. *(Picture my face squashed against his back.)* He grunted as our bodies collided, and then he turned quickly to wrap his arms around my shoulders to steady me.

His dark eyes were inches away from mine and I thought of what Cammie had said the night before. She was absolutely right. It was his eyes that pulled me closer. It was his eyes that made my breath pause as I tried to take them in as quickly as possible. It felt like I was getting a glimpse into a world that didn't belong to me, but I wanted more. Just a little bit more.

"Don't you have other shoes to wear?" he asked, pushing me back to stand on my own.

I was a twenty-seven year old woman and Jason had an uncanny ability to make me feel like I was five again. With a hard scowl and a whip of my blonde hair, I brushed past him and made sure to walk as sexy as I possibly could on my high-heels. I'd wear them every day if I wanted to; he could go fuck himself.

I heard Derek chuckle on the other end of the stable, but Jason didn't say a word as he followed me back to the house.

I'd assumed we'd go up to the third floor to write. I knew that's where he kept his instruments because they weren't anywhere else in the house. But instead, when we made it to the second story landing, he pointed to the wraparound porch.

"I'll meet you out there. Get some paper and a pen," he ordered before he took the third-story stairs two at a time and disappeared.

I purposely ignored his instructions and went out on the porch with my hands empty and chin raised. Jason might rule over everyone else in his life, but he wasn't my boss and he sure as shit wasn't going to order me around and expect me to follow his instructions blindly.

The porch, of course, was styled like the rest of the house with dark brown wicker furniture topped with plush white pillows and cushions. I chose a small two-seater couch and relaxed back into the cushions just as Jason pulled open the porch door. I glanced up to see him with a guitar in his right hand, a pad of paper in his left, and a pen stuck behind his lips. Even if he was annoying me, the sight was too cute not to elicit a smile. Even just a little, private one.

He sat across from me so that we were separated by the coffee table. It was a smart move considering how much tension was brewing between us. He threw down the pen and paper onto the coffee table, adjusted his guitar over his lap, and then finally glanced up to find me empty handed.

"Did you forget to pack a single pen in all of your twelve suitcases?" he asked with an arched brow.

"Nope," I answered. "But I don't need one."

He smirked. "Is that so?"

"I have a good memory."

He grunted and then reached for his pen and pad. Silence hung before us and then he glanced back up to me.

"So I'm assuming they want us to write a love song."

I laughed, a bark of a laugh, because the idea of co-writing a love song with Jason seemed like the funniest idea in the world.

"My thoughts exactly," he replied, tapping his pen on the paper.

"We could write a break-up song?" I suggested.

He nodded, staring out beyond the porch. "That could work."

"Are we actually agreeing on something?" I joked, trying to lighten the mood.

Jason didn't respond. He picked up his guitar, absentmindedly strumming the strings. I felt an instant pang of envy. I'd been taking guitar lessons for the past ten years, and I was good, good enough to play on stage, but Jason was a natural. His fingers worked the guitar strings like he was born to do it.

"Okay, let's just start throwing out some ideas, things we'd want the song to sound like," I suggested.

He arched a brow, his fingers eternally strumming the guitar. "That's not how I usually write."

I smiled tightly. "Well, we're going to have to compromise."

"Sounds good. You go in the other room and talk to yourself and I'll just write the song by myself," he said with a confident smirk. *Oh, wasn't he just the funniest thing ever.*

"Let's write a song about a guy who is an arrogant asshole," I said.

He shook his head with a smug, unimpressed look.

There was a knock on the porch door and then a moment later, a perfectly coifed LuAnne stepped out wearing her standard preppy. Her hair was curled and poufy like she was hosting a southern dinner party, but she pulled it off well. In her hands there was a polished silver tray with tea and snacks arranged artfully on a china plate.

"How's the writing going?" she asked with a wide smile as she glanced between us. Her smile faltered when she saw our matching scowls.

"Really well," I lied, reaching for the glass of water.

"Great," Jason said.

LuAnne's eyebrows shot up. "Really? What do you have so far?"

Jason grunted, but I smiled at LuAnne, "We're going the love ballad route, but I'll have to write most of the song considering Jason has no heart."

LuAnne laughed and shook her head at us.

"Good thing there's still a month to get the song done, right?"

"Mhm," I mumbled as I took a sip of water.

"Thanks for this, Lu," Jason said, reaching forward for one of the apple slices.

"Of course," she said, patting his shoulder. "I'll see you guys for dinner later," she said, heading back for the door.

When the door was shut tight, and I knew LuAnne was out of earshot, I glanced back at Jason.

"One month should be plenty of time to get this done," he said, turning back to his guitar. "Of course, if you'd let me work alone, I could have it done in a week."

I rolled my eyes dramatically. "Does your cockiness have a dimmer switch or is it always set to 'high'?"

"Guess you've figured me out, huh?" he asked, as the strumming of his guitar came to an abrupt halt.

I gulped down a comeback, feeling like I may have pushed our game too far.

When I didn't reply, he pushed up off the chair and headed toward the door, leaving the food, drinks, and his paper pad behind.

"That's enough writing for today," he said, not bothering to look back at me before he slammed the door closed behind him.

I sat frozen, running the last few minutes over in my mind. The only conclusion I came to was the fact that Jason and I were a ticking time bomb, destined to explode over and over again. I sighed and pushed up off the couch, but the morning light highlighted the black scribbles written on the top of Jason's notebook. Even though I shouldn't have, I looked at it.

His penmanship was terrible, and the scratched out lyrics were distracting, but it was the first time I'd caught a glimpse of his writing process:

She never liked the way I tried to make her smile
But I said I'd ~~change~~ try harder

She never liked ~~the way I wrote~~ my music, my style, my
prose
But I said I'd ~~change~~ ~~break~~ rewrite it all

~~I thought I'd fix it all, but then she walked away~~
~~She told me to~~
She taught me everything I needed to say,
But still those edges started to strip and fray

I read and reread the lyrics, trying to decipher how long ago he'd written them. There were dried coffee stains across the paper and some of the lines he'd written in pencil were completely faded. It was tempting to tear the page off and take it back to my room so that I could keep studying it, but the moment I bent to grab the pad, I heard footsteps on the gravel drive below and I jumped back, fearing someone had seen me snooping. After a minute of holding in my breath, I decided to take the food tray inside, but leave his notepad. He'd come back for it and I didn't want him to know I'd read it. Even if it was just the front page. Those lyrics felt personal, more personal than Jason probably intended to be with me.

LuAnne thanked me for the tray when I brought it to her in the kitchen and I spent the rest of the afternoon lying on my bed, breaking apart his lyrics until my mind started to unravel each word.

I wanted to know who he'd written those lyrics about— if they were real or fiction.

Chapter Nine

"We had our first writing session yesterday," I said into the phone's receiver.

Cammie hummed, "Aaaand?"

"Umm," I stared up at my white ceiling, trying to find a one-word answer to that question. There wasn't one. "It was pretty terrible. Our performance will probably be worse than a Kanye-Taylor-Swift duet. *"Imma let you finish"*, but we had the worst chemistry ever."

"I see," she said, drawing out the "e" sound like a psychic reading a fortune. "Did you get any lyrics done?"

I laughed, "Not a line."

"Wow. You two are destined for greatness, I can tell."

Choosing to ignore her statement, even if it was pretty accurate, I rolled out of bed and headed toward my closet to pick out an outfit for the day.

"How's your school stuff? Have you given Grayson a call yet?" I asked, sliding sweaters and jackets aside before landing on a black tunic dress that would keep me warm enough if I paired it with my fitted leather jacket and knee-high boots.

"It's going well. I finished that model last night, so now—"

"Oh, that's funny. I finished off a model the other night, too."

"Oh, god. Are you talking about that Colombian guy?"

"Um, he was Brazilian and he has a name. I just don't happen to remember it."

"Gross. Well, I hope you washed your hands since then. Anyway, now I'm drafting plans for an urban, mixed-use development."

"Huh, that urban model had plenty of mixed-uses, too."

"That's the last sexual, architecture-based pun you get to use for the day," she warned.

"Alright, fine. I don't even know what half those words mean anyway."

She laughed, "Basically, it's a building with restaurants and shops on the bottom floor and apartments on top."

"Ah. See, you should just talk to me like I'm a toddler and I'll totally understand you."

"I already do that so, no worries."

"Har Har. Hey, you never told me if you called Grayson," I reminded her.

"What? Oh weird, can't hear you. The phone is cutting out, koshcshckshhhhh."

"I can hear you just fine."

"What? Nope. Sorry, no habla ingles."

Then the phone went dead because my little sister is a total liarface.

I didn't bother calling her back. If she wanted to be weird about the Grayson situation, I'd let her. It was her future career, not mine. I'd call Grayson in a few days and check with him. Maybe if he called her, she would realize that he didn't hate her like she thought he did.

I was still contemplating that thought when I heard a knock on my door followed by another two. I glanced down to the pajamas I'd worn to bed and froze. My boobs were definitely on display, like somehow they'd fallen out of my tank top during my sleep. It's not like I was a buxom wench from some renaissance fair, but I had my fair share of cleavage.

"Hold on!" I called as I flew toward the bathroom to grab the robe that was hanging behind the door.

Once I was wrapped up, I opened the door to find Jason standing there. He'd been staring out the window at the end of the hallway, probably annoyed that I'd made him wait all of five seconds. When he heard the door open, he turned toward me and scanned down the robe that ended at my mid-thigh. His eyes blazed over my skin, and I swore I saw a hint of interest in his eyes, hidden deep behind his mask of cockiness. I looked down, trying to take in the view from his angle, but then my eyes landed on my toe nails and I laughed.

Of course.

The day before I'd left, Cammie and I were hanging out in my condo and she'd volunteered to do my toe nail polish. I didn't even think much of it, but when she was finished and I glanced down, I'd wanted to kill her. She'd taken the liberty to paint my toes bright pink. (Not the worst color in the world.) But then she added letters onto each one of my toes nails so that it spelled out: "I <3 J. Biebs!!" Don't get me wrong, I have nothing against Justin

Bieber, but I'd have gone with Jamie Dornan or David Beckham. *I mean, c'mon.*

I hadn't removed the message because the pizza we'd ordered had arrived soon after and I got distracted. *Shoving pepperoni pizza in my face ranks above all else.*

So, anyway, Jason was staring at my toes, and I was blushing hard at the fact that he now thought I wanted to do a fourteen-year-old kid. When he finally glanced back up to my face, he was wearing a small smile.

"I took you for a One Direction girl," he said, his smile widening even more.

"Yeah, yeah, my sister did it as a joke," I explained, knowing he probably wouldn't believe the true story anyway.

"You don't have to explain yourself to me," he said with a smug grin.

I rolled my eyes. "Did you need something?" I asked, my tone conveying how annoyed I was with him.

"We have a song to write and I'm sick of being in this house. Let's go up to a coffee shop in town."

I pursed my lips in thought. In LA I would have never been able to write at a coffee shop. There would have been paparazzi with their lens pressed to the windows and curious fans interrupting me at every moment. I loved my fans, but sometimes it became too much of a good thing.

"No one will recognize you there, princess," he said as if reading my thoughts. "Be ready in ten minutes."

He turned on his heels and I watched him walk toward the stairs in sweaty workout clothes. He must have just gone for a run. (I didn't *want* to check him out as he walked away, but I was powerless to help it.)

I would have protested to his demands, but the thought of going into town was too enticing. I'd seen a bit of the town square when Derek has driven me to the ranch, but I wanted to see it during the daytime when people were out and about. Once I'd thrown on my outfit, brushed my teeth, thrown my hair into a ponytail and applied a bit of make-up, I had a minute to spare, so I shot Cammie a death-text.

Brooklyn: Jason just saw my Justin Beiber toe nails. You are dead to me. And are henceforth excommunicated.

Cammie: You'll be back. You alllwaayyysss come back.

"Brooklyn, let's go!" Jason yelled from the bottom floor.

"Okay, I'm coming, Mr. Bossypants!" I said, dropping my phone into my cross-body bag and trotting downstairs. LuAnne was standing next to Jason with a little smile.

"Morning, Brooklyn. You look adorable in that get-up," she said as I stepped forward to kiss her cheek.

"Thanks, Lu," I replied with a smile. "Tell me, does Jason always have his panties in a wad or is that just around me?"

Jason crossed his arms, but Lu threw her head back and laughed, clearly enjoying my sauciness.

"I can't believe that label of yours thought a duet with you two would be a good idea. They clearly haven't seen you two together before."

I grunted, "Oh, they saw us together all right. I don't think they cared much though."

Jason shook his head and walked toward the front door, brushing past me so that our arms touched. The static electricity jumped between us, zapping me enough to make me take a hesitant step back. *Don't even go there. He zapped you because it's cold. Don't read into it, weirdo.*

"I'll be in the car," he said, leaving the front door open behind him.

LuAnne met my gaze and I could see a little glow of mischief in her eyes. I knew she could see past Jason's exterior, but she wasn't going to help me out. I was all on my own. *Team Brooklyn is currently accepting new members. The only requirement is that you also loathe Jason Monroe.*

With a sigh, I headed out the front door and reluctantly climbed into the passenger side of Jason's Jeep Wrangler. To his credit, he'd opened the door for me. Well, okay, it was cracked open a few inches, probably by accident. *That counted, right?*

Jason kept the radio off the entire way to the coffee shop in Big Timber, but not because he wanted to chat. We sat next to one another in complete silence as I watched his hand on the gear shifter. I pretended I was looking at my nails, but in actuality I was taking the opportunity to study him. His fingers were long and callused from years of working guitar strings. There was a scar that ran from the knuckle of his thumb down to his wrist. The paleness of it stuck out in comparison to his tan skin.

"Bike accident in college," he said, having caught me staring.

I raised my brows. "College boy, eh?"

"I went to the University of Montana for two years before I got signed to a record label. I finished the last two years up online."

An image of a younger Jason Monroe serenading girls on a college campus made me laugh.

"I bet the girls loved you on campus with that guitar and all," I said, trying to ease the quiet tension that seemed to follow us everywhere. I couldn't place its origins, but it probably had something to do with the fact that I had the urge to straddle his gear shifter.

His gaze hovered on the road in front of us as he answered, "Just one."

That's as far as he cared to elaborate, and for the rest of the ride we remained silent.

Suffice to say, Jason and I would not become lifelong soul mates.

• • •

When we rolled into Big Timber, I was expecting to see signs of life. Maybe a few kids in miniature cowboy and cowgirl attire, some old men sitting out front of a barber shop reading a newspaper, a woman selling jams on the corner of Main Street. *Isn't that what happens in small towns?* Instead, it was nearly as deserted as it'd been when Derek had driven me through it the first time.

Jason found a parking spot (there were about 100 available ones, unlike in LA) outside of a coffee shop that sat between a butcher shop and a shoe repair place. The awning was a little tattered, but the windows were painted with a giant coffee cup and scrolling cursive letters that spelled out Big Timber Brew.

"Looks like we've found the mecca of city life," I joked as we hopped out of the car. I fully expected a tumbleweed to roll by and take me out, it was *that* quiet.

Jason's mouth quirked up but he didn't offer a reply. I was starting to learn that everything about him was a challenge. He didn't offer laughter or words just to fill the silence. He laughed when he thought something was genuinely funny and he spoke only when he genuinely had something to say. My head would explode if I tried to do that. I'd talk to a brick wall if it meant I didn't have to sit in silence.

He held the door open for me and a little bell chimed over my head as I walked inside the dim shop. The smell of coffee hit me in a wave and I took a deep whiff. *Better than crack, I tell you.*

"What'll you have?" Jason asked, retrieving a wallet from his back pocket. Oh, Mr. Silent was going to pay for my coffee.

"I'll come up there and order," I said, mostly because I didn't want him to make fun of me for my complicated coffee choice.

A portly woman with a bob, the likes of which I hadn't seen since Rachel on Friends, was manning the counter. Her green apron accentuated all of her curves, but her wide lip-sticked smile was what caught my attention.

"Morning, Jason," she crooned, her eyes twinkling as she took him in behind me.

"Hey, Marcy," he replied with a tip of his head. If he'd been wearing a cowboy hat, I bet he would have tipped that forward, too. There was something about Jason that just seemed old-fashioned even if he wasn't that way on the outside. "This is Brook—"

"Brooklyn Heart!" Marcy exclaimed, putting her hands over her mouth. "I don't live under a rock, dummy!"

She rushed around the counter and came toward me with her arms outstretched. There was just enough time to give Jason a worried glance before her arms were around me. *Mmm, coffee.* Her hair smelled like a mocha Frappuccino and I liked it.

"You are the cutest thing I've ever seen," she said, releasing me and holding my hand up so I was forced to spin in a circle. So far, I was two for two when it came to Montana women. Maybe it was just Montana people in general. My LA fans were just as excited to see me, but the people I'd met in Montana just seemed more genuine, like they wanted to adopt me into their family and feed me Sunday dinner.

"We came in here to write for a little bit, if that's okay?" Jason asked behind me.

Marcy finally dropped my hand and glanced toward him. "Of course it is! Y'know, I've always told you I had some good ideas for a song."

I smiled at Jason, but he was eyeing the menu board behind the counter. The scruff on his chin looked trimmed, and if I could do it without him biting my hand off, I would have reached out to run my hand from his chiseled cheek bone down to his jawline. I knew it'd be a little scratchy at first, but I'd get used to it.

"Okay, what can I make for you?" Marcy asked, drawing my attention back to her.

I stared into her honey-brown eyes, and rattled off my drink of choice. "Small vanilla latte with almond milk and an extra shot of espresso." The moment I got it all out I heard Jason chuckle softly behind me and I suddenly felt self-conscious about my order. "Er, if you have it," I finished, wrapping my hand around my stomach to grip my other arm.

Marcy's smile fell slightly, "Um, we don't have almond milk. I can get you—"

"Coffee is good," I said with a smile, cursing myself for making Marcy feel less than adequate.

"Same for me," Jason said, setting a twenty on the counter when Marcy turned to fill two coffee mugs with a dark brew.

She slid the mugs toward us on the counter and tried to give Jason his change. He held up his hand in protest and then turned to find a seat before she could push the issue.

"Guess you take your coffee like you take everything else," Jason said. "Complicated as hell."

Was I supposed to feel bad for wanting almond milk? "Yeah, and you take yours black like the color of your soul," I said, genuinely annoyed that he thought so little of me. "Are you always this judgmental?"

Jason sat back in his chair, his jaw clenched tighter than usual. After another moment of contemplation, his eyes hit mine and he exhaled. "I'm sorry. That was rude of me. You can have whatever damn coffee you want," he said, looking down at his mug as soon as the words were out. Then he smirked, just slightly so that the left side of his mouth lifted in a sexy, private manner. "Besides, I like my coffee with cream and sugar."

I grunted and rolled my eyes, tossing a sweetener packet his way.

He didn't like being wrong and it didn't look like apologies were his favorite either. I already knew Jason was a proud man, but maybe he had a soft side, too.

"So, do you want to get started?"

We were the only people in the coffee shop, but we were sitting far enough from the counter that Marcy couldn't hear us over the soft music playing overhead. The table Jason had picked was old and wobbly. Kids had scratched their names on it over the years so that there were hundreds of phrases like: "Kaley loves Alex" and "Ava + Nick 4ever".

"My name is on one of these somewhere," Jason admitted, leaning forward to inspect the graffiti.

"Seriously?"

He nodded. "I've lived here my whole life. That's why I kept the ranch even though I stay primarily in LA now."

I'd assumed as much since Derek had said he'd met Jason in high school, but it was an interesting piece of information nonetheless.

"What does your graffiti say?" I asked, tracing a pink heart that was scribbled next to my coffee cup.

The edge of his mouth curled up. "I think it said something like 'Jason Monroe is a douche'."

If I'd had coffee in my mouth, I would have spit it out everywhere. Instead I just started cracking up.

"What? Really?"

He smiled wider. "I was an ass in high school. I thought I was too cool for this place and all the girls who lived here."

"Shocker," I said, reaching down for my coffee.

He chuckled and shook his head of the memories.

Feeling a shift in the conversation, I reached into my purse and pulled out a blank pad of paper and a pen.

"So, do you want to start brainstorming about the type of song we want to write?"

He contemplated the question for a moment, staring at the pad of paper.

"I guess so. It seems weird to think of it like that. I usually just write what's on my mind."

I nodded, "Same here. But since we're two heads and not one, we're going to have to communicate on things we normally wouldn't."

He nodded. "Okay, so we never decided the actual topic."

"I don't normally do that. I think of most songs like a fictional story, especially since there's hardly ever real song-worthy drama going on in my life," I said, staring out the window to watch a black sedan pull up in front of the coffee shop. Like a clown car, paparazzo after paparazzo hopped out with their giant lenses attached to cameras around their necks. I bristled at the sight of them. They were expected in LA, but the few days I'd been in Montana had apparently reset my bullshit meter because I was not happy to see them.

"Marcy?" Jason called with a sharp tone, glancing over to where she was standing behind the counter, eyeing the paparazzi.

"I didn't call them," she swore, her gaze sliding to me with a plea. Poor Marcy. I wouldn't blame her for their presence. They probably had drones or something by now.

The paparazzi weren't allowed to come into the establishment, but they could stand outside and pound the glass in an attempt to get Jason and me to look over at them.

"Fucking ridiculous," Jason said, downing the rest of his coffee in one swallow.

His anger surprised me, and my need to keep the peace surfaced immediately.

"It's okay. Let's try to get some ideas on paper and then we can head back to the ranch."

"Let's just go now," Jason said, scooting his chair back so that it screeched against the concrete floor.

I reached my hand out to cover his and he paused immediately, staring down at my fingers. "Please. I like it here and the paparazzi will always be there. Let's ignore them and just enjoy the moment."

He swallowed hard, and hesitated for a moment before pulling his hand back. "Okay."

"I'll get you some more coffee," I said with a smile, trying to ease the tension.

"You know what," Marcy began, "I can pull those front drapes down. That ought to help block their pictures, too." She walked to the front and untied black curtains from the front corners of the shop. "Usually I use them to block the afternoon sun, but this is perfect."

The curtains were almost sheer so that they didn't block the early morning sunlight, but it definitely did the trick. I'm sure their cameras could still get a quality photo of us, but at least I didn't have to see them.

Thirty minutes and two cups of coffee later, Jason and I had three words written down on the note pad: "love" and "in love". So, I guess, technically only two words, since love was repeated twice. And did "in" really even count? *Dear god, we were so screwed.*

I stood up to go refill my coffee even though I knew I'd start to get jittery if I kept downing cups.

"How's it going?" Marcy asked as she refilled my cup with a bright smile.

"Oh, pretty good," I lied, returning the smile.

I was about to reach for the cup when the bell over the door chimed and I heard an audible gasp.

"Oh, my dear god!" a voice yelled behind me.

Chapter Ten

When I turned around to face the coffee shop's door, there was a teenage boy standing there with his wide eyes pinned on me. Everything about him screamed "high school". He had all the classic signs: jeans that didn't quite fit, a loose polo shirt, spiky hair that was probably the biggest trend at the moment.

"This can't be real," he said, still in a daze.

Marcy laughed beside me and I was left standing there, trying to process the situation.

"Logan, calm down. She's just a person," Jason said, standing up to pat the boy's shoulder.

Still, the boy, Logan, couldn't process the fact that I was standing in front of him. I'd met super fans before. They were harmless (most of the time), but it was funny to see one in a random coffee shop in Montana. I felt like I should have started tap dancing or doing something that was actually worthy of his attention. I was just standing there, with my hand outstretched for my coffee cup.

Jason sighed and pushed the boy toward me. "Logan, this is Brooklyn Heart. Brooklyn, this is my cousin, Logan."

I reached my hand out toward him, but Logan didn't move to take it. Instead, he made a strangled sound that resembled a strangled animal.

"Hi there," I smiled, dropping my hand back to my side when it was clear that hand-on-hand contact would have given him an aneurysm.

Jason rolled his eyes at his cousin and nudged him forward. That finally seemed to do the trick because Logan blinked twice and smiled wide. Up close I could see the handsome features waiting to emerge. He had Jason's lips and cheek bones. I knew he'd grow into himself in the next few years, and if he was even half as handsome as his older cousin, Logan would be just fine.

Oh god, why am I calling Jason handsome? And why are we all just standing here looking at each other?

"Shouldn't you be in school right now?" Jason asked, glancing down at his watch.

Logan pulled his gaze off me for a moment to look at Jason. "I have a free period in the morning, and Mrs. O'Doyle lets me sneak out and come here if I promise to bring her back a cup of coffee." Then he looked back at me to clarify. "I work here after school," he said with a proud smile.

"Cool job," I nodded.

His eyes widened at my approval.

"Okay, Brook, let's get back to work," Jason said as he turned toward our table. I inwardly groaned at the idea of sitting back down to our ideas. Our juices weren't flowing and I felt like we should just call it a day and move on. There were only so many combinations you could make

105

with the three words we'd written down: in love love, love in love, love love in. None of those sounded like the next bestselling pop-song to me.

"You call her Brook? Are you guys good friends?" Logan asked, glancing back and forth between us.

"Logan, grab your coffee and go back to school," Jason said, promptly ending Logan's interrogation.

Logan gave me one last smile as he walked past our table toward the counter. I felt his eyes on me the entire time he was in the shop, but I didn't want him to realize it. At one point, while pretending to text, he tried to take a sneaky picture in the reflection of the chrome cappuccino machine. He cursed when the flash went off. I tried hard to stifle a laugh.

After the bell chimed, marking his exit, I glanced back to Jason. "Your cousin seems nice," I said.

"He is. He's a really good kid, and apparently your number one fan." He said that like it wasn't a good thing.

"Jealous, Monroe?" I goaded.

His brown gaze met mine. "Maybe a little," he said with a small smirk.

HOLD THE PRESSES, EVERYONE, JASON MONROE WAS KIDDING AROUND.

"Let's just go back to the house, my attention is shot," he said, scraping his chair against the concrete floors.

I agreed, and after thanking Marcy for allowing us a place to hangout, we pushed through the door. As soon as they saw us, the paparazzi swarmed forward. There had to have been a dozen of them, and as they rushed toward us, I stepped back against Jason. He wrapped a protective arm around my bicep and kept me against him.

"We'll pose for a few seconds and then you guys need to back up," Jason said, handling the paparazzi like a pro.

They just needed a good photo of us and then they'd be on their way. *Hopefully*.

"What is the relationship status between you two?" one of the men asked.

"Ten," Jason whispered in my ear, sending a shiver down my spine.

"Are you exclusive?" another chimed in and soon they were like a flock of squawking birds.

"Nine," he whispered again, this time a little closer, his breath hitting my ear. "Eight."

"Are the two of you collaborating?"

"Seven."

"How do you like Montana, Brooklyn?"

"Six," he counted.

"Are you here to meet Jason's family?"

"Oh, fuck it," he said, wrapping an arm around me and pushing us through the crowd of photographers so that he could open his passenger door for me. As quickly as possible, I slid into the car. He rounded the front of it and then locked us inside as he pulled away from the coffee shop.

"I'd tell you I'm sorry, but I know it's probably like that for you all the time in LA," Jason said, giving me a sidelong glance.

I shrugged. "It's worse because we're together and they have no clue what we're doing. They think we're dating."

Jason laughed and I shifted my gaze to look out the window. *Was is that insane to think we were a couple?*

I guess so.

We pulled up in front of his house, he killed the engine, and then he turned toward me.

"I think I know why we're having a hard time getting started on the song," he said, rubbing the stubble on his chin.

"Oh?" I asked.

"Yeah, I think we need to get to know each other a little bit better," he began.

"I guess that makes sense," I replied, trying to quell the excitement firing up inside of me. You'd think he'd just told me he thought I was prettiest girl in the world with the way my body was reacting. *Take a chill-pill, heart.*

"I have some work to finish up this afternoon, but if you're up for it we can go on a ride tomorrow morning."

That sounded like an invitation for a date, but I knew better. "A horseback ride?"

He smiled, "Yeah."

"I can't believe you'd want to go horseback riding with me. I didn't even think you liked me all that much," I admitted.

He shrugged and stared out through the front windshield. "Truthfully, I just need to take Jasper out on the trails, get him accustomed to the terrain out there."

Liar. Liar. Fucking pants on fire. Okay, maybe that's not how that rhyme went, but whatever. I wouldn't call him out on his assholery this time.

"Lovely. Well enjoy your afternoon," I said, hopping out of his Jeep. I didn't bother waiting to see if he'd respond. He'd just turned a perfectly good morning sour with his inability to function as a normal human being. Even if he did want to go horseback riding with me, he'd never admit it. Gah! The man was grueling. I just wanted to shake him and learn all of his stupid dark secrets. *I bet they weren't even all that good, either.*

I stormed through the front door, grunting a hello to LuAnn who was sitting at the kitchen counter. With enough attitude to warn away any bear within fifty miles, I pulled out the ingredients for a sandwich, practically ripping the lettuce to shreds as I positioned it on top of the turkey.

"That poor condiment never did anything to you," LuAnne joked as she watched me stabbing my knife into the jar of mayonnaise.

"The mayo is substituting as the person I'd like to be stabbing," I muttered, recapping the jar and stuffing everything back into the refrigerator.

Jason walked into the kitchen as I grabbed my plate. I glanced at him over my shoulder, watching him drag his hand through his hair. He looked tense, like a coiled wire ready to spring open, but I brushed past him with my plate before he could speak and make the situation worse.

After taking lunch up to my room so that I wouldn't have to talk to Jason while I ate, I dialed Cammie's number.

"Whattup, cutie?" she asked after picking up. And just like that, I was in a better mood. The girl was better than Buddha.

"I can't tell you how happy I am to hear your voice," I admitted, falling back onto my bed and letting the blankets envelope me.

"Ew, easy on the cling. What's going on?" she asked.

"Oh nothing, just everything sucks and Jason is a dickhead. What's new?"

She laughed. "Hold on, let me step out of the studio so my classmates don't overhear me and try to sell the story to the tabloids."

"Didn't they just hear you say that?" I asked.

The distinct sound of a door opening and closing was followed by the sound of traffic in the background. "No. I sit next to a foreign-exchange student that doesn't speak English. She can design a house in like ten seconds flat though, so whatever."

"Maybe she just pretends to not speak English so that she doesn't have to talk to you all day," I quipped.

"Wow, someone ordered spicy mustard on their gluten-free panini today. Or is the 'tude because Jason has your vayjayjay worked up?"

"Oh my god, I can't handle your slang. Vayjayjay sounds like a bad rapper name."

Cammie cracked up. "Objection sustained."

"How's your project going?"

"Same ol' same ol'. I'm counting down the days until I get to come to see you. I have seven days until I present my final project and then I get to come stay with you for three days. Montana better call in the National Guard because we're going to whore it up big time."

I covered my eyes and smiled. "Oy vey."

"So have you been collecting boys for me to hang out with while I'm in town?"

I ran through the mental checklist of people I'd met in Montana so far. "Well you can take your pick between Jason the rockstar assface, Derek the cute, but cliché cowboy, or Logan, Jason's cousin who isn't a day over fifteen."

"Sounds like you're only a construction worker and a Native American short of a Village People cover band," she said.

I laughed. "The real gem, though, is LuAnne. She runs the place while Jason is gone and I've had more fun with her than anyone else so far. Last night we finished off a bottle of wine and she showed me her tramp stamp of a black stallion." I couldn't quite figure LuAnn out. She seemed so proper, and then out of nowhere she'd whip out the wine and talk about her glory days. I'd decided she'd been quite the flower child.

"Wow. So you've gotten farther with the housekeeper than you have with People's sexiest man alive 2013?"

"I'd totally swap teams for LuAnne. The woman would make me garlic mashed potatoes for every meal."

"Oh damn, I'd swap teams for some mashed potatoes right now, too. But, seriously, are we going to get to the pertinent info here or are you just going to distract me while I should be busting my ass in the studio?"

I laughed, "You make it sound much worse than it probably is."

"Last night half of us slept at our desks. I woke up with an indentation of my keyboard on my face and my nose had typed 149 pages of m's."

"Cammie, that's not right! Give me the number to your advisor so I can call and yell at them."

She groaned. "Yeah, no thanks, psycho. It's part of the system. Everyone has to go through it and we end up stronger architects in the end. Like Spartan warriors."

"Really? Or do you just end up with back problems and poor hygiene habits?"

"Brooklyn Josephina Heart, enough. Tell me what's bothering you or I'm hanging up."

Josephina was not my middle name.

I finally caved and filled her in on the last few days of Jason nonsense. I told her all about the failed attempts at writing and his comment in the Jeep on the way home.

"So you guys are going to go horseback riding tomorrow, yes?" she clarified.

"Yup. To get to know each other."

"What's your end goal there?" she asked.

"Umm, for him to realize that I'm not a terrible person and maybe for him to actually like me," I admitted. *Were those outrageous goals?* No.

"My advice is to wear some tight riding pants and make sure he gets an eyeful of dat ass."

"Yeahhhh," I drawled playfully. "I'm not sure that advice aligns with my end goals."

"Okay, yeah, you're right. Instead you should douse yourself in water while you're riding, but make sure you're wearing a killer bra and a white shirt."

"Still not correct."

"Oh, right. Okay, I think you should pretend like you can't get up onto the horse on your own so that he has to give you a boost... and maybe his hand slips... and maybe... you don't have underwear on..."

"Cameron!" I yelled into the phone, forcing her to pause.

She cracked up in response to my reaction, but I'd had enough of my little sister for one day.

"Oddly enough, I don't miss you anymore," I joked.

"Lies. I'm your best friend. Mom and Dad would be proud," she said lightheartedly. I smiled at her confidence. We used to not talk about our parents very often. After the car accident eight years ago, we'd both ventured through dark periods in our lives, dealing with grief in our own ways. Cammie had gone through a wild phase, and I'd focused on my music. For a while, I wasn't sure Cammie would surface from her depression. For two years, I hadn't said my parents' names for fear that it would awaken those sad feelings again.

"You're right. They would be. Good luck in the studio and please don't sleep there again."

"I won't. Good luck with Jason and definitely *do sleep there*. Haha, did you see what I just did?"

She laughed all the way up until I hung up on her.

R.S. Grey

Chapter Eleven

I decided to take part of Cammie's advice while getting dressed the next morning. Obviously, I didn't wear riding crops because I didn't just have those lying around, but I opted for a tight pair of yoga pants. I noticed Derek checking out my ass on my way to the kitchen for breakfast so I knew they'd do the trick.

I sat down at the kitchen table and LuAnne placed a cup of granola and yogurt in front of me. I smiled up at her.

"Eat up. I heard you're going on a ride this morning," she said, patting my shoulders before heading back to flip over the pound of bacon sitting in the frying pan. I hadn't quite figured out how Derek could survive on his all-bacon-all-the-time diet.

"You goin' on a ride?" Derek asked as he poured himself a cup of coffee.

"Yeah, Jason is taking me out after breakfast."

Derek nodded. I opened my mouth to continue, but I didn't get the chance to expand on the subject because I

114

saw Jason walking down the stairs out of the corner of my eye. He was freshly showered, his damp hair a shade darker than usual. He was wearing worn jeans that I hadn't seen him in before, a white button-up, and an army green Patagonia down-vest that looked like it'd keep him warm during our ride.

When LuAnne cleared her throat, I realized I'd been watching him with my spoon hovering half-way to my mouth while drips of yogurt were spilled over onto the table in front of me.

"You okay there, Brook?" LuAnne asked me with a teasing grin.

I didn't bother answering her, I threw her an indifferent shrug and for the next ten minutes I focused on my yogurt like it was the most interesting thing in the world. Which wasn't easy considering Jason sat directly across from me after he'd grabbed his breakfast. I could feel his leg against mine under the table and I had to fight the urge to move mine away. I didn't want him to think I cared that he was touching me. But I really, really cared.

"That must be some good yogurt," Jason joked, forcing me to look up at him. I should have staved off because when I met his gaze there was no denying my interest. Hello, heartbeat, *yes*, I know you're pounding extra fast because Jason is freshly showered and I can smell his body wash and his hair is drying in this perfect way that makes me want to reach over the table and lick him.

Oh, right, he'd spoken to me.

"Huh?" I asked like a weirdo.

He smiled and shook his head. "You were just concentrating pretty hard on that bite."

Recover. Don't let him know that you're basically in love with him.

"Ah, yeah. I was probably just thinking about how I'd rather have some of your pancakes instead of this." Nice, Brooklyn. That sounded at least *half*-true.

He nodded and went back to his breakfast, but right before he was finished he offered me his last bite on his fork. Oh my god. Jason = hot. Jason feeding me pancakes = nuclear. I forced my body to react so I could lean forward and take the bite off his fork. I didn't bother trying to be seductive with it. I would have probably poked the fork in my eye or something.

"Ready to go?" he asked after I'd sat in silence for a few minutes, my plate and bowl empty in front of me.

"Yup," I said with an overly enthusiastic smile.

He tucked his head in agreement and then sauntered down the hallway, assuming I'd just follow after him like a puppy.

LuAnne pursed her lips to keep from laughing when I shot her a knowing glance.

"I think that's your cue," she joked.

"Wish me luck. Maybe send out a search party in a few hours if we aren't back," I said, only half joking. Seriously, there was about a 50% chance that I would annoy Jason enough to where he'd just leave me in the woods to fend for myself. I'd have to figure out how to drink my own pee and stuff. Nope. No, thank you. I'd rather be eaten by a leopard. Wait, we're in Montana... so a mountain leopard? *Whatever, something with sharp teeth.*

"Coming?" Jason asked as he opened one of the closets in the hallway. He reached in and retrieved a vest that matched the one he was wearing, only it was dark brown instead of green. "I don't want you complaining about being cold the whole time we're out there."

I huffed. "I think somewhere in there you were trying to be sweet, but then you ruined it with your mouth."

A private smile played on his lips. "That's the first time I've been told that my mouth ruined something."

"Oh my god, did you seriously just say that?" I asked as he opened the vest so that I could spin around and slip my arms through the holes.

He looked back at me with an arched brow as he pulled open the front door. "It's the truth."

I puffed out a breath of air as I sauntered past him. *Of course it is.*

In brooding silence (because that's really the only way Jason did things), we made our way toward the stable to get the horses ready. Jason strapped on the saddles for each of us and I took a few minutes to get to know Dotty. I didn't know much about horses, but if this girl was about to haul my ass through the forest, I figured she at least deserved a few pats before we got started.

"You're cute, Dotty," I told her, rubbing my palm down her long neck. "Maybe when we get back, I'll braid your mane."

Jason grunted across the stable. When he turned to grab something off the wall, I stuck my tongue out at him.

"Shh, don't tell," I whispered to Dotty, and in response she stomped her hoof. *Look at us, we were already besties.*

"When did you last ride?" Jason asked, walking toward me with Jasper in tow. The dark horse was at least a few inches taller than Dotty, and he filled out those inches in a way that made me glad I wasn't going to be riding him. When he puffed air out of his snout, I took two steps back just in case I looked like a juicy apple or a big ol' sugar cube.

"Umm, let's say I was wearing a training bra and braces at the time."

Jason frowned. "Alright, well we'll take it slow out on the trail. Dotty shouldn't give you too much trouble."

I patted Dotty. "Nah, she and I have an understanding."

"Is that right?" he asked, arching a dark brow and taking two more steps toward me.

I nodded with a smug smile. "Yup. She's on Team Brooklyn now."

He chuckled lightly. "I didn't realize we were on teams."

"Yeah, well, I guess that means I'm already winning." Dotty snorted and stomped her foot again. She was probably ready to get on the trail, but I took it to mean she was definitely Team Brooklyn.

"Let's walk them out and then I'll help you get up."

Despite my best efforts, I still blushed thinking about my conversation with Cammie the night before. I was *not* going to let Jason get to third base on the side of a horse. I mean maybe on the back of a horse... No. *No base running during this horse ride.*

Once we stepped out of the stable, I inhaled a breath of fresh air and took in the scenery before me. A short mountain range spanned the horizon on all sides, but the base was hidden behind rows and rows of pine trees. A gravel path led from the stable out into the woods, but only the first few yards were visible from where I stood. A blast of wind brought with it a chill and the sharp smell of pine. I wrapped Jason's vest tighter around me. It was too big, but

The Duet

it smelled like him, *or so I assumed.* It had a spiced, captivating scent.

"Okay, are you ready?" he asked. He'd tied Jasper to a post so he could come help me mount Dotty.

Before I could answer, his hands were at my hips, sliding beneath the vest. A thin layer of black spandex separated his warm palms from my panties and I knew without a doubt he could feel my thong. *Why hadn't I just gone commando?* Oh right, because Cammie had scarred me last night.

"Yeah, okay. Sure, let me just—" I was rambling, but I had no clue how to mount a horse. I'd used a step-ladder when I was younger.

"Hold onto the horn of the saddle and I'll lift you up."

I nodded and then he counted down to one. Our timing was off though, and I freaked out when he lifted me off the ground. He ended up placing me in the saddle on my stomach with my chest on one side of Dotty's body, and my legs hanging off the other side.

"You're supposed to lift your leg up and straddle her," Jason said as if I didn't actually know that.

"Oh, really? I thought everyone rode horses with their asses in the air."

"Well, technically it's in my face," Jason corrected with a tad too much amusement for my taste.

"Oh my god, stop looking at my ass and back up so I can swing myself around."

The jerk just laughed as I performed the awkward task of adjusting my body on top of Dotty. I decided that was probably the moment when Jason finally thought, *"Yeah, I will never be dating this psycho."*

"Sheesh, sorry about that girl," I said to Dotty when I was finally sitting up like a normal person. Once I was positioned correctly, it wasn't so bad. My feet reached the stirrups okay. I slid my sneakers into the straps, and after Jason adjusted a few things on my saddle, we were ready to go.

Jason hopped up onto Jasper easily, which ruined the jokes I'd started to stockpile about him failing. *I should have known Jason Monroe didn't fail at anything.*

After a few instructions about how to use my heels to communicate with Dotty so she'd know if I wanted her to speed up or slow down, we were off on the trail, winding through the woods. The gravel path gave way to dirt and the smell of pine grew even stronger.

"This is so beautiful. I'd come out here every day if I could," I said as I dipped my head low to avoid colliding with a tree branch coming up on our left.

"Glad you like it," Jason said, turning to peer at me over his shoulder.

Jasper and Dotty carried us across a shallow creek and then we turned down a new trail that was even thinner and less cleared out than the one before. Every few feet I had to dip my head to duck under a branch, but it was too fun to turn back.

"So were you planning on getting to know me or did you just want to lead me out into the wilderness for fun?"

He laughed, "Isn't this part of getting to know someone?"

I rolled my eyes. "No. We have to actually make an effort. How about we each get to ask five questions or something."

"I'd rather just let it come naturally," he replied, not bothering to turn around.

"Well, sitting here in silence isn't really going to help us."

He groaned. "Fine. Ask away."

I decided there was no point in shooting the shit. This ride wouldn't last all day and if there was any hope for us, we had to break down a few walls – not with a hammer, but with a wrecking ball. (Sorry to put the image of Miley in your head.)

"What's your deepest, darkest secret?" I asked.

Jason threw his head back and laughed, clutching his stomach with his hand. I'd never seen him so relaxed. I couldn't help the smile that spread across my face, until I realized that he was about to get smacked in the head if he didn't push an upcoming branch out of the way.

"Jason!" I yelled, but alas it was too late. He sat up at the precise moment when he was supposed to dip beneath the branch. He got a pine branch smack-dab in the forehead and I couldn't do anything other than howl with laughter. I couldn't even stop long enough to muster speech.

"You good back there?" Jason mocked, rubbing the spot on his forehead that would no doubt have a red welt in a few minutes. Aw, man. *Now I kind of feel bad.*

I forced myself to get it together.

"Hold on, let me take a look and see how bad it is," I said, pulling Dotty up alongside Jasper on the path. The horses slowed to a stop as I reached out to pull Jason's hand away from his forehead.

"Like I'm going to trust you. I'd be bleeding down my face and you'd still be laughing," he said with a sense of teasing.

His words made my stomach twist with guilt. "Oh my gosh, I'm sorry. I swear. You can trust me," I said, holding his arm down with both of mine so I could get a good look. That was a mistake. There were pine needles stuck to his forehead, like twenty of them haphazardly displayed above his eyebrows.

I couldn't stop laughing for a solid five minutes.

"I'm," laugh, "so," laugh, "sorry."

Jason grinned and shook his head at me before reaching behind him to grab a handful of pine needles from the tree.

"Hey!" I tried to duck out of the way as he threw them, but most of them found their way down my top and into my hair.

"That's a good look for you," he joked.

I shot him an evil glare as I shook out my shirt. "Are we even now?"

He smirked. "Not even close. And now it's my turn to ask a question since you wasted yours." He tapped his heel against Jasper's side so that the horse started trotting down the trail again. Dotty and I were left in the dust as I tried to get pine needles out of my bra.

For the next few minutes we rode in silence. I wasn't sure if he was trying to come up with a good question or just ignoring me. With him, it could have easily been either. Then finally, he turned back to glance at me.

"Do you write your own songs or does the label hire a song writer for you?" he asked with a serious tone, his dark eyes staring straight into mine.

WHAT?

I jerked my head back as the muscles in my neck stiffened. "Are you kidding me?"

His eyes widened in reaction to my anger.

"Of course I write my own songs," I responded through clenched teeth. "You can look that up yourself."

He shook his head, "I wanted to know the truth, not what the Internet had to say."

I narrowed my eyes on him and enunciated every word as sharply as possible. "I write every single one of my songs. They're *my* songs."

It wasn't out of the norm for singers to have writers feeding them music. Some bands still produced their own songs or used a mix of original content. I'd always wanted to stay true to myself. I wanted to get up on stage and perform my lyrics, my melodies, for my fans. And for Jason to ask that question, in a way in which he *clearly* thought he had me figured out— it absolutely boiled my blood.

I had the sudden urge to thump my heel into Dotty's side so she'd take off in a gallop and we could leave Jason behind, but I wasn't sure how strong of a rider I was yet. So instead, I took a few calming breaths and tried to forget about it. For the length of my entire career, I've had people question my authenticity. I should have had a thicker skin about it, but it'd always be a soft spot. Especially when people like Jason Monroe brought it back up.

I knew Jason wanted to apologize, to explain himself. He kept peering back at me with solemn eyes, but I wasn't going to let him. Let the asshole stew for a bit.

Finally, he cleared his throat.

"I shouldn't have suggested that you don't write your own songs. I'm sorry."

I grunted, unable to loosen the grip on my annoyance with him. But when the silence became too much to handle, I caved.

"Longest time you've gone without sex?" I asked, trying to break the tension.

He might have passed over that question ten minutes earlier, but he knew he had some ground to make up with me.

He only hesitated for a moment before replying. "Two months, maybe a little bit more. I've never really counted. You?"

I swallowed. Did Brazilian model count? *Technically.* "A year," I answered honestly.

"Seriously?"

"Are you using up one of your questions?" I asked with a tilt of my head.

He laughed and shook his head.

"Have you ever been broken up with?" Jason asked.

I smiled down at my saddle. You had to actually be in a relationship to go through a break-up. I decided he didn't need to know the gritty details, so technically, I told the truth when I replied, "No."

"Have you?" I asked as an afterthought.

I almost didn't hear his reply, "Once."

We came to a clearing in the forest where the grass had overtaken the trees for a few yards. There was a small pond in the center with water so clear that I knew it'd come from a spring. We hopped off the horses and let them rest and get a drink for a few minutes. I sat back on the grass, stuffing my hands into the pockets of my borrowed vest.

"Oh, I have a good one!" I exclaimed, picking up a pinecone and tossing it across the clearing.

He nodded for me to go ahead.

"Would you rather experience love firsthand or write about fictional love in your songs?"

His eyebrows furrowed and then released. "Those are my two options? I either live it or write about it?"

I smiled. "Yup."

I could feel his gaze on me, his jaw tight, and his arms crossed. I knew if I turned to look at him, our eyes would meet and I'd see more of Jason Monroe than I ever had

124

before. But I didn't turn. I kept my eyes trained on the water.

A moment later, he answered with a quiet, hard tone. "Write about it."

My mouth fell open. "Are you serious?"

"The written word will be my life's mistress," he answered with a mocking tone.

"Oh, please," I answered, rolling my eyes and leaning back onto my elbows in the grass. "You sound like a pretentious ass."

He winked. "What about you?"

Obviously, it was a no brainer. Up until that point, I'd never known the real thing. "I'd want to live it."

"You'd give up performing forever?" he asked, our gazes locking as he stared down at me.

"Of course. Why write about something you'll never experience?"

Chapter Twelve

Holy cow, was my vajayjay (as Cammie liked to call it) sore after riding Dotty all day. I never knew that area could be so sore from non-sex related activities, but note to self: put some bubble wrap down there next time.

I sat in the bathtub for a solid hour after we got back, washing the smell of pine, sweat, and horse out of my hair and off my body. The more I relaxed, the less I ever wanted to leave. I'd just live in the bathtub forever and LuAnne could sneak me in food. Unfortunately, just as my fingers really started to prune over, my phone started vibrating on the tile next to the tub. In spite of my better judgment, I peered over the ledge to see Summer's purple hair and smiling face staring up at me. She'd programmed a picture of herself holding up a sign that said, "answer this call!!!!" when she'd first started working for me, and now the image was taunting me.

I groaned and laid back against the back of the tub. There was no way I was talking to Summer while I was taking a bath. I made a mental note to call her back after I finished and then I closed my eyes as the jasmine bath salts started to fade. I either had to get out or add more.

Obviously, I was going to add more.

Except, I never got the chance.

The second I opened my eyes, I saw a big, black spider hanging directly above me on the ceiling and before I could process how big it was, I let out a guttural scream. A shudder ran down my spine as I pressed against the back of the tub, splashing nearly half of the water over the sides. Footsteps pounded in the hallway and then the door to the bathroom burst open.

I blinked rapidly to find Jason standing in the doorway, breathing hard and staring at me like he was seeing a ghost.

"What the hell is wrong?" he asked, not even bothering to avert his eyes. To his credit, with my knees bent to my chest, he wasn't actually seeing anything.

I couldn't look back up to the spider. I pointed to the ceiling and squeezed my eyes closed.

"Kill it, please. Kill it before it drops in the tub with me. I'm serious. I am not a spider person. I don't even like Spider-Man, not even when Toby Maguire played him. He almost made it worse."

The moment I stopped rambling, I realized Jason was laughing, but not just light giggles. No, he was bent forward and wiping his eyes he was laughing so hard. I peered back up at the ceiling and realized that my big, fat spider was actually really small— *embarrassingly* small.

I sighed. "Yeah, okay, you can stop laughing now. It was surprising, and to my credit it looked a *lot* bigger at first."

He stood back up and tried to wipe the smile from his face.

"Do you still want me to kill it?" he asked, taking a step forward as he stared up to ceiling.

"Wait! It's wet!" I yelled, watching in slow motion as Jason stepped forward and slipped into the pool of water I'd splashed out of the tub. He went from standing and staring at the ceiling to crumbling back against the floor, landing with a thud on his back. I held my hand over my mouth as I bolted up to see if he was okay. I scanned his body, looking for blood, but, luckily, I think his shapely *derriere* caught most of his fall.

"Are you okay?" I asked, parting my hands over my mouth so that he could hear me.

"Peachy," he groaned, staying on the ground. "But just so you know, your spider friend just fell into the bath."

I screamed and jumped out of the tub as fast as I could. I didn't care if Jason could see *everything*. I'd flash a whole subway if it meant I didn't have to swim with spiders. I hopped over Jason as quickly as I could, careful not to slip in the same puddles that he had. I reached for the robe behind the door and tugged it around myself, tying the belt in one smooth gesture.

"Just so you know, I'm not even mad about falling anymore because I just got the best view of my entire life," he explained with a smug grin on his face. I would have helped him up, but that little comment had earned him about ten extra hours in the doghouse.

"Erase it from your memory. You were not given permission to check out my goods."

"But they were oh so good," he said, dropping his hand over his heart like he was wounded. The content smile on his lips told me he was far from it. I kicked him in the side playfully, and then reached down so he could grab onto my hand and stand up.

"Thanks for coming in to rescue me," I said, my cheeks red with residual embarrassment.

"It was my pleasure, but just so you know, you're now the boy who cried wolf. I'm not going to come running in next time you scream while you're in the bath," he swore, shaking his head.

"That's fine. I hope you got a good look because you're never going to see this ass ever again," I joked.

Jason's amused smirk turned into something a little more dangerous. He stepped forward and gripped my robe, just below my hips, and bent down so his mouth hovered over mine.

"No worries, Sweet Cheeks. I've been told I have quite the memory," he said as I held my breath. He left me there in limbo as I waited for him to tear through the wall between us. It was pure torture, like someone dangling an ice cream cone in front of your mouth when you're trying to stave off a sweet tooth.

He leaned forward two more inches, his chest pressing against mine, and then he stole a kiss. His free hand gripped my wet hair, tugging me closer. It was quick, over before it even began. But his supple lips were on mine, and for one brief second I felt like I was drowning in him.

When he pulled back, I fluttered my eyes open and actively fought off a moan. Without a word, he let go of me and exited my bathroom like he was the King of Siam. I would have said something, formed a retort to his earlier teasing, but the mood had already shifted. He was like an unpredictable summer storm. One minute he hated me, one minute he wanted to kiss me. And as he fled from the room, I assumed his pendulum was already swinging away from me once again.

I stayed where I was, running my finger back and forth across my bottom lip. It'd been a *really, really* good first kiss. To put it in perspective, any kisses that I'd had before *that kiss* were just a waste of facial muscles. I should have been saving up all my energy for Jason Monroe because I had a feeling I was going to need it.

I stood there fanning myself for a solid ten minutes before I realized that Mr. Spidey could still be somewhere in the bathroom. *Nope. Nope.* I rushed out and closed the door. Guess I'll just never go into that room again.

Problem solved.

• • •

Thirty minutes later, after I'd called Summer back and parts of my dignity were finally seeping back in, I padded down the stairs in search of food. My call with Summer wasn't long, but she'd informed me that the next day a car would arrive at 8:00 A.M. sharp to drive me to Billings, Montana. The meetings and photo shoots I'd been avoiding while in Montana had finally caught up to me, and I was booked solid for two days. There was a photo shoot for a fragrance line and a swimsuit company wanted initial designs approved for the "Brooklyn Heart Collection." It was only two days, but the thought of leaving the ranch, of leaving Jason, didn't sit well with me.

I trotted down the rest of the stairs, trying to shake the confusing feelings playing out in my head. Maybe I was just hungry. That was usually the culprit to any bad mood.

"Hey, Brooklyn," Derek called out as soon as my feet hit the bottom stair. He was standing in the doorway of the kitchen with a playful smile. His tight t-shirt was dirty from work and his hair was patted down at an awkward angle from being stuffed under a cowboy hat all day. In all, he was still pretty cute.

"I heard you're quite the screamer," he said with a cheeky smile. My gaze darted to where Jason was sitting behind him at the table. His dark hair concealed his eyes as he stared down at his phone, and even though he wasn't contributing, his wicked smile told me he was enjoying Derek's teasing all the same.

Before I could reply, LuAnne twisted away from the stove with her dishtowel to smack Derek on the back of the head. The loud clap of the towel rang out in the kitchen and Derek leaned forward to get out of her reach.

"Brook, don't you worry about these two boys. They never grow up, I swear," she said, giving me a 'what are we going to do' shrug as I stepped past the doorway.

"Which is exactly why I'm glad I'm headed to Billings for two days," I announced, giving Derek a playful glare. *Maybe I was actually happy to get a break.*

Derek's bottom lip stuck out like a five-year-old. "Really?"

I nodded. "Yeah, my assistant has me booked with meetings for a solid 48 hours."

Without a word, Jason scooted his chair back so that the wooden legs scraped against the hardwood. All three of us turned to stare at him, but he didn't offer any response. Instead, he went to the fridge and pulled out a bottle of beer from the bottom shelf.

"Want one, Derek?" he asked, already reaching for a second bottle.

"Sure thing," he replied.

"Oh, no thank you. I'm fine," I teased, resting my hip on the kitchen island and pretending to not check him out as he bent down again, retrieving a third bottle.

When he handed it over to me after popping the top off, his brown eyes met mine. "My apologies. Didn't figure you for a beer fan, Princess."

"Aw, he calls her princess," LuAnne said, peering over at us from the stove.

Derek and Jason chuckled while I rolled my eyes.

"It's not a term of endearment, let me assure you," I answered.

Jason held up his hands in defense. "Who said it wasn't?"

Before I could answer, the doorbell rang. I nearly jumped at the noise, considering I hadn't heard it ring in all the days I'd stayed there.

"Who's that?" I asked as Jason turned to answer it.

"It's Logan, and he's just in time for dinner," LuAnne said. I watched her moving around the kitchen. In one quick motion she took a pot of boiling pasta off the stove and dumped it into a strainer in the sink. Meanwhile, Jason opened the front door for his teenage cousin who looked just as shell-shocked as he had been at the coffee shop the day before.

"Is she here?" he asked Jason as he stepped through the threshold, probably not intending for his voice to carry through the house as well as it did.

Jason patted his back, "Hello to you, too, cuz."

I smiled, watching them approach. When Logan saw me standing in the kitchen, his eyes traveled over my loose cotton dress, down to the beer in my hand, and back up to my face in a matter of seconds.

"Hi Logan," I offered with a smile, hoping to ease his nerves.

It didn't work. His eyes widened when I said his name and then he took two awkward steps forward.

"I brought you these," he said, skating over a formal greeting in an attempt to shove whatever it was he was holding into my hand.

When I glanced down at the bag I saw the Big Timber Brew logo.

"They're chocolate-covered coffee beans," he explained.

"Oh!" I flipped the bag over to get a better look at the candy. "I love these, thank you, Logan." I stepped forward to give him a quick hug and my eyes met Jason's over Logan's shoulder. He tipped his beer to me with a thankful smile before he took a long sip.

"Who's hungry!?" LuAnne hollered as I stepped out of Logan's embrace.

I overheard Logan whisper, "Oh my god, my shirt smells like her now," as I went to take my seat at the table.

Logan sat across from me, anxiously fidgeting in his seat, and Jason sat beside me, casually resting his hand on the back of my chair in a way that completely confused me. LuAnne set out a big bowl of spaghetti with a fresh salad and breadsticks. The food smelled divine, and I even let myself enjoy the pasta knowing full well my trainer would kick my ass for it in the morning. He'd taken to calling me on Skype so we could continue our sessions as usual while I was in Montana. At first, I contemplated holding up a stick-figure of myself working out to fool him, but then I'd go back to LA ten pounds heavier and he'd only kick my ass more. *The life of a public figure.* Every time I glanced at a rag magazine while I waited in line at the grocery store (yes, celebrities do that, too) they'd have my picture next to a bold statement: "Too thin?", "Too Fat?", or my personal favorite, "Seriously, does she ever stop eating?"

"So the coffee beans were kind of an attempt at buttering you up," Logan said, breaking me out of my bread-filled daze.

"Were they now?" I asked.

Logan's gaze darted to Jason, and then back to me. "I have this request and I'm sure that you'll be too busy or whatever, but I thought I'd ask because I'd be an idiot not to ask. Every guy in school would be so jealous if you actually said yes."

His ramblings were piquing my interest.

"Said yes to what?" I asked with a tilt of my head.

Logan took a deep breath. "Would you go to prom with me?"

Derek's howling laughter filled the kitchen until I heard an audible kick beneath the table. Jason's foot had undoubtedly left a nice indention on his shin.

"Prom?" I asked, trying to clarify his question in my mind.

He smiled wider. "Yup."

I hadn't attended my senior prom. At the time, I was dating an older guy and he didn't want to go, so I'd skipped it and we'd had sex in the back of his car. It wasn't so bad; I mean I got some serious carpet burn on my back from his shitty seats. At the end of the night, after he'd dropped me back off at home, I'd felt a pang of regret about not going to prom for at least a little while. Especially since, if I recall correctly, that car sex had lasted all of two minutes in total.

When Logan cleared his throat, I realized I needed to answer.

"Logan, I'd love to," I began, but he cut me off with a fist pump and a "Yes!" before I could continue. "I just have to check my schedule with my assistant, and also, I think Jason should come with us, too."

Yes, that second part was a nice touch.

Jason's brows nearly shot to the ceiling when I threw him into the mix, so I continued. "I'm sure there's a girl in your school who would love to go to prom with Jason. So let's figure that out. Until then, why don't you give me the date and I'll coordinate everything with Summer."

Logan probably didn't hear a single word I said after "I'd love to" because his eyes were glazed over and his smile was so wide it almost split his face in two.

"Would you do that, Jason?" Logan asked with an air of hope.

Jason wiped his mouth with the napkin in his lap, stalling for time, but when he saw the joy on his cousin's face, he nodded, just one. "Yeah. Okay."

I hadn't realized I'd been holding my breath until I exhaled with his reply. *Why did it feel like I was in high school and I'd just asked Jason to my senior prom?*

Jason's hand slid onto my leg beneath the table and he squeezed once, just above my knee. I glanced over, appreciating his secret smile.

"I think Brooklyn and I will have fun reliving our high school years," he spoke as his thumb slid over the sensitive skin on the inside of my knee.

In true eighteen-year-old girl form, my next thoughts went something like this:

OH MY GOD, I NEED A DRESS!
Is he going to take my virginity?
Oh wait...

Chapter Thirteen

The next morning a car was waiting for me outside on the gravel drive just as Summer had promised. Everyone was already up and doing their own thing. I'd seen LuAnne briefly at breakfast, but I really wanted to see Jason once before I left. Two days without seeing him had started to feel like it would last a lifetime.

I lingered in the kitchen after breakfast. I took extra care to drag my bags downstairs as slowly as possible, but still he was nowhere to be found.

When the driver honked twice, I knew I didn't have any more time to linger. I sighed and opened the front door, resigned to the fact that I'd have to settle for seeing him when I returned in two days.

Just before I stepped out, I heard him say my name.

"Brook," he called behind me. I spun around to see him standing in the doorway of the kitchen with gray pajama pants slung low on his hips. He'd forgone a t-shirt and shoes and his hair was deliciously mussed up from sleep.

He didn't make a move to walk toward me, but he held his cup of coffee up in a silent salute. I returned it with a small bow, enjoying the low chuckle it warranted from him.

"Come back safe," he said, turning back toward the kitchen. That image of him standing in the doorway seared into my memory as I closed the heavy front door behind me.

• • •

"Are you almost done in there?" Summer called from the other side of the bathroom door. I was at my first photo shoot of the day, one that I hadn't known about until I was handed a tiny piece of string they thought could pass as a bathing suit.

I groaned. "Yes, but just so you know, I thought we were going over bikini designs today. I didn't know I'd be modeling them for the campaign."

With one last glance in the bathroom mirror, I pushed the door open to find Summer sitting on a chair in my private dressing room, flipping through papers on her lap. She was sporting a new eyebrow piercing and dark, shimmery eye shadow at 9:00 A.M. *My eyelids would have revolted.*

"I thought I told you about it," she said, not bothering to glance up from her work. "Oh, well, good thing you've waxed recently or they'd have some serious retouching," Summer said, pulling me back to the moment.

"Ew, god. It's not that. I gorged myself on Italian food last night and now I'm about to take photos that will be plastered on billboards and magazines," I complained, turning in a circle to inspect the bikini from every angle in the dressing room mirror. *Damn you, bread. Must you taste like heaven?*

There was a tap on the dressing room door and then a soft voice called out, "Brooklyn, we're ready for you!"

After the photo shoot I had meeting after meeting until eventually, I didn't care what things I was signing up for: you want me to host baby pageants? *Great.* You want me to hula dance while performing on The Voice? *Awesome.* It all became a blur and I relied on Summer to ensure that I wasn't signing myself up for anything too ridiculous.

When our last meeting concluded, it was a little after 6:00 P.M. and I was about to take a bite out of the car console I was so hungry.

"How about we freshen up at the hotel and then go out to dinner?" Summer asked from the across the backseat of the town car.

The idea of food had me instantly agreeing, and then for the one-hundredth time that day, I checked my phone for missed calls or texts. I had plenty, don't get me wrong. My agent, my manager, and Cammie usually kept my phone's voicemail perpetually full, but I was looking for something from a *particular* person. A person who had kissed me the night before and who had stood in the kitchen doorway that morning looking sexy as sin. I told myself that if I didn't actually think his name then I wasn't really obsessing about him.

Jason.

No!

Jason-Jason-JASON! *Jason-Jason-JASON!* My traitorous brain had paired his name with a Cha-cha-cha rhythm.

"So how has it been living with Jason Monroe?" Summer asked, turning her sharp eyes on me.

Had I just said his name out loud?

"Are you psychic?" I asked with an arched brow.

She laughed, "Not that I know of. Why?"

"I was just thinking about him," I answered, purposely staring at Summer's black nail polish. Her nails couldn't judge me like her eyes could.

Summer dropped her phone and gave me her full attention. "Yeah, you and half of the women in the western hemisphere. Go on."

I laughed. "There's nothing to add. I was just thinking about him."

"What part of his body, specifically, were you thinking about? His abs, his butt, his big ol' di—"

"Summer!"

The driver fidgeted in his seat, probably doing his best to ignore our conversation. Good grief. Summer was going to give the man a heart attack and then we'd all be dead on the side of the road.

"I wasn't thinking about any of his body parts. I was just thinking that he's become a nice friend."

Summer groaned and rolled her head back against the seat. "Oh, please, you are so full of shit."

"Am not!"

"Does he have that sexy V in his abs or do they Photoshop it on him for the billboards?"

"Oh, it's there."

"Case closed. You little sleaze," Summer said just as our town car pulled up outside of our hotel. The paparazzi were there as usual, but thanks to hotel policy they'd been exiled to the other side of the street. The boutique hotel's front entrance was set up with privacy in mind. There were hedges along the front of the street and a wide awning that gave the hotel a French look.

Summer and I rushed inside and I instantly relaxed once we were behind the hotel doors. We didn't talk about Jason anymore as we rode the elevator to the top floor, but that was probably because I pretended to be on a phone call the whole time. I'm not proud, but Summer is the snoopiest snoop I've ever met and she'd see right through my defense system.

Nope, this shit was going on lockdown. Jason Monroe was getting buried where I kept all my other cravings: deep, deep, deep down below. *Right next to mint chocolate chip ice cream.*

I smiled, confident in my newfound resolve as the elevators chimed on our floor. I clapped my hands together and stepped forward as the doors swung open.

"Let's get ready quick. I'm hungry!"

• • •

Two rounds of sushi and a bottle of sake later, I was sitting in the backseat of the town car headed toward a club with Summer. She insisted that we were going to the "top club" in Montana, which really didn't do much for me. However, when I started to protest, she turned her big eyes toward me and yammered on about how much she'd missed me the last few days.

"Fine, whatever," I told her. "Let's go."

If she wanted to drag me to Montana's premier nightlife destination, I'd let her. Plus, if I went home, I'd just think about J-A-S-O-N. (I decided that if I spelled his name out then it didn't actually count as thinking about him. Sometimes, I'm a bona fide genius.)

"How much sake did we have back there?" I asked as Summer dragged me past the club's doors and into the dim lighting. I blinked quickly, trying to process my new surroundings. Denim. So much denim everywhere. And wood. Everything in Montana was made of wood and denim.

"If I wrote a song about Montana, it'd be called 'Denim Denim Wood'," I told Summer as she made room for us at the bar. I noticed a few people giving us second-glances, mostly because my body guard was posted a few feet away from us, standing out like a sore-thumb in all black with an angry scowl. (I made him smile once. Best day of my life.) He wasn't staying with me at Jason's ranch, but he'd flown in with Summer for the few days I'd be staying in Billings. He clasped his hands together and leaned back against the bar, watching the crowd around us.

Other than good ol' Hank drawing attention, I didn't think people recognized me. The lighting was dim and the setting was so off that there's no way I had any fans inside the club. I reveled in the anonymity as Summer ordered us two Vodka sodas. I was still processing all of the Saki from dinner, and was definitely on the verge of seeing double, but I didn't want to be a party-pooper.

While we waited for our drinks, I glanced down at my phone again. The only thing waiting for me was a text from Cammie.

Cammie: How's the wild wild west treating you?

I smiled and shot her a reply.

Brooklyn: I'm toasted thanks to Summa.

Cammie: I approve.

"Cheers!" Summer said, passing me one of the drinks as I pocketed my phone.

When I glanced back up, two guys wearing suits that screamed, "WE'RE LAWYERS" headed toward us with confident smiles. While their suits were well pressed, their ties were loose, and their five o'clock shadows had started to appear. Not bad. *Not bad at all.*

"We were about to offer to buy you ladies a drink, but it looks like you beat us to it," the one on the left said, pointing to my drink in hand. In my inebriated state, the only real difference I could find between the pair of them was that one was blonde and the other had dark brown hair. Maybe they were related. Maybe they were twins!

"Are you guys twins? Did your parents always dress you the same?" I asked, skipping over introductions. I didn't want them to know my name and I didn't want to lie and make up a fake one.

They laughed and exchanged a glance. Summer snorted. "They look nothing alike, Tipsy Tina."

The guys laughed and the blonde one took a step closer to me. "Is that your name, Tina? I'm Collin."

I had a few seconds to try and think of what my answer should be, but in those seconds I was focused on sipping my drink. Oops.

"Yeah, that's me. Tina is the name... that I have."

He laughed like he didn't quite believe me. Maybe he knew exactly who I was but he was willing to play the game as much as I was.

"Tina, after you finish that drink, we should dance."

Collin was confident; I'd give him that. And I couldn't remember the last time I'd danced with someone in a club. I was usually too self-conscious to let myself go.

"Well, then, maybe you should shut up so I can finish quicker," I slurred with what I assumed was a casually seductive smile. Chances are, *it wasn't*.

He laughed and turned to the blonde guy to chat about things I didn't care about, so I pulled my phone back out. Except, instead of texting Cammie back, I thought I had come up with the best idea known to man-kind. Drunk texting. *I should definitely text Jason so that he knows that I haven't forgotten about him*. I bet he would definitely want to know that I'm okay since we're kind of…sort of…friends. Okay, let's put it this way: if I were inside of a burning building, he probably would *think* about saving me. That's something. Two days before, he probably wouldn't have even called the fire department. *Progress*.

I thought about what I should text him for one whole second. I wanted it to be organic and not too structured. Organic, yup, that's what I wanted to sound like.

Brooklyn: I'm in a Montana honky-tonk bar and I'm going to dance with a guy named Cullen. He's not twins or even related to the other guy he came with, isn't that weird?

I smiled down at the text, proud of what I'd thought up. To me, I seemed aloof, charming, and seductive. But just to be sure, I attached a selfie of me winking and holding up my drink, just so he'd know how adorable I was.

"Did you just send that picture to someone? Because you looked like you had something poking your eye and you had some drool on your chin," Summer said, trying to snatch my phone out of my hand.

Silly Summer didn't know what she was talking about.

"How's the drink coming along?" Cullen asked. *Wait, was that his name? It seemed so right, but wrong at the same time.*

"Fantastico," I replied just as my phone buzzed in my hands.

HALLELUJAH. J-A-S-O-N had texted me back.

No. Crap. It was just my little sister.

Cammie: You better not be drunk texting anyone. This is a warning. Do not drunk text anyone.

Brooklyn: fffffuuuuucccck youuuuuu.

Cammie: Oh god, you already have. Haven't you? What'd you send?

I attached the selfie so she'd know that I was perfectly fine and doing great.

Her reply was simply: hahahahahahaha

I figured she was laughing because I'd said something funny, but I couldn't remember what I'd said. I was always saying funny things.

"I think Ms. *Tina* might be too drunk to dance," Summer said, peering over at me with amusement in her eyes.

"Aw, c'mon. It'll be fun," Callum said. *Why had his parents named him that? It was a hard name to remember.*

"Yeah, listen to him, Summer. I'm going to dance and no one in this bar is going to stop me. Not you, not Hank, and not Callum."

"My names Collin," he said with a laugh.

"No one asked you, Callum," I said, taking his hand in mine and dragging him to the dance floor.

He followed after me and started following my lead. I had no clue what song was streaming through the crackling speakers, but it was easy to dance to and I swayed my hips back and forth while he stared down at them.

"You're kind of feisty," he said, stepping closer. "I like it."

He sounded nothing like J-A-S-O-N so I just ignored whatever else he said as we danced together. The country song faded into a rock song, and then the opening beat of one of *my* songs came on. Of course it wasn't the first time I'd heard my songs on the radio or at a club. But for some reason, the fact that people in Montana played my songs in honky-tonk bars was extremely exciting.

"Oh my gosh! This is my song!" I screamed, looking to Summer to see if she was as excited as I was. Her mouth was attached to Callum's twin so she couldn't see me, but I knew she was excited on the inside.

Callum shrugged and tried to grab my arm so he that could pull me toward him. "Uh yeah, this is a good song. I think that Brooklyn Heart girl sings it."

"That's me!" I said with a laugh, pointing to my chest like a little boy trying to prove he was telling the truth.

Callum's eyes widened for a second, but then he narrowed them and studied me.

"Sure, okay. It's your song," he said playfully as he stepped back toward me. He didn't believe me at all and for some reason that made me impossibly sad.

Why didn't he trust me? I puckered my lower lip and my eyes welled up with tears.

"Whoa, are you okay?" Callum asked as I felt tears run down my face.

That's when it hit me. I was drunk, not just cute and tipsy, but full-on drunk crying in the middle of the dance floor.

"He didn't even text me back," I said, crying harder.

Carl tried to comfort me as he led me off the dance floor, back toward my friend. Poor guy, he thought he was going to have a normal night and instead I took him straight into Crazytown, USA. *Population: Tipsy Tina aka Brooklyn Heart.*

"I think your friend should head home," Carl said to Summer when we reached them at the bar.

Hank stepped forward and politely asked Carlos to remove his arms from my shoulders.

"Uh oh, it looks like Tipsy Tina has had enough fun for one night."

I kept crying. "My name's not Tina!"

Hank stepped forward and wrapped his a protective hand around my elbow. "Brooklyn, it's time to go. I'll have the car brought around." I saw him give a stern warning to Summer, and she swallowed hard and nodded.

The night was over.

"Holy shit, she wasn't lying. That's Brooklyn Heart," Carlos said as Summer and Hank led me out of the bar. "I just danced with Brooklyn Heart! She cried on me!"

Shut up, Carlos. I wanted to be crying on Jason. Well, not crying, but doing something on him *at least.*

Chapter Fourteen

A small alien civilization had set up shop inside of my brain and I think their sole purpose was to cause me pain. Lots and lots of pain.

"Brooklyn, you're going to have to wake up soon. We have a meeting with the fragrance people in an hour," Summer *thought* she was whispering as she leaned over my hotel bed, but the aliens in my head rioted in response.

"If you don't leave this room in two seconds, I will drop-kick your face," I said, barely moving my lips enough to get the words out.

She laughed and backed out, closing the door as loudly as possible. "I'm giving you another two minutes, but that's it! Also, I want a raise, and hazard pay!" Summer yelled through the door. I responded by reaching down and chucking my high-heel at the door.

She was technically giving me two more minutes but I could hear her voice on the other side of the door, talking to someone on the phone. Maybe the hotel people were kicking me out after my dance performance in the lobby at

2:00 A.M. the night before. *I can't help the fact that the tile floor was perfect for break-dancing.*

"Yeah, she's okay."

Silence.

"Nah, we left pretty early and she slept it off."

Silence.

"Yeah, her body guard, Hank, was with us."

Who was she talking to?

"Okay, bye."

"Who was that?" I yelled through the door.

"The president."

"Lies."

"You're right, it was Kanye West. Now get up."

I wanted to care about the fact that she wouldn't tell me who was on the phone, but I had no more room in my brain for caring. The moment I sat up, my brain switched over into anti-throw up mode. I walked to the bathroom like a small, frail hunchback and then did my best to avoid the mirror. But there was a smell in the air that I couldn't place. I sniffed my shirt and my armpits, and while they weren't a field of roses, they were at least recognizable. Then I pulled my hair to my face and smelled it. Soy sauce. When I glanced in the mirror, I realized I had what looked like a quarter bottle of soy sauce in my hair... which meant that I'd left the restaurant and gone to the club like that. *Had I poured soy sauce on myself at sushi? Why?*

Summer was going to die. Slowly and painfully.

After a shower and roughly one million cups of coffee, I staggered through my day, trying to be as present as possible. The meetings were interesting, but no amount of Advil would quell my pounding headache, so I just succumbed to the pain. I became one with it.

It wasn't until lunch when Summer brought up the night before.

"Did you ever check your phone to read your drunk texts?" she asked as I poured dressing over my Greek salad.

I scrunched my brows in thought. *Drunk texts?* I didn't recall any of those. I didn't even think I had my phone after the restaurant.

"No, why?" I asked nonchalantly, taking a big bite of salad.

Summer's eyes widened. "You remember doing that, right? Sending the text to Jason?"

I had to fight not to spit lettuce and tomato all over Summer's face. After a painful swallow, I took a deep breath and reached for my phone. Summer was just playing a joke on me. I wouldn't have texted— *oh Jesus. Mother Teresa.* I did.

There was a selfie of me with my drink in my hand. I was contorting my face into what I probably thought was a wink but more closely resembled a massive stroke. I had the soy sauce in my hair, and *yup*, definitely drool on my chin. Sloppy. I was a sloppy monster and I'd willingly sent this photo to Jason. I could only pray he hadn't sold it to TMZ yet.

Two deep breaths later, I peered up at Summer. "From this moment forward, we will never discuss last night again. I'm going to erase it from my memory."

Summer smiled and nodded. "Whatever you say, Captain."

I tried to tell myself it didn't matter, that everyone does embarrassing stuff, but it really wasn't the selfie that was bothering me. It was the fact that Jason hadn't bothered texting me back. *Didn't he care enough to see if I'd made it home okay?*

By that afternoon, I had convinced myself to concentrate on work and ignore the lingering thoughts of Jason. I had to repress the urge to replay our encounters over and over again. Even still, for the remainder of the trip, I'd close my eyes and think of his kiss in the bathroom. It was so easy in fact, that I'd imagine him and relive our time together for what felt like hours until I realized what I was doing. Then I'd reprimand myself and fill my head with the conversations from my mundane meetings. It would last for ten minutes, maybe fifteen, and then I'd slip, and the cycle would start all over again.

It was no use. I was going insane, with thoughts of Jason pushing me over the edge.

• • •

Two *long* days later, I found myself back at Jason's house just after midnight. They'd left the door unlocked for me since apparently no one gets robbed in the middle of the woods in Montana. The house was quiet when I let myself in, but I welcomed it. It meant I wouldn't have to face Jason just yet.

I'd had one last day of meetings and then I'd endured the ride back to Big Timber by myself, since Summer was scheduled to fly back to LA from the Billings airport. I tried to take a nap during the ride back to Big Timber, but instead, I'd opened and reopened my text messages wondering why I still cared that Jason had never texted me back. I suppose it gave me a definitive answer concerning Jason. The friendship I thought was slowly forming between us was most definitely *not* forming. We were still at square one. Except, we weren't even enemies anymore. We were absolutely nothing. Not even worth a text back.

Awesome.

• • •

The next morning I headed downstairs with what I thought was a very positive attitude. I'd pushed the negative thoughts that had clouded my brain for the last twenty-four hours aside and focused on better things, like my favorite pair of jeans – the ones that made my ass look "outta this world" (*thank you, sales girl who talked me into purchasing them with that line*). I styled my hair into soft curls, and swiped on some bright red lipstick. *This day was about to become my bitch.*

When I stepped into the kitchen, LuAnne whistled from where she sat at the table, flipping through a magazine. Her poufy blonde hair and bright smile were just what I needed.

"Welcome back, Brooklyn. This place was boring with you gone," she said, winking up at me.

I leaned over the table to kiss her cheek, leaving a bright red stain behind. She laughed, but wouldn't let me wipe it away.

"I needed a little color on my cheek," she joked.

"Where are the boys?" I asked, heading over toward the kitchen island. There was warm breakfast food laid out, the likes of which would bring a carb-conscious female to her knees, but I piled my plate with fruit and warm, scrambled eggs. *Because I was in control of my life. I didn't need French toast, and I definitely didn't need Jason.*

"Oh, Derek went out to work a while ago and Jason hasn't come down yet. He stayed up in that room the whole time you were gone. I think I maybe saw him for five minutes in total," LuAnne said with an admonishing shake of her head.

"Songs don't write themselves," a deep voice declared from the hallway.

The hair on my neck stood on end and I whipped my head toward that soulful voice so fast I nearly sprained my back. I didn't bother wincing at the pain because Jason was standing there in the doorway, running a hand through his mess of hair and stealing back my resolve like it'd never belonged to me in the first place. His facial hair was longer than I'd ever seen it, but it only emphasized his dark, grizzly man appeal. His song-worthy eyes were already on me when I met his gaze, but there was nothing behind them. No anger. No excitement. *Nothing*. He was the Fort Knox of people and I was sick of trying to read through his expressions. Clearly, I wasn't very good at it.

"Hello Jason," I said, hoping I sounded as formal and annoyed as I intended to.

"Hi," he said, stepping forward to fill his own plate with food. He could have gone on the other side of the kitchen island, but no, he came to stand directly next to me so that our elbows bumped when he reached for the bacon in front of me. His body wash filled my senses in the most annoyingly sexy way.

I grabbed my plate and took the seat next to LuAnne before he accidentally touched me again. But, that traitorous whore stood up as soon as I sat down.

"Well, I'll let you two enjoy breakfast. Come find me later if you want to chat, Brooklyn."

No, I had no plans of chatting with her. I had plans to murder her for leaving me with Jason.

I once went on a blind date where in the span of one meal, my date had called his mom, cried, made me pray for ten minutes when our food arrived (I kid you not, ten minutes. My linguine was cold by the time he'd decided his prayer was long enough.), and then he yelled at our waiter when the steak he'd ordered wasn't rare enough. It was the worst date I'd ever been on, and yet, as Jason sat across from me at the table, I found myself longing to go back to that night.

Nothing was worse than sitting at that table with Jason in absolute silence. Painful silence. Every scrape of my fork on my plate, every time my glass clinked against the table. It made me want to scream.

Jason stood up before I did, finishing off his eggs and bacon like a ravenous dog. I watched him clear his plate off in his sink, letting my gaze slide down his body. He was wearing loose black sweatpants and a white t-shirt, but I still thought he looked edible.

"Come find me when you're done. We have work to do."

He didn't even look at me as he offered that line. He was looking past the sink, out through the kitchen window, and then he turned and headed back upstairs, taking them two at a time.

"I'll come when I find the time!" I yelled because that seemed like a smart thing to say. How dare he think that he could just order me around like that? Maybe I didn't feel like writing right now. Maybe I had other, more important things to do.

Ten minutes later I realized I actually had nothing to do. I'd already called and checked in with Summer and

Cammie. I'd returned all my emails before breakfast. I'd even managed to work out already because my insane-ass trainer had called me at the butt-crack of dawn. So, I took the stairs really slowly, trying to show Jason that I'd come up when I was good and ready, thank you very much.

Mid-way up the stairs, I leaned over the banister and hollered to LuAnne. "Do you need my help with anything? Cleaning? Dusting? Flipping through magazines!?"

"No, you go on ahead and get your writing done. I'm all good," she said, and then she turned the vacuum on, drowning out any possibilities of using her as an excuse. Dammit. She'd been my last option.

With the speed of a barely-mobile elderly person, I grabbed my guitar from the case in my room and then went out to look for Jason on the patio where we'd tried to write the first time. He wasn't there. For a second, I was confused and assumed he'd ditched me for greener pastures, but then my eyes widened. *His room*. He was in his room and I'd finally get to see it. I practically ran to the third floor, tripped up the stairs, and then softly knocked on the door with as much composure as possible.

"Come in," he said.

I turned the handle and pushed the door open, holding my breath in anticipation. I knew that taking a look inside Jason's room would be like getting a peek inside of his soul. It was where he created music, where he sat and thought and wrote and played for hours at a time, and when I stood in the doorway, I wasn't disappointed in the least. It was *so* Jason. The furnishings were all dark-oiled wood and clean, modern lines. The drapes were drawn to let in the early morning light from the large window that led to the third-floor balcony. To call it a room didn't do it justice.

On one side there was a giant four-poster bed that was, of course, unmade. I stared at the pillow where his head had undoubtedly rested the night before and I had a strange longing to lie down in that exact position so that I could get a sense of how he slept.

Next to his nightstand, there was a bookshelf half-full of books and half-full of random trinkets that looked like they were souvenirs from various places around the world. There was a miniature Eiffel Tower holding up a guitar manual and an oriental elephant painted rich, vibrant colors.

Across the room, where the window opened to the balcony, there was a small sitting area. Jason was already leaned back on a leather couch, facing the window. There was an overstuffed armchair across from the couch, and since he made no move to greet me, I walked over and took a seat there. I could feel the sun on the back of my neck and I knew the view from where Jason sat would have been amazing, but I was *not* going to sit on the same couch with him. He'd probably push me off.

"I started playing around with a few opening bars that I think could work for a duet," he said, absentmindedly playing his acoustic guitar as he watched me take a seat. He was strumming a rhythm, soft and smooth. His guitar's body was faded around the sound hole and pick guard, but the sound was clean. I wondered how many years he'd played on that guitar, how many songs he's created using that fretboard.

I started nodding my head to the rhythm he repeated over and over. It was simple, with a beat and pulse I could feel. He hit the bass string, followed with an upstroke, downstroke, upstroke. He held the note for one extra beat and then opened to a *C* chord. *Am, Em, F, C, G.* Chord after chord, and I was completely mesmerized by the finger-picking pattern he repeated on the strings.

I couldn't unlock my guitar case fast enough. Two more times listening to him strum the same rhythm, and then I started strumming along, mimicking his chords and picking the strings of my guitar until we were both working off one another.

We started and restarted a hundred times, experimenting with the rhythm he'd created. Then finally, he closed his eyes and started singing softly. His gritty, soulful voice sent a chill down my spine.

Don't want you to stay
Can't tell you to go

He kept his eyes closed and I kept the rhythm for the two of us, praying he'd keep singing.

But if there's one thing you outta know
You're a designer queen
A corporate machine
A cold-hearted crow

His lips twisted up after his last line and I knew he was teasing me.

"Wow, tell me how you really feel," I laughed, continuing to pick my guitar strings. "How about I go now?"

He opened his eyes and smiled. The first real smile he'd given me in days. "Go for it."

I waited for the chords to repeat from the beginning while my mind sought out lyrics. This wasn't how I usually worked. My songs were crafted, slowly and thoughtfully, but there was something fun about drawing lyrics from the tip of my tongue, seeing what I'd produce. I licked my bottom lip and swallowed, preparing my voice before I started to softly sing.

You want me to go
You hate the status of my quo

He smiled wider. His dark eyes watching my fingers move over the strings with noticeable admiration.

Now I'm at an all-time low

I glanced down at the fretboard, trying out a lick that fell fluidly into the bars we'd already created.

I'd go if I could
Oh, yes I know I should
You've got me misunderstood

I bit my lip to keep from smiling.

You're a judgmental cow
Bet you feel so good now

Neither one of us stopped playing as we laughed at our pitiful attempt at a song. I didn't know what we were doing— we sure as shit weren't writing our duet— but there wasn't half as much tension in the room as there had been when I'd first walked in and that counted for something.

"That was really terrible," I said, strumming my fingers down the neck of my guitar before letting it rest on my lap.

"The bars or our lyrics?" he asked.

"No, I loved the chords. I meant my lyrics."

He rubbed his lips together as if considering my answer. Thoughts clouded his gaze, but he kept them locked away.

"I didn't mean those lyrics. Maybe I did when I first met you, but not anymore," he said, staring out through the window over my shoulder.

I smiled. "Oh, I definitely meant mine."

He laughed and we continued to strum for the remainder for the morning. We didn't write any lyrics that day, but we continued playing together, creating what would eventually become the melody of our duet. The roots were being laid with chords that fell together like the leaves from a tree.

Creating the chords to a song was a process that never got any easier. In the beginning my fingers would sit on the fretboard as my mind worked in overtime, trying to fuel my creativity. I'd strum and strum, pick and pluck, until things started to work together.

I'd start with one chord. That's all it took. And when I finished, and played back the song, it felt like that's how those chords were always meant to be.

A good song never felt like it'd been struck into creation by my own hands. It felt like fate had willed the song to be and I'd merely chiseled away at the clutter around it, breathing clarity into the infinite combination of sounds.

Jason and I didn't get to that point on the first day we played together, but I knew we'd get there soon. I'd never felt the clutter fall away quite as fast, or quite as easily, as it did when Jason and I played together.

Chapter Fifteen

If I had one piece of advice to bestow upon you, it would be: Never wear a pair of high-heels to a stable. *Leave your Prada sling-backs in LA.*

The next morning I found myself wandering out toward the barn and stable with a cup of coffee in hand. The morning air was cool, but I had a wool wrap to keep me warm. My heels were wobbly on the gravel path, but I did just fine getting to the door of the stable without spraining an ankle.

I hadn't seen Dotty since before I'd left to go out of town so I was anxious to pay her a visit and sneak her some of the sugar cubes I'd tucked into my pocket at breakfast. I set my cup of coffee on a rock outside of the stable door and used both of my hands, and pretty much all of my body-weight, to pull open the heavy stable door.

"Jeez." I exhaled as soon as I'd pulled it open wide enough to step inside.

The stable had natural light from the windows on the roof so I didn't bother turning the light switch on. I didn't want to jar the horses if they were still resting. Just like last time, the smell hit me first. It wasn't too strong, just a reminder that I was in a stable and not a five-star hotel, but then I saw Dotty standing in her stall as if she'd been waiting for me all night.

I smiled and stepped forward slowly, letting her get used to me before I reached out so she could sniff my hand and rub her muzzle against my palm. She pushed her head and neck out over the top of her stall so that she could sniff my hair.

"Dotty, you are looking like a stunner this morning. Bet you have the stallions going crazy," I said, rubbing her cheek and neck.

She sniffed my coffee first and then bent her head low to try to get to my pocket.

I laughed and pulled out the sugar cubes, feeding them to her one at a time. I could have stayed out there all day, writing next to her stall, but I had a Skype call with my agent in thirty minutes and I doubted Jason's Montana internet signal reached the horse stable.

"I'll come back later today," I promised her, rubbing her neck until she emitted a low rumble through her nostrils.

I turned to leave the stable, careful to pull the door closed all the way once I was outside. But when I turned toward the house, my heel caught on a rock in the path and since my bottom half was facing the stable and my top half was twisted toward the house, I went down flailing aimlessly. Scalding coffee flew onto my hair and shirt. But no worries, I only got mud in my mouth, hair, eyes, ears, and nose. *Nowhere important.* Oh, and my Prada heels that cost me more than what I used to make in a month at my high school job? Broken, so broken that the mud in my vagina took a backseat. (Just kidding, sometimes life just demands a little dramatic embellishment.)

I wobbled back into the house with one heel intact and the other, less than intact, and passed every single person on my way to the kitchen. Derek was walking out the front door, LuAnne was finishing up some dishes in the sink, and Jason was sitting at the table trying so, so hard to keep from cracking up.

When I spoke, my voice was eerily calm, but I could hear myself getting close to cracking.

"LuAnne, could I borrow a car to head into town after I wipe the mud, and what smells like shit, off my face?"

"Oh god, Brook. How'd you manage to do that to yourself already? The day just started."

I shook my head, and took the towel she held out to me. *Pretend it's a mud facial; pretend your skin will be flawless once you wipe it off.*

"I think it had something to do with those shoes she's wearing," Jason said from the table. His tone was a little too light and happy for my taste, so when I wiped the towel down my face again, I made sure to hold up my middle finger. His chuckle told me he was more than aware of my gesture.

• • •

Thirty minutes later, I pulled up outside of Callahan's General Store in downtown Big Timber. The parking lot was completely empty other than an old busted-up truck. The store itself looked old, but the white paint on the outside was new and a big wooden sign blew back and forth in the wind. It was cut out into the shape of a pair of cowboy boots with "Callahan's" written in white calligraphy.

I had faith that I'd be able to find what I needed here.

A bell chimed when I pushed open the door, and a grizzly looking man stood behind the counter with his palms resting on the glass. His black eyes stared straight at me.

"What can I do for you?" he asked, his voice an octave lower than I even thought possible. This man was a bear in human form. His white beard hung low, past his chin, and I wondered if there was anyone else around to help me find a pair of boots. This guy looked like he wanted to eat me for lunch.

"Hello. I umm…I need a pair of boots," I said, scanning his merchandise before glancing back at him.

For two seconds he didn't say a word, but then he leaned forward, pushed off the counter and walked around toward me. "Well, then you've come to the right place."

Oh dear god, I thought that was going in a drastically different direction. This man looked like he wanted to kill me, stuff my body and put me on display next to his taxidermied squirrels. I kid you not, there were like four of them sitting on the counter. *One was wearing a top hat.*

"I bet you're about a seven and a half," he said, looking down at my feet, clad in the only pair of sneakers I'd brought with me for the trip. I wore them to work out, but after the mud-in-the-face debacle, I wasn't about to ruin another pair of heels.

"Yes, that's exactly my size," I gaped. "How'd you know that?"

"Ain't the first time I sized up a foot, honey."

Hold the phone. Did this behemoth of a man just call me "honey" like my hair stylist did back in LA? I narrowed my eyes on him, but he was glancing over the racks of boots on the wall and I couldn't get a very good read.

"Try these. They'd look good with just about anything, although I'm a bit over the boots and short skirt trend myself, I'm sure you'd be able to pull it off well."

I couldn't even process his words. It's not like I pride myself on my gay-dar or anything, but c'mon. This man screamed heterosexual male. I mean, he had on a camo-print shirt for Christ's sake. Oh my god, that's when I saw the Hermes belt buckle peeking out from under his shirt. He was wearing camo because it was trendy, not because he lived in the country.

"Are you going to take these boots, or keep staring at my belt like you're wishing I had it in your size?" he asked, pursing his lips and tilting his head.

"You are the most interesting person I've ever met," I blurted out as I took the red cowboy boots from him.

He laughed and shrugged. "Don't judge a book by its cover. I moved out to Montana to open up a chic bed and breakfast, but not many people travel out here for that. So I have the store as well."

An hour later, I walked out of Callahan's General Store with a smoking hot pair of red cowboy boots, a new pair of cutoff jeans shorts, and a coffee date with Paulo. Yes, that was grizzly man's name. *Paulo.*

• • •

A few hours later, after I'd returned from town, I went up to Jason's room wearing my daisy dukes and my red cowboy boots. I had my guitar in my right hand, so I knocked gently with the left, pressing my ear to the door to see if he was inside.

"Come in," he called out.

I pushed his door open and stepped in, expecting to find him in the same spot on the couch, but he was pulling his black acoustic Gibson from its stand. When he turned and glanced up to take in my new outfit, he paused for a second, trying to conceal a private smile as his gaze slid over my bare legs.

"You're channeling a little Nancy Sinatra," he quipped, taking in my appearance nice and slow. For the first time, his interest was clear to see. It was written across his face from the way he took a deep, savoring breath, to the way his lips seemed to unconsciously part. Perhaps the signs had been there from the start, but I'd been too distracted concealing my own interest to notice his.

"More like Jessica Simpson. But thanks."

I sat down in the overstuffed chair and waited for him to take his seat on the couch. He'd trimmed off his beard overnight so that only short stubble remained. His black long-sleeved shirt was unbuttoned on top. I could see more of his tan neck and chest then I'd ever seen before.

He cleared his throat as he sat down, positioned his guitar over his lap and crossed his bare feet. We'd been in the same situation before, but today, the tension was back, igniting the air between us.

There was a pen stuck behind his ear and his writing note pad sat with a blank page open on the coffee table between us.

It was time to write.

Wordlessly, we started playing the opening bars of the song we'd been working on the day before, but no lyrics came. I could feel them, trying to break through, but I wasn't used to the nerves pushing them back down my throat. I wrote alone. Always alone. I never had to worry about someone thinking my lyrics were silly because, by the time I shared them they were perfect. Maybe that's why neither one of us spoke up.

We kept strumming, playing on and on, with silence twining around the sounds of our guitars. I kept catching Jason's gaze on my legs... my arms... my neck. He'd focus on me for just a moment, always glancing away when I looked up. But I could feel him, feel the tension multiplying. I noticed every breath he took, the desire building in my body as his heated gaze stayed glued on me.

"I don't usually get writer's block," Jason spoke up a few minutes later, after clearing his throat.

I nodded, staring down at my fretboard. "Neither do I."

"How should we get over it?" he asked.

I thought for a moment. "We could just say the first few things that come to mind, no matter how silly."

He nodded, but didn't reply.

"We could start with a word, a single word and move on from there."

Still no reply.

"Or we could just have sex," I added, just to make sure he was listening.

His guitar strings rang out sharply before they stopped all together.

When I looked up at him, his dark eyes were focused right on me. Not my guitar, not the window behind me— they were pinned on my face as if he was trying to read between the lines. I've never been someone who filters what comes out of my mouth, but in that moment I was left wondering why I'd joked about something like that. Jason and I were not close enough to understand each other's humor. Or actually, I wasn't sure Jason had a sense of humor at all.

"I like that idea," he said, letting a smile slide over his beautiful mouth.

I swallowed hard. That's the last thing I expected him to say.

Then he continued, "We obviously still feel nervous around one another. You're too scared to sing even though I can see you've got lyrics brewing."

What in-all-that-is-holy is going on? Are we actually talking about having sex right now? My eyes stayed glued on my fingers sliding back and forth along my guitar string. Do not look at him. Do not look at him.

"So, it's purely a business thing," I suggested, trying to think of any possible excuse to get this man in bed. I'd tell myself it was for world peace if that's what he wanted to hear. *That's right, I'd have an orgasm for world peace, because I'm noble like that.*

"You can look at it like that," he replied, rubbing his stubble.

"So, we should have sex— right here, right now?" I asked, meeting his eyes.

He wet his bottom lip, flashed me a confident grin and then,

it began.

Chapter Sixteen

We were like animals. Whereas our minds had writer's block, our bodies had no trouble improvising. Our guitars were tossed aside as Jason came around the coffee table and I was peeling my shirt up over my head at the same time that he bent to kiss me. Our lips parted when my shirt got in the way, but I didn't care. I was already working at his belt buckle. There was no foreplay. There was no two-hour make-out session before we finally pushed past the invisible boundary.

In its place, there were small bites, and nails scraping against skin. His stubble scratched my face, his arms wrapped around my waist and then he was carrying me over to his bed in the corner of the room. It was still as unmade as it'd been the day before, but I liked that. I didn't have to worry about messing it up even more.

My heart was beating so fast I was scared it'd break through my rib cage. I couldn't recall the last time I'd felt this way, maybe with a past boyfriend, but I doubt I'd ever felt this *rushed* to feel someone else's skin. Once his shirt was gone, I dragged my palms down over his chest and abs. He was a musician and his body reflected that with toned, sinuous muscles that weren't as bulky as some of the men I'd been with before. But Jason could move; his hips had a mind of their own and the way he rolled against me made my mind splinter into two.

"Holy fuck," I groaned as I felt his warm skin against mine.

"This can't turn into something more," he said, breaking the sound of our heavy breathing as he scooted down the bed to slip off my boots.

"The sex? Or us?" I asked.

He tugged off my jean shorts with half of the care that he'd shown my boots, leaving me in my black panties. His eyes raked over my thighs and stomach, and then he finally glanced up to my face.

"Us."

I rolled my eyes. I didn't give a shit what happened with us. Just because I was the girl didn't mean I had to care what happened after we had sex. Cuddling? *Who needs it?* Talking? *Overrated.* This was going to happen and I was going to enjoy every second of it. And after? *I couldn't even think that far.*

"Great. Can you stop talking now?" I asked with a grin as I gripped his biceps and pulled him back up so that his body covered mine.

He laughed and shook his head, obviously surprised by my response. But then his lips found mine again and his hips dug into me at the same time that his tongue slipped into my mouth. I think I orgasmed on the spot. He was so skilled and I hadn't had a proper orgasm in far too long.

My body was overly sensitive, ready to spring to life beneath his deft touch.

When he pulled his boxers off, he took my underwear and bra with them and we were left completely naked, staring at one another in awe. If there were time, I would have pushed him onto his back and sat atop him to get my fill of every single patch of skin. I wanted to know how he felt, take my time touching his biceps, his chest, his abs, his thighs.

But there was no time. I needed him.

He reached past me for a condom in his side drawer and I tried to ignore the fact that he could unroll that bad boy like he was competing in "Condom Application" on an Olympic level. This man had clearly had quite a lot of sex in his life and I was about to benefit from all that experience.

I had to hold back a squeal as he repositioned us in the center of the bed and parted my legs. *Dear god, if you're up there, please don't let me pass out from excitement before he even gets it in.*

Thankfully, God or whoever, definitely heard my prayers, because when Jason sank into me, I experienced heaven and let me tell you, it looks like a musician's room. And it feels like Jason's bed. And it smells like Jason's body wash. And it tastes like his mouth over mine, dipping into me and making me whole.

I let him take the lead since I wasn't actually able to use my brain for anything other than generating soft moans. His thumb found my most sensitive spot and I bit my lip, arching my neck off his pillow.

There's a moment just before you orgasm when your toes curl and you know it's coming. You can feel it rolling through you. It'd been so long for me, I wanted to prolong the agony, ride the anticipation for as long as possible—just feel the moment and realize I was three seconds away from the best orgasm of my life.

"I – can't – even," I said, unsure of where I was going with that sentence.

I never got the chance to find out because a second later, my body shook with uncontrollable pleasure as Jason brought me to an orgasm that seared my soul. I took his face between my hands and kissed him with every ounce of passion that he'd given me, and then I watched and listened as he finished after me. It was so sexy to behold, someone deriving pleasure from you, from the sheer act of being inside of you.

A moment later, when he was done, he collapsed onto my chest, breathing against my ear. We stayed like that for a few minutes and then he whispered a few words into my ear. His mouth tickled my skin, but I strained to hear what he was saying. The words were faint and I could hardly hear them, but I did. And I wasn't sure I was meant to.

Loving you would be as easy as taking a breath
But to look at you, that's a dance with death

He'd written the first lyrics to our duet.

And in doing so, he'd stolen the first part of my heart.

I gave myself ten seconds to stay on his bed, beneath his weight, while I collected as many memories as possible: he'd liked when I tugged on his hair, his sheets smelled fresh and masculine, the moan he'd emitted as he'd come undone inside of me was the single most delicious sound I've ever heard.

As soon as the ten seconds were up, I took a breath, and sat up. Silently, I rolled off the bed to find my clothes.

Jason mimicked my actions on the opposite side, his eyes cast toward the ground.

"I meant it when I said I don't want anything serious right now," he explained, running a hand through his hair, agitated about something he clearly didn't want to tell me about. Maybe he was just upset he'd had sex with me. *Perfect, just what a girl wants to think about after she just had her legs wrapped around a guy like a python in heat.*

"Seems to me like you're the one hung up on it. Like I said, we agree on that subject," I said, still breathing heavy from our... *whatever it was we'd just done.* It definitely wasn't lovemaking, but it wasn't just sex either. I tried not to mull it over since he'd just nailed home the fact that he wanted nothing to do with me.

"Things are *complicated* for me," he started to explain, holding his head between his hands. I wanted to jab my fist into his mouth so he'd stop ruining the moment.

"I get it. So, just let it be," I said, realizing that I was a simple person. I just wanted good chocolate, my guitar, and maybe some sex every now and then. Maybe Jason and I were perfect for one another.

He looked back at me as I slid on my bra and tugged my shirt overhead. Staring back at him made me realize that the millions of thoughts swirling through my head before we'd had sex were suddenly silenced. I felt calm and sated, and when the lyrics came to me, I smiled because maybe Jason and I had been right after all. A little sex never hurt anyone, especially when it got the creative juices flowing.

I retrieved my guitar from the couch and grabbed a pen so I could record the words he'd whispered into my ear and add a verse of my own. I didn't overanalyze them or

172

ponder where they'd come from. I wrote them down, gave Jason a nod, and exited his room to give him some privacy.

I'd risk it all,
For you I would
You'd make me fall,
And fall I would

Chapter Seventeen

I woke up the next morning craving Jason Monroe. Not him as a person, I didn't want his past or his future. I wanted another thirty minutes of heaven. The craving was something I knew I couldn't fight. I'd never been addicted to anything in my life, save for caffeine, but I'd heard that it only took one time to become addicted to a drug.

Great. I was officially a drug addict.

I rolled over in bed, trying to ignore my trainer's Skype call ringing out in the background of the room. I should have been up and at it an hour ago, but I couldn't leave my bed for fear of starting the day. I had wanted a one-night stand with Jason and that's what I got, but now I wanted more. A two-night stand. *Surely, that's a thing, right?*

I decided to get Cammie's advice about the subject because she never steered me wrong. (Well, most of the time. She did tell me that I wouldn't regret dyeing my hair black when I was fifteen. Also, she let me try out the bang trend.) I sent her a text in case she was working in the studio.

Brooklyn: Heyyy. Just for conversation's sake... Would it be wrong to have sex with Jason?

It took her five, long minutes to reply and I was going crazy the entire time.

Cammie: Good morning to you too. It would be wrong *not* to. Are you going to have sex with him? I didn't even think you guys were friends?
Brooklyn: Oh, we aren't.
Cammie: Do it. #YOLO. There couldn't possibly be any consequences....

Her sarcasm oozed all the way from California.

Brooklyn: You're right. I should come back to LA and just write with him over the phone or something.
Cammie: No. Just relax and enjoy life for once. Jeez. You're not allowed to come back yet, and don't forget that I'm coming to visit you in a few days!
Brooklyn: Okay. Have you talked to Grayson yet?
Cammie: Gotta go. Studio started.

I rolled my eyes at how childish she was being about the Grayson thing. I swore to call him myself as soon as I finished my workout and shower. With a groan, I sat up and stretched, changed into workout clothes, unrolled my yoga mat in the center of the room, and called my trainer back.

"Since you didn't answer my first call, you're doing an extra set of everything," my trainer said with a cheery voice as soon as the video call connected.

"Peachy," I said with a note of sarcasm. Okay, fine, maybe it was more than just a *note*.

• • •

After my trainer made me cry, (it might have just been sweat dripping into my eye, but still, it stung) I headed downstairs. I poured myself a steaming cup of coffee and sat at the table to dial Grayson's work number.

After two rings, the call connected and a woman answered with a clipped tone. "Cole Designs, this is Beatrice. How can I help you?"

Grayson must have gotten a new secretary. His old secretary was named Katherine, or so I thought. It was hard to keep up with the rotating door of young, beautiful women in his office.

"Hi Beatrice. This is Brooklyn calling for Grayson."

"Oh, um, just hold on one second please," she replied, obviously flustered. I wasn't sure if she recognized my name or if she was nervous to tell Grayson I was calling. Maybe he'd told her not to interrupt him. It wouldn't have been the first time I'd forced one of his secretaries to connect me to him via hard threats. If the man had it his way, he'd never talk to anyone and just work on his designs all day. *Hmm, who did that remind me of? *Cough* Jason.*

Speaking of the devil, while Grayson's hold music filtered into my ear, I watched Jason walk down the stairs and head into the kitchen. When he saw me sitting at the table he nodded and smiled, staring down at the hint of cleavage peaking out of my tank top for a second longer than necessary. *Well, well, well... maybe I wasn't the only one craving round two.*

"Yes. Hi Brooklyn, Grayson says he's very busy right now and can't talk."

What a shocker.

"Beatrice, could you tell him it's an emergency?" I asked, knowing that would get him. I used that trick at least once a month, but it never ceased to work. He never wanted to ignore me on the off chance that this time it could *actually* be an emergency.

Jason glanced over his shoulder, eyeing me up and down. Once the hold music kicked on again, I shook my head at him. "It's not a real emergency."

He laughed. "Of course not."

I watched him spoon some sugar into his coffee before he came to sit across from me at the table. Apparently since I was making a call in the middle of a kitchen, I didn't deserve any privacy.

"Can I try a sip of your coffee?" I asked. He'd added a little bit of milk once he'd sat down, and for once I thought it might taste better than my black version.

He eyed me curiously, but then slid the cup over. Holding the phone to my ear with one hand, I used the other to grab the mug and took a sip. The second it hit my tongue I could feel my taste buds shriveling up from how sweet it was.

"Jesus, did you put the whole cup of sugar in there?" I asked, handing it back over.

He grinned. "Are you asking me or Jesus?"

I rolled my eyes. "That is such a dad joke."

"Hello, Grayson speaking."

Oh, shit. I waved my hand at Jason to let him know to stop talking, but he just readjusted in his seat, making it so his foot was resting against mine. If I weren't on the phone with another man, it'd feel like we were enjoying a breakfast together like a couple or something.

I gulped down the idea.

"Brooklyn? Are you there?"

"Oh, yes. Hi Grayson!" I tried to focus on the phone call.

"Tell me, are you missing a leg or an arm?" Grayson asked.

"No," I shook my head, realizing Jason could hear every word of our phone call.

"Did your car explode?"

"No."

"Are you stranded in the desert somewhere?"

"Haha, I get it. This isn't a real emergency."

Oh god, Grayson was pissed with a capital P.

"You do realize that I'm running a company, right? So when you call me at ten in the morning, I'm going to be in a meeting with a client or out on a job site."

I felt like a little kid getting reprimanded. Jason might have been quiet and broody, but Grayson was seriously intimidating when he wanted to be.

"I'm sorry. I swear I won't keep you long. I just really, really need you to call Cammie. She's nervous about graduating and she's been in that studio working twenty-four-seven."

He cut me off. "I don't see how that concerns me."

"Grayson Cole," I said with all of the courage I could possibly muster.

"I've got to go, Brook, but if I have time, I'll give Cameron a call soon. Bye."

With that, he hung up, leaving me glancing down at my phone like it was about to chew my hand off. Maybe I *didn't* want him calling Cammie. *Would I really want her to have a boss like Grayson?* She'd probably end up spending even more time in the office than she was currently spending in the studio.

"Friend from home?" Jason asked with his eyebrows perked up.

"He's an old friend that I've been trying to connect with my sister."

"For a date?"

I snorted. "God no. Just so he could maybe mentor her a little bit, possibly give her a job once she graduates in a few weeks."

He nodded. "Don't you think she could figure out a job on her own?"

I glared at him across the table, but he just sat there with his calm mask, sipping away at his sugar-filled coffee.

"Don't you think you should learn how to drink your coffee black? That sip tasted like I was taking a bite of a candy bar."

Jason flashed a perfect, white smile. "Never had a cavity in my life."

I dropped my phone on the table so I could give him a sarcastic round of applause.

That's how our breakfast went. We teased each other, chatting when we felt like it, staying quiet when we felt like it. We checked our email on our phones and took calls. The only thing we didn't do was discuss the day before or anything involving our sexcapades. And the weird thing was, I didn't care.

"The award show is getting close. We only have another week or two here before we head back to LA so we can practice on stage," Jason said, looking up from his phone. He'd probably received the same threatening email from our record label that I had. On the surface it'd seemed nice and formal, but I could tell they wanted to make sure we knew how serious this duet was.

"Well then, let's go work," I said, standing up and grabbing both of our coffee cups. "If you grab my guitar, I'll top off our coffee and meet you upstairs."

A few minutes later, I kicked open his bedroom door, careful not to spill any of the hot liquid on my hands as I maneuvered toward the sitting area. My guitar was propped on the armchair, but when I passed by his bed, I recognized a pair of my underwear— a lacy red thong— lying on his pillow.

"Did you go through my stuff?" I asked.

He turned around, glanced at the panties, and then up at me with a devilish smile. "I saw those on the top of some folded clothes and I figured we needed some inspiration to get through the morning writing session."

I laughed. "So if we get some lyrics down, then what?"

I walked over to hand him his coffee, but before I could step away, he gripped the back of my thigh and slid his hand higher along the seam of my pants. "Then we get to reward ourselves."

Most of what we wrote down that morning was complete shit. Lyrics that could have been written by a five-year-old if such a five-year-old wasn't even trying very hard. I was concentrating as best as I could, but every time Jason started playing, strumming the strings on his guitar, I became enraptured by his hands. I thought about the calluses on the tips of his fingers, the way they'd felt on my skin, the way they'd dipped into the grooves of my hip.

"Are you concentrating on music or something else?" Jason asked, cutting the song off and eyeing me with suspicion.

"I am—" I paused and looked around his room. "Really admiring what you've done with the place. Especially that pile of clothes next to your bed. Very hobo chic."

Jason laughed and dropped his guitar next to him on the couch.

"I think that's enough for today, don't you agree?" he asked, walking around the coffee table and taking my guitar out of my hands.

"Gentle with her," I chided as he set my guitar next to his. When he spun around his brow was arched in amusement, but I stayed put. I was safe on the armchair. On there, I was just another musician, trying to write a song. But then Jason decided to strip that feeling from me in one easy move.

He propped his hands on the arms of the chair and dipped down to steal a kiss from me. I was caged in against the soft fabric, with his biceps on either side of my chest. I wrapped my arms around his neck and tugged him closer so that he had to bend his arms to oblige.

If the position were reversed I would have crawled onto his lap, but Jason kept his weight propped up, tantalizing me with the distance. When his tongue slid across my bottom lip, asking for entry, I obliged by reaching down for the button on his pants.

"These look hot. We should take them off," I said, as my fingers tugged the zipper down.

"How polite of you," Jason teased, tugging my shirt up the sides of my torso.

"I'm just looking out for you here. Don't want you to get overheated," I laughed, letting the pants fall to the ground and then smiling at the pair of black boxer briefs staring up at me. *Let's have a round of applause for that sight, ladies and gentlemen.*

"Ah, I feel better already," he said, before standing and tugging his shirt over his head.

I fell back against the armchair and propped my arms behind my head. "My my my, how the tables have turned," I joked.

He grinned. "You have three seconds to stand up and strip or this show ends."

"What?! That's not fair. I thought you were going to do a little dance for me. I want to see you shimmy. We might be able to work it into our Grammy performance."

"Three," he began, his arms crossed and his brow arched.

"Oh c'mon, shake that butt for me."

"Two," he continued, adding his fingers into the mix.

"NO!" I said, jumping off the couch and ripping my shirt off over my head. I heard threads splitting, but I'd tear the shirt apart with my teeth if it meant I got to sleep with Jason again.

"One and a half," he teased as I tried to slide out of my jeans.

"Stop counting! This isn't fair!" I was literally hopping around on one foot. Fuck you, jeans. *How dare you come between me and my orgasm?* I fell back onto the floor and wiggled as fast as I could. *That's what I get for wearing skintight jeans. From now on, I'm only wearing mom jeans that go up to my boobs.*

Jason helped me rip the jeans from my ankles and then gripped my biceps to lift me off the ground and toss me back onto the bed.

"Whoa, caveman action. I like it," I teased scooting back until I hit the center of his bed. Per usual, the blankets were crumbled into a mess and half his pillows were tossed to the side. He must be a kicker when he slept... or maybe he slept spread eagle. *In the nude. With whipped cream.*

He shook his head and stalked toward me.

"Good, good. Now beat your chest like Tarzan," I added with a wink.

"I think if you're still making jokes, I'm not doing a good enough job," he said, dipping his knee onto the bed and crawling over me.

"You're right. I think this mouth could be put to better use—"

I'll give the guy credit, with a line like that, I was kind of asking for him to shove his you-know-what in my mouth, but instead, he kissed me. Hard. And he didn't stop kissing me for the next thirty minutes. I could almost feel my lips bruising. I knew that when I walked out of his room later it would look like I had had an allergic reaction to something I'd eaten because the man had kissed me senseless, but I didn't care. I just needed more.

His hands explored every curve of my body, adding feather light touches to each sensitive spot: the groove of my knee, down the center of my chest.

I dug my fingers into his thighs as he rolled the condom on, enraptured by the sight.

"I really, really need you inside of me," I told him as he tossed the empty condom wrapper on the floor behind him.

His gaze found mine, and for a moment, he froze, staring back and forth between my eyes with a clouded expression. But then he blinked, and bent forward, biting the skin in the groove of my neck at the exact moment that he pressed deep inside of me. *HELLO HEAVEN, I'VE MISSED YOU.*

I heard myself release a throaty moan, like I was literally relaxing every muscle in my body all at once. And then the shudders began and I was completely helpless. I tore at his sheets and he licked and sucked and kissed every patch of my skin he could find.

It was as if the world was apologizing for the months, and months, and months I'd gone with zero sex. As if the HR department of the world had caught their mistake and were scrambling around to fix it.

Well, I tip my hat to you, HR department. You nailed it with Jason Monroe.

After what felt like hours, I laid back on Jason's sheets staring up at his ceiling with a dopey smile on my face. He was humming the melody of the song we'd created and I kept replaying the lyrics we'd come up with the day before in my mind.

When the idea hit me, I sat up in bed, grabbed my bra and panties and slid them on as I walked to the armchair. The lyrics were coming and I wanted to get to my guitar while they were still fresh. I positioned the guitar on my lap and plucked the strings, humming to myself as I worked the

words in my mind until they'd formed into complete lines.
And when they did, I sang soft and low.

Loving you would be as easy as taking a breath
But to look at you, that's a dance with death

I'd risk it all,
For you I would
You'd make me fall,
And fall I would

Loving you would be as easy as taking a breath
But to lay with you, that's a dance with death

"I like that," Jason said, sitting up in his bed.

I repeated the last verse three more times before the
next lines came to me.

I thought once was enough
You turned to me and called my bluff,
Maybe I should have walked away
but I couldn't resist, I needed replay after replay

Chapter Eighteen

A few nights later, I found myself checking emails in my bed. It was only 8:00 P.M., but I'd opened the window in my room to feel the soft breeze a few hours earlier and promptly decided I wasn't going to get out of bed again for the rest of the night.

Well, that is, until Derek interrupted me.

"Brooklyn, you decent?" he asked after tapping his knuckles on the door.

"Uhh, hold on!"

I quickly stashed the remnants of a candy bar and the romance novel I'd been devouring inside the drawer of my bedside table. It's not that I'm embarrassed to read romance, but this particular book's cover was a little over the top, even for me. Ripped hunk with billowy white top, tearing the corset off some damsel in the distress. i.e. the stuff dreams are made of. LuAnne had lent it to me.

"Okay! You can come in," I said, sitting up and folding my legs like pretzel.

The door opened and his blonde head poked through the gap.

"I was going to go into town and grab a beer. Wanna come with?"

The invitation seemed easy enough, but then I thought about the fact that Hank wasn't there to escort us.

Before I could even ask about security measure, Derek pushed the door open all the way and straightened up. "I know Hank isn't here, but I can be your security guard for the night, and believe me, no one in this bar will recognize you anyway. I swear." He puffed out his chest and flexed his biceps for good measure.

I laughed and rolled out of bed. My smutty read would have to wait until I got home. I had a craving for a cold beer.

"Do they have darts there?" I asked.

"Yep," he smiled. "And the first game is on me."

"I'm in," I said, moving to my closet so I could change my top. I'd spilled spaghetti sauce on it at dinner and hadn't bothered changing yet. "Give me two seconds and I'll meet you downstairs."

"Got it," he said, backing out and closing the door behind him.

After finding a loose peasant blouse (that looked oddly similar to the cover model's shirt on my book), I freshened up my make-up and trotted down the stairs. Derek was standing in the entryway twirling his car keys around on his thumb, and when he saw me coming down he smiled wide.

Seeing him standing there by himself made my smile falter. I'd assumed everyone would be going to the bar, but the fact that it would just be Derek and me left a tinge of guilt in my stomach.

Sure, Jason and I weren't anything official, but we were having sex and we were becoming really good friends. I think. The sex was definitely happening, unless I was imagining that too.

"Did you ask Jason if he wanted to go?" I asked, trying to sound just the right amount of interested in the question.

"Nah, LuAnne said he was busy writing or something," Derek said, stepping forward to guide me to the front door.

A part of me wanted to twist out of his arms and go up and talk to Jason myself, but maybe this was a good test. If things were truly the same between Jason and I— if we were simply colleagues— then I could go out and get a drink with Derek without having to worry about a thing.

Right?

• • •

Once the bartender had slid an ice-cold Corona with lime across the bar, everything seemed peachy keen. Derek challenged me to round after round of darts. In the beginning, *most* of my darts actually hit the dartboard. However, as the night progressed, and the Coronas kept coming, my dart-flinging abilities took a nosedive. (I stopped when one errant dart managed to wedge itself between the ceiling and the wall.)

"Pitiful! Just pitiful, Brooklyn," Derek teased, walking forward to grab the darts out of the board while shaking his head. "You're making me look bad in front of my all my friends."

I turned around to inspect the small bar. There was one bartender and three patrons in total. One of which was Paulo, who looked to be on a date with a well-dressed man.

"There's no one here, you liar! You're just sad because you don't know how to play my version of darts."

Derek tipped his head back and cracked up. "I'm sorry. What version is that?"

I smiled confidently, but the beer was starting to get to me so my facial muscles weren't quite cooperating. "Ceiling Darts. I just invented it."

Derek squeezed his eyes closed, holding in his laughter. "Oh boy, it's time to get you home. Jason is going to kill me. I already know it."

He set the darts down back in their holder, snatched my Corona from me mid-sip, and dropped it into the closest trashcan. "Whoa! Party foul. Give me back my drink. And why will Jason be mad? Can he not play ceiling darts, either?" I asked.

He shook his head and laughed. "Let's go."

Somehow, Derek managed to get me out of the bar even though I insisted that Paulo really wanted me to come and say bye to him. I even shouted out to him, but Derek kept pushing me out the door, apologizing to everyone as we went.

"He's not sorry, because I'm awesome!" I yelled right before the door closed behind us.

"That doesn't even make sense, Brooklyn," Derek laughed.

He opened the passenger door for me because Derek was a gentlemen. A cowboy gentlemen with big muscles and a nice smile. I couldn't remember why I didn't go for Derek. Probably because he wasn't Jason. Jason was everything. Derek was... I felt sick.

I slept most of the way home but stirred awake when he turned onto the uneven gravel drive. Derek moved to carry me to the house, but I guffawed (yes, guffawed) and hopped out of the truck by myself. I would have promptly eaten shit had Derek not been there to steady me. The porch light flipped on, and a second later, I heard the sound of the dead bolt turning and the front door opening.

There, silhouetted in the darkness, stood Jason. His arms were crossed and his dark eyebrows were tugged together.

"Uh oh, Mr. GrumpyGus looks mad," I said, trying to catch my footing on the loose gravel. *Why did the ground keep shifting out from underneath me?*

Derek didn't think that was funny, and neither did Jason. Tough crowd.

"She had a few Coronas. I didn't realize what a lightweight she was," Derek explained, as if he was trying to defend his actions.

I held up my hands. "No. No. I'm an independent woman, like Ms. Beyoncé. I did this to myself. So there's no one to blame here except Beyoncé," I said as I brushed past Jason and entered the house. I tried to head up the stairs but they seemed to never end, so I decided to sit down halfway to the top and catch my breath.

"Phew. When did you add these extra steps to the house? We were only gone for like two hours." I laid back so my head rested on the landing in the center of the stairs. *I could just sleep here.*

"Should I?" Derek started to ask, but Jason cut him off.

"I got it. Night Derek."

"Captain's orders, Derek!" I said, thinking my jokes were dead on. Seriously Derek should have left me at the bar so I could have performed stand-up for everyone. *Paulo's date would have loved that.*

I felt a presence walk past me on the stairs, but I didn't open my eyes to confirm the hunch.

"Princess, you just going to lay there the whole night?" Jason asked.

His voice was dark and deep, but there was something new in it: annoyance. Surprise, surprise. Jason hated me again. *What's new?*

"I'm thinking about it," I answered. "You just go on up and I'll take the first watch for the night."

I had no clue what I was talking about, but I figured that if I sounded like I knew what I was doing, he'd leave me alone.

The next thing I knew, there were two hands gripping my biceps and forcing me to sit up. Then my body was tossed over his shoulder like a sack of sugar.

I wasn't sure if sugar came in sacks that were my size, but if they did, Dotty would have loved it. He carried me up the stairs and my head bobbed back and forth right in front of his butt. He was wearing flannel pajama pants, but I could still see the outline of his derrière perfectly. It looked so appetizing.

"Did you just bite my butt?" he asked.

I had.

I wanted to know what it tasted like.

"No. Shh, I'm trying to sleep."

Then I proceeded to fake snore. (Like I said, *comedy gold.*)

Once we were in my room, Jason kicked my door closed and set me back down on my feet. Then, without bothering to ask, he pulled my blouse over the top of my head and unbuckled my pants. There was no romance in his movements so I knew we weren't about to have sex, but I still wanted out of my clothes anyway. They smelled like the bar, and I wanted to smell good so that Jason would like me.

Once I was standing there in my panties and bra, Jason came out of my closet holding up an oversized "New Kids On The Block" t-shirt and helped me put it on.

I don't remember if he helped me brush my teeth or wash my face, but I do remember the feeling of falling face first onto my bed and sinking into the soft blankets.

"I never want to leave this place," I whispered right before slipping into a deep, drunk slumber.

When I woke up at 4:00 A.M. with a splitting headache and the driest mouth known to man, I rolled over in the darkness and tried to sit up. Before I could get far, I saw the figure sitting in the corner of my room. Jason. He was on the chair next to the closet that was I usually reserved for dirty clothes. His elbow was propped up on the chair's arm and his head was resting in his palm. It had to have been the worst sleeping position, but I supposed it had afforded him a good view of me sleeping in bed.

His hair was sticking up in every direction and he was snoring softly, but that only made the scene more endearing.

I laid there watching him for a few minutes, wondering why he hadn't joined me in the bed or gone back to his room once I'd fallen asleep.

When I woke up again later that morning, he was gone.

• • •

Jason was quiet when I stepped into his room the next day so that we could continue writing. I took a deep breath in the center of the doorway, but he didn't look up when I strolled in. He was strumming his guitar with his head down. His guitar pick was wedged between his lips as he concentrated on his instrument.

I stood back, watching him. The chords he was playing weren't part of our song. I'd never heard the harmony before. It had a gentle, smooth sound, but the moment he noticed me standing there, he clapped his hand down on the sound hole and pulled the pick from his mouth.

"Morning," he said. His tone was as distant as it'd ever been.

"Hi," I spoke softly before taking a sip of my tea. I'd skipped the coffee, opting to ease my vocal chords back into action with a little honey and jasmine blend. "How'd you sleep?"

He shrugged, his eyes focused on his guitar. "Not great. You?"

I smiled at the memory of him in my armchair. "Okay."

He set his guitar down on the stand beside the couch and then folded his hands between his legs. "Have fun last night?"

There it was.

The furrowed brow, the slight frown.

He was pissed that I'd gone out with Derek.

But that wasn't part of our rules. We were the king and queen of living in the present. We didn't talk about the past and we didn't talk about the future. For the last week, Jason and I lived like someone had told us that if we wanted to write the next big hit, we had to have sex *everywhere*. *All the time*. It wasn't even a surprise anymore when I felt him join me in my bed or when I walked into his bathroom in the morning. I'd wait patiently for him to finish brushing his teeth so that I could tear his clothes off. Pretty much every surface of the upstairs needed to be disinfected or blown up. We were getting a little ridiculous, but let me explain something. The way Jason sings, that soulful, deep, crooning — that's how he had sex. Every time we fell into bed together it felt like he was making love to me, digging the heels of his hands into mine, twining our legs together, teasing every surface of my body until I was sure I'd slipped into a coma.

But then when it finished, *we were finished*. It felt as if someone flipped a light switch as soon as the sex was over. Either he'd gather his clothes and leave, or I did. We never stayed because it wasn't part of our silent set-up. We were treasure hunters, thrill-seekers, adrenaline junkies.

So when he asked me that question, it was the first time I was forced to acknowledge what we were doing beyond the moment we were actually doing it in.

"Yes. Derek took me out for drinks," I answered hesitantly.

He chewed on his bottom lip and stared out through his massive bedroom window. The bottom panel was pushed up and I could feel the breeze blowing through. We sat there in silence for a few seconds and then he nodded.

"Right, let's get started," he said, his gaze hovering somewhere far off in the distance.

And that was that. Whatever confusion, anger, or doubt he'd been feeling moments before were completely gone. When he glanced up at me, his brown eyes weren't clouded over. Rather, they were crystal clear.

Which meant we were back at square one.

Except maybe I wasn't quite as content with square one as I'd been five minutes earlier.

Chapter Nineteen

Saturday morning, two weeks after I'd first arrived in Montana, Cammie was scheduled to visit and I couldn't contain my excitement. I'd paired my red boots with cut-off shorts and a white blouse, and I'd even added some matching red lipstick. The outfit, plus the fact that I didn't bother with my hair in Montana, made me look like a full-on country singer. My dark blonde curls were going every which way as I stood outside of the airport, but I didn't care. *Snap away, paparazzi.*

"If you try and step closer again, I'm calling airport security," Hank warned the group of photographers positioned on the other side of the street. Like a flock of scared pigeons, they scooted back a couple of feet.

I gave him a small smile, but he of course, just nodded curtly as if to say "it's part of the job, ma'am." Seriously, I was going to set Hank up someday with a woman who loved the strong, silent type. I laughed just thinking of how terribly awkward their dinner conversations would be.

The airport's automatic doors swooshed open as another round of travelers dispersed in various directions. Some of them lined up for the taxis; some ran into the arms of loved ones. I was watching as one couple reunited— the man was clad in Army camo and the girl was crying. Big, heartfelt tears ran down her cheeks. I could have written a song about that exact moment. A soldier's reunion with his loved ones was always a sight to behold.

"Hello! Earth to Brooklyn!" a voice snapped in front of me.

When I pulled my gaze away from the couple, I found my sister standing in front of me, looking like a ray of sunshine on a cloudy day. She had on white converse, skinny jeans, and an off-the-shoulder t-shirt that had a brand's logo on it. Of course, I didn't recognize it because at twenty-seven, I was already an old fart compared to her. She'd pulled her long dark brown hair up into a loose bun and her smile practically touched the corners of her light brown eyes.

"Cammie!" I squealed jumping forward to wrap my arms around her.

After spinning her in a circle nearly fifty times, she finally protested.

"Oh my god, I'm going to puke all over your cowboy boots!"

"NO!" I yelled, dropping her and stepping back. *No one touches the red cowboy boots.*

"I'm so excited!" she said, glancing around at the slices of Montana visible from the airport entrance. Two weeks without my sister was a lot harder than I'd thought it would be. Even though we talked on the phone and texted every day, I'd still missed her.

"Ladies, what do you have planned in Montana?" one of the paparazzi yelled.

Hank practically snarled at the man. Usually, whenever one of them spoke up, the rest followed suit, so Hank stepped forward and ushered Cammie and I to the town car waiting for us on the curb. Once the doors were closed and the tinted windows were rolled up, I sat back in the seat and just took Cammie in.

After our parents passed away, it would have been easy to slip into a parent role for Cammie, but I'd always tried to maintain our relationship as sisters. Seeing her in the car, looking as grown-up as ever (because well, she was) I had a "proud parent moment" even though I'd probably done nothing to contribute to her success.

Cammie was intelligent and driven. She'd always pushed herself to excel at anything she did and I admired that about her.

"Are you going to stare at me like that the entire drive over? Because if so, I'm pulling out my iPad and ignoring you," she threatened with a small smile.

I shook my head and let out a deep breath, trying to push past the emotions roiling up inside of me. Cammie needed me to be normal, not a pile of blubbering craziness.

"What do you feel like doing when we get to Big Timber?" I asked, pulling out my cell phone. There were lots of emails and messages from industry people, but of course, nothing from Jason. I'd been with him the night before, when we'd "tested out" the patio furniture and attempted to be as quiet as possible. (It'd worked out quite terribly considering how painful wicker is on bare skin. Let's just say wicker-imprints on your ass last longer than you'd think they would.) He hadn't been awake when I'd left to get Cammie, and for all I knew he didn't even remember she was coming to visit for the weekend.

"Hmm, do they have a sushi place? I'm craving some spicy tuna," she answered.

I gave her a pointed stare. "You do realize how far away we are from the ocean, right?"

Cammie smiled. "Alright fine. I'll just take a triple scoop of thick 'n' hearty Montana cowboy, please."

Derek's easy grin flashed in my mind and then I thought about the fact that Cammie and him were closer in age than he and I were. *Greeeatttt.*

"There actually is a guy who works for Jason. I don't really know what all he does. I think he helps with the animals and stuff."

"Huh," Cammie smirked. "I guess Jason has been keeping you busy."

My eyes widened in fear. I hadn't told her about my true arrangement with Jason. It wasn't a conscious decision; I'd just decided to keep the situation closer to my heart. Maybe it was because I didn't know what was going on myself, or maybe it was because I didn't care to hear her judgment. Either way, it'd been my little secret.

My silence spurred her to continue. "You know, with song writing and stuff," she clarified, casting me a suspicious glance.

"Oh, yeah. That. We've been writing a lot. I think we'll be done with our song in a few days."

Cammie clapped. "That's perfect! That means you can come home early. LA sucks without you. I've been hanging out with people in my studio and the only thing they ever want to talk about is architecture. If I have to hear one more debate on modernism versus classicism, I'll stab someone with a Doric column." She made a pretend barfing sound and I laughed.

"Well, I guarantee, if you even say the word 'Doric' again while in my presence, I will fall asleep instantly."

Cammie smiled. "Perfect."

"Are you all done with your projects?"

She nodded and let her head fall back on the headrest. "I presented two days ago, cleared out my studio yesterday, and now I'm here. I'm finally done!"

"So the only thing left is your graduation next weekend?" I asked, trying to get my schedule worked out in my brain.

"Yes, and then I have to start job hunting."

I opened my mouth to ask her about Grayson, but then stopped myself. I'd done enough with that situation. If she didn't want to call him and he didn't want to call her, there was nothing more I could do. Cammie would find her own career path.

The rest of the car ride back to Big Timber, we planned out everything we'd do over the weekend. Most of it involved stuffing our faces and wearing pajamas, but I knew we'd find some kind of trouble to get into before the weekend was done.

• • •

We arrived at Jason's ranch right around lunchtime, but LuAnne was the only person who greeted us at the door.

"Oh my gosh! You two could be twins if not for the hair and the eyes. Like delicate little snowflakes from the same cloud, you two are," she said with her hands clasped in front of her mouth. *Oh, LuAnne.* Her gaze darted back and forth between the two us for nearly a minute before she realized she was blocking our path into the house. "Oh! Come in, come in. I just set out some sandwich stuff on the kitchen table."

She ushered us inside and I watched Cammie take in the ranch.

"This is really cool. I think I was expecting more of a cabin in the woods or something," she said, probably admiring the architecture much more than I had.

The two of us made our way into the kitchen and sat down at the table with LuAnne. As we devoured her chicken-salad sandwiches, she explained that the boys had run into town to grab some lumber to repair the side of the barn. Just thinking about Jason and lumber made me cross and re-cross my legs. *Why was it so hot imaging a man around wood?*

"Did you hear me, Brook?" Cammie asked pinching the back of my arm.

I flinched back and yelped.

"Jeez, that hurts!"

"Sorry, LuAnne was asking if you wanted to show me the stables and you were staring off into lala land."

I wasn't in lala land. I was in Jason Land.

"Sure, let me finish this sandwich and we'll go."

In reality, I needed to cool my jets and stop imagining Jason in compromising positions or my knees would give out when I stood up.

The air was warming up when we finally stepped out to inspect the barn and stables. I smiled down at my red boots and the matching pair that I'd gifted Cammie after lunch. I knew she wouldn't have any footwear that was appropriate for tromping around a barn, so I'd picked her up a pair from Paulo earlier in the week.

"I feel like a northwestern version of Dorothy," she said, tapping the heels of her boots together as if she were wearing ruby slippers.

I shook my head and tugged her toward the path that led around the side of the house. Since I wasn't sure where the guys were doing repairs on the barn, I decided to skip over it and show her the stable first. Dotty would be eager to sniff out the sugar cubes in our pockets anyway.

"How many horses do they have here?" Cammie asked as I bent forward to pull open the heavy door.

"Five. Two mares and three geldings. Dotty is the first one on the right," I said, pointing her out once we stepped inside. She'd been lying on the hay, but the moment she saw us step inside, she pressed up onto her hooves and came over to greet us with a soft rumble from her nostrils.

"She's so pretty! I want to give her all the sugar cubes," Cammie said, unfolding her hand toward the horse. In three seconds flat, all of her sugar cubes were gone.

"Cammie, you can't just let her take them all at once," I laughed, patting Dotty's cheek.

"Maybe she wouldn't scarf them down so fast if you guys weren't so stingy with them," Cammie protested. "Don't worry, Dotty, I've got your back."

"Hey. Are you guys in the stable?" a deep voice called from a few yards away. When Cammie and I turned toward the door, a sweaty Derek stepped through the threshold with a warm smile on his face. By the looks of his raised brows, he was pleasantly surprised by Cammie. *Yeah, yeah, cowboy, she's quite a looker.*

"Hey," he said, cleaning his hands on a towel he had stuffed in his back pocket. "I'm Derek."

Cammie took the hand he had outstretched towards her and smiled. "Nice to meet you. I'm Cameron Heart."

Derek glanced toward me. "The little sister! I didn't realize you'd be visiting." The touch of mischief in his eyes was impossible to miss.

Footsteps behind him drew my attention to the stable door right as Jason stepped inside. I didn't want him to, but still, he stole all of my attention. His hair was pushed back out of his eyes probably from the sweat that had also gathered across his neck and chest. His flannel shirtsleeves were rolled up to his elbows and the top few snap-buttons were undone. He had on a pair of dark brown leather work-boots and some faded Levi's. Holy shit. Mr. Brooding Musician looked edible.

Just like everyone else, Jason's gaze flashed back and forth between the pair of us before finally pausing on me. A slow smile unfolded as he stepped toward me, but he paused a few feet away. I didn't expect him to wrap me up in a hug or a kiss. He never touched me when other people were around. *Another unspoken rule.* But it still hurt to realize that we looked like two passing strangers. I had to pretend that I didn't want to tackle him, that I didn't know what he looked like beneath that flannel shirt.

"You look just like you do on TV," Cammie said, beaming at Jason. She wasn't one to get star struck usually. We'd been around enough celebrities in LA for her to get used to them, but apparently Jason Monroe was a different story. Her cheeks were flushed and she was beaming from ear to ear. She looked absolutely gorgeous and for the first time in my life, I wanted to push my sister into the pile of horse poop sitting inside Dotty's stall. *Wow. Territorial much?*

Jason stepped forward to shake Cammie's hand, and I stared at their hands touching, wondering what the hell was wrong with me.

"We'll be out here the rest of the afternoon, but maybe we can all do something fun after dinner," Derek said, beaming at Cammie.

"Yeah, sure, sounds great," I said, moving toward the door. I hated the dark, twisted feeling settling into the pit of my stomach. I hated caring that Jason might think my little sister was hot. I hated wondering what the hell was going on between us. And I hated not being able to look him in the eye as I passed by him for fear that he'd see all my emotions written across my face.

It was probably time to tell Cammie the whole truth.

Chapter Twenty

"Tell me something I didn't know, slut monkey."

My mouth dropped open. "Are you serious?"

Cammie rolled her eyes and sat up on my bed across from me.

"I'm your sister and your best friend. Well, pretty much your *only* friend, let's face it. Of course I knew there was something going on between you and Jason. There's no way you'd be able to resist while living with that man."

My mouth dropped open even wider and I wondered if my jaw was about to become unhinged.

"The problem is, I can't figure out exactly *what* is going on," she said, narrowing her eyes on me.

"Just sex," I answered quickly, clarifying that fact for her and for myself.

Cammie pursed her lips and rolled her eyes. "Okay, great. So you won't mind if I try and hook up with him next, since it's just a sex thing?"

"That's not even funny, Cammie," I said with a sharp tone.

"My point exactly," she said.

I pushed off the bed and straightened my blouse, suddenly pissed off at the world as a whole. "I'm going down to help LuAnne with dinner," I said, leaving my bedroom and closing the door behind me with a sharp slam. My heart was beating a mile a minute, so I pressed my back against the doorframe and rested there for a moment, collecting my feelings and shoving them back down where they belonged.

Jason had made it perfectly clear that things were complicated for him and that he wasn't interested in anything beyond sex. Which meant, if I wanted things with Jason to continue, I had to follow his rules. But in that moment I realized that my body and my head were no longer on the same page. I wasn't sure how much longer I could keep playing this game, pretending that I wouldn't end up as the sole casualty when everything was said and done.

A moment later, the front door opened and closed. I jumped off the wall and pushed my hair behind my ears, trying to get ahold of myself in case Jason was about to walk up the stairs. I held my breath, waiting for footsteps, but then I heard Cammie moving around in my room, and I knew I had to move. If she came out to see me standing there, she'd know something was wrong.

LuAnne put me to work in the kitchen right away and I enjoyed every second of it. The busy work made time pass quickly and it kept me focused on chopping vegetables. Once I was done with my first task, LuAnne put me on chocolate cream pie duty and I, of course, obliged. I'd never made one before, but she gave me a recipe that was easy to follow. I was gathering ingredients from the pantry and refrigerator when I felt Cammie's arms wrap around my stomach.

"I'm sorry. I'll stop trying to pry into your love life," she whispered before letting me go.

I smiled and turned around so I could hug her back. "I'm sorry, too. Let's just not talk about it anymore." I almost added a please but I didn't want her to know how desperately I wished we could drop the subject forever.

She nodded, and then together, we made a chocolate cream pie. Life was always better with my sister by my side, even when she tried to push issues that I didn't want to talk about.

"That pie smells so good," LuAnne said just before she tugged on a pair of oven mitts and pulled out a roasted chicken from the oven. The kitchen was instantly filled with the most delicious smell of rosemary and thyme. As if on cue, my stomach rumbled and the boys flew through the front door.

"Go shower, dinner's ready in ten!" LuAnne yelled out to them. They grunted back with what I assumed were actual words before I heard their feet clamber up the stairs.

Jason was inside the house.

He was about to be naked and in the shower.

Why were my hands so freaking sweaty all of a sudden?

"I'm just going to go use the restroom really quick," I said to Cammie and LuAnne as I stepped out of the kitchen. There was a small bathroom downstairs that sat just below the staircase, set back into an alcove, and it was the perfect place to give myself a tiny pep talk before dinner. I straightened out my blouse and fluffed up my hair. Good news: I smelled like chocolate cream pie. Or maybe that wasn't a good thing? *Shit, what if Jason hates chocolate?*

I rolled my eyes at how ridiculous I was being and then pushed off the bathroom sink. As I turned to leave, I heard a light tap on the bathroom door, and then a second later, the door handle turned and Jason pushed his way into the small space. I didn't even have time to offer up a timid "Someone's in here!" because he was already "in there" invading my space and pushing my back to the sink's countertop.

"What are you—"

Before I could get the question out, he kissed me senseless, sealing his body to mine. His lips were demanding, and his kiss was impossible to keep up with. He was sweaty; I could smell the musk from his day of hard labor, but the heavy blend silenced my questions even more.

When he pulled away and I fluttered my eyes open, I knew I looked as flustered as I felt.

"Someone could hear us," I whispered.

He kept his hand tucked beneath my hair, just at the base of my neck as he shook his head. His gaze was pinned on my lips, filled with blood from his kiss. "You looked so sexy earlier but I couldn't do a damn thing about it with Cammie and Derek around."

"So now you're…"

He smirked. "Doing something about it."

With that little cooler-than-cool statement, he unbuttoned my jean shorts and pushed them down my legs. He started working on his jeans, but I couldn't find words as I realized that we were about to have a standing-up bathroom quickie. I stared at him as he slid his boxer-briefs down. Kept staring as his fingers slid gently up my inner-thighs. Then suddenly, I wasn't looking at anything. I clamped my eyelids closed and pressed back against the cold bathroom counter as he gripped me tighter.

His attentive fingers were more than enough to prepare me and it was impossibly hard to remain quiet as he slid into me. I bit down on his neck as he fisted my hair. My nails scratched his back and he scraped his teeth along my skin, teasing me, but never biting. The sex was rough and carnal and I couldn't help but feel a little used.

My head fell back against the bathroom mirror as I came hard, just moments before he whispered my name against my lips as his own release followed.

As soon as we were finished, he zipped up his jeans and pulled my shorts back up so that he could button them for me. Without a word, he turned and exited the bathroom like he hadn't just taken a blowtorch to my heart.

I squeezed my eyes shut, surprised to find a tear trickling down my cheek.

• • •

"So what do you two have planned for your visit, Cammie?" LuAnne asked as the five of us sat down at the table for dinner. Jason had placed himself across from me, but I prided myself on not looking at him at all during dinner, especially after what had just happened in the bathroom. My eyes followed a strict fork-plate-chicken-fork-plate-chicken route so that I wouldn't stray and glance up at him. *Although I think I just looked like a cyborg.*

"I'm not sure. I think we'll go explore the town tomorrow. Brookie told me there were a few shops that we could check out," Cammie replied.

"That prom thing is tomorrow," Jason said casually.

My eyes jumped up to him. Dammit. *Look away!* I glanced back down to my plate.

"Logan's prom?" I asked, eyeing my green beans.

"Yeah. I figured your assistant would have reminded you about it."

I cringed. "She would have had I actually told her about it. I completely forgot."

Cammie feigned shock. "Brooklyn, you got invited to the *senior prom*? I'm so proud!"

I gave her an annoyed glare. "It's a long story, but yes, apparently, tomorrow night I'll be hanging out with a bunch of eighteen year olds."

"Can you imagine the sheer amount of suppressed sexual tension in that one place?" She shivered as if she could feel it right then. "I do *not* envy you."

I cringed. "Thank you for that, Cammie."

"Do you have something to wear already?" she asked, before cutting into a piece of chicken.

Crap. Of course I didn't have anything to wear. I hadn't thought to pack an evening gown in my suitcase when heading to Montana. When Cammie saw the panic flash across my face, she clapped her hands together.

"SHOPPING SPREE!"

Derek and Jason laughed, but I just sat there wishing I could trade places with the chicken on the table. I'd rather have someone stick a fork in me than see Jason dressed up in a tuxedo.

My heart couldn't handle it. My hoo-hah probably couldn't either. Maybe I could carry an icepack around in my underwear. To y'know, cool it off down there.

• • •

The next morning Cammie and I met up with Paulo, the fabulously grizzly taxidermist, at the one shop in Big Timber that sold dresses that you could get away with wearing to prom. We'd called ahead and had them open the shop an hour early so that there wouldn't be any security issues. You'd think that wouldn't be necessary, but teenage girls can be really scary. One time a fan jumped on my back while I was at a restaurant and my face fell forward onto my plate and I literally thought my steak knife was going to stab me. So yeah, I don't fear dark alleys. I fear teenage girls.

"Dress me up, bitches," I said as I followed Paulo and Cammie into the shop. I had a thermos of coffee in my left hand and a pair of high-heels in the other.

Paulo shot me one of those "girl, please" glares, but I just winked.

"We need to find their sluttiest dresses," Cammie mocked as we perused the store. It was small, and the entire front half was stocked with western wear and casual clothes, but in the back there were racks upon racks of formal dresses. Apparently it was the only dress shop in town.

"I think you should wear this," Cammie said, pulling out a pink taffeta disaster.

I flipped her the bird and turned toward another rack.

"You've got a nice butt and some decent tits. You should show them off," Paulo said, holding up a red dress that should have been placed in the underwear section of the store. It was completely see-through save for the thin patches covering the crotch area and the breasts. I looked past the dress, to glare at Paulo who was wearing a fitted black blazer and a handkerchief tied around his neck. Most of his mischievous smile was hidden behind his beard, and once again I was left wondering how exactly a person like him existed in a place like Big Timber, Montana.

"You can't be serious," I said.

"Yup! Two to one. You have to try it on," Cammie said, taking the hanger from Paulo and draping the "dress" over her arm.

I should have kicked the two of them out right then because for the next hour, they just got progressively worse. I think they found every dress in that store that would make me look like a lady of the night. I was left scouring through the racks to find anything that would do a decent job of covering up my boobs. I wasn't trying to give Logan a heart attack at his senior prom.

Near the back of the store, there were a few dresses that were glitter-free, sequin-free, and that wouldn't cut off halfway down my ass. That's where I found a simple black dress that had a low-cut back and a hemline that hit my ankles. The material wasn't what I was used to from the designers in LA, but it had a traditional cut, and I knew it would fit my frame well. I grabbed my size and snuck away to the dressing room while Cammie and Paulo took turns trying on tiaras and practicing their coronation waves.

"Boo, you whore. Come out and show us the dress you just snuck in there," Cammie said as soon as I closed the dressing room drape.

"Did you just quote Mean Girls?" I asked, pulling my shirt over my head and unbuttoning my shorts.

The drape flew open and Cammie stood there with her hands on her hips.

"Cameron! Jeez, a little privacy please."

She tilted her head down in annoyance. "Paulo isn't buying what you're selling and I've seen your body before. So just show me the dress already."

To her credit, the shop owner was blushing and trying to hide her face in the magazine she was reading at the counter. But there was no point in fighting Cammie, so I let my shorts fall to the ground and then reached for the dress.

"Let the record show that Brooklyn Heart actually wears some killer panties," Cammie said, as she and Paulo applauded. I curtsied and then spun in a circle, because if you can't beat them, *join them*.

"Zip me up," I said as the soft dress material cascaded over my skin. It fell to the floor around my feet, but I knew it'd fit better once I slipped the heels on. Cammie pulled the zipper up the side, where it lay hidden beneath my arm, and then she stepped back and I turned to the mirror.

Damn. *Not bad at all*. I was used to wearing tailored gowns created by famous designers, but apparently Hawte Country Couture could design a decent dress.

"It's so gorgeous on you," Cammie said.

"Agreed, but you can't wear a bra with that back," Paulo said.

Cammie laughed. "Are you going to let Logan cop a feel while you guys slow dance?"

I groaned. "I don't think kids slow dance anymore. I think it's all dry humping and heavy petting. Which is why I will be stationed by the punch bowl with the parent chaperones." *That was the plan at least.*

"Whatever, party-pooper. Let's pay for this dress so we can go home and figure out how to style your hair."

Paulo perked up and smiled wide. "Will you let me do it?"

I coughed and tried to resist the urge to say, "hell no."

"I used to style hair when I lived in New York," he explained.

Cammie and I both turned to him with shocked gapes. "Are you serious?"

He nodded. "That's where I lived with my partner, but when I moved out here, he stayed behind to run the salon."

"Aw, I'm sorry Paulo."

He grunted. "Don't be. I plan on moving back to New York once the bed-and-breakfast and the shop are up and running."

It shouldn't have, but the idea of Paulo leaving Big Timber for good made me sad. Maybe it was the idea that everyone would eventually be moving on from Big Timber. Cammie and I would be going back to LA, Paulo would head to the New York, and Jason would go wherever it was he planned on going next. I wouldn't know because we didn't talk about the future. I wasn't even sure when he was heading to LA for the award show. He'd be there for the event, but for all I knew he was leaving again as soon as it was over.

So our future was set. We'd have our time together at his ranch and then when I left, our little fling would be over.

We'd be over.

Chapter Twenty-One

I learned three things while getting ready for the senior prom:

　　1. A twenty-seven year old woman should never say the above statement.

　　2. Paulo could work a curling iron.

　　3. Cammie couldn't keep a sex secret to save her life.

　　"So do you think Jason and Logan will have a fight over you during the senior prom?" she asked, while Paulo finished my make-up, because yes, he could also do make-up. *I'd found a big, burly, tattooed fairy godmother.*

　　Before that moment, Paulo hadn't realized there was anything going on between Jason and I outside of our music, but now he definitely did. Thanks to Cammie.

　　"Like maybe Logan will pull you out onto the floor for a slow dance and Jason will be overcome with jealousy. They'll fight over you and everyone at prom will stop to watch. Then they'll tell Jason that he's retroactively expelled and can't graduate until he repeats senior year as a twenty-eight year old."

Paulo gasped in feigned horror.

"Are you guys almost done writing cheesy 90s sitcom scenarios?" I asked, glaring at Cammie over my shoulder in the mirror.

She reached forward and gripped my shoulder. "Brookie, no matter what you do— Use a condom. You don't want to become a teen mother."

Her and Paulo completely lost it after that and I was left finishing up my own damn make-up after I'd kicked them out of my room. I looked at myself in the mirror and tried to get Cammie out of my head. *(I also thought that I shouldn't have been so hasty to kick Paulo out. Only one of my eyes was finished and I couldn't do my own make-up for shit.)*

With a sigh, I went to work, reminding myself that the night was about the two high schoolers that Jason and I were escorting: Logan, and another senior named Jessie.

When the school had heard about Jason's offer to accompany a girl to the senior prom, they'd held a creative writing contest. Quite a few senior girls had written in and Jason had picked Jessie's story out of all of them. He hadn't let me read it, but I had a feeling he'd made a good choice. So it was all set. A limo would arrive in thirty minutes and then we'd go pick up Logan and Jessie to head to the dance.

I hadn't spoken with or even *looked* at Jason since our bathroom romp. So when I stepped down the stairs, holding up the bottom of my dress so I wouldn't trip, I was not at all prepared to see him standing at the very bottom in a tailored black tuxedo.

I inhaled a sharp breath and paused. For the first time since I'd met him, his chin and neck were completely clean and smooth. His hair was slicked back and my breath was coming in painful, short spurts. That strong chin was usually hidden behind stubble. Those eyes were usually hidden behind disheveled hair. Yet there he was, looking like the most beautiful man I'd ever seen, and he wasn't even my date.

Jason held his hand out for me to take once I'd gathered my wits enough to step down to him.

"You guys have fun and don't worry about curfew!" Cammie yelled.

I glared over my shoulder and she shrugged. "Last one, I swear."

I blew her a kiss and a wink before Jason whisked us out to the limo.

"Your sister is a lot like you," Jason said as he held the limo door open for me so I could slide in. The interior was dimly lit and there were a few sodas chilling in an ice bucket below the far window. Although there was plenty of space for the two of us, Jason slid in next to me so that his thigh pressed against mine. The driver closed to the door for us, and soon we were pulling away from the ranch on the uneven gravel drive.

"Is she?" I asked. He wasn't the first person to tell me that Cammie and I were alike, but I loved knowing why people thought that. Everyone had a different reason: our personality, our looks, our mannerisms.

"Yeah, I mean she looks like you a little bit. But she's got a lightness about her. It's surprising to find that in people who've dealt with loss like the two of you have."

His words completely took me by surprise. Sure, Jason knew about me losing my parents, but the fact that he'd given it a second thought shook my emotions awake. The emotions I was trying to shove back down.

"She's always been my anchor and I hope I've been that for her as well. She can make me laugh like no one else." I could feel his dark gaze concentrated on me, so I continued. "Not at first, of course. We had to work to get our humor back after everything that happened. But I remember the first time we laughed. The first time we told ourselves it was okay to be happy again."

He reached out for my hand and held it between his palms, but he didn't offer any words. For a moment, I stared at the physical connection, completely shocked at his silent support. We sat like that until the limo pulled up outside of Logan's house. It was a small redbrick home with a wrought-iron star positioned over the garage and a Ford truck parked in the driveway.

I'd barely knocked on the door before it opened, and there was Logan, beaming ear to ear. He was wearing a tuxedo that hung off his shoulders and gaped around his waist, but he looked so handsome with gelled hair and a nervous smile. In that moment I knew I was doing the right thing by going to prom with him, even if it wasn't exactly my idea of a fun night.

"Your carriage awaits," I joked.

He glanced at the limo over my shoulder and then nodded quickly. "My parents want to take a few photos if that's okay," he explained with a shrug as his confident smile started to wane. I knew that there would be a few photos taken of the event, but my goal in going to the prom with Logan wasn't for a publicity stunt. I didn't want the photos to end up in a magazine. Still, I found myself smiling and stepping into his house.

A few minutes later, after Logan's litter sister had asked me to literally sign every item in her room, we headed outside to slide into the limousine. Jason was on his phone when we slid back in, and to my dismay, he'd moved over to the side bench so that Logan and I could sit by one another. As much as I wanted to protest, Logan deserved to have my attention for the night. *Well, I could at least sit by him. Actually pulling my attention away from Jason in tuxedo just wasn't feasible.*

I forced my gaze out the window as the limousine pulled out of Logan's neighborhood and crossed the main road in Big Timber, toward a rougher looking area of town. When we pulled off onto a dirt road, a sign hung loose from its chains overhead. It read: "Big Timber RV Park". Jessie's home was at the farthest end of the park, surrounded by trees, with small garden in the front yard. She was already sitting outside on the wooden stairs in front of her door, waiting for us with a big smile on her face. Her dark hair was pulled up into a simple up-do with a gemstone-covered barrette securing it all in place. I recognized her dress from the shop in town, a light purple poofy thing, but she looked like a princess in it, and as Jason exited the limousine, she looked like she was looking up at her prince. There was no one to take pictures of Jessie and Jason, so before they turned to climb back into the limousine, I hopped out with my iPhone and posed them next to the garden with the trees in the background.

She was a quiet girl, obviously shy around Jason and I, but when we returned to the limousine and I told her that I liked her dress, her apprehensiveness started to fade.

"Thanks! It took forever to pick the perfect one," she said, looking down at the material and smoothing it out between her palms.

"You look great," Jason said, with a small smile.

You would have thought he'd just told her she won a small island off the coast of Jamaica. Her eyes widened and she visibly stiffened. Jason met my gaze and I smiled to let him know he'd done the right thing.

• • •

The senior prom was held in the cafeteria of their high school. I didn't know how the room was normally set-up, but the prom committee had done a good job with decorations. Save for that quintessential school smell, I'd have thought we were in a fancy ballroom in downtown LA. Multi-colored lights flashed overhead and there were balloons and streamers everywhere. A young DJ was up on stage with a laptop set-up on a black table. His music pounded through speakers set up around the room.

To the left of the stage there was a line forming to have professional photos taken with a blue backdrop. Couples stood beneath a white plastic arch with fake ivy twined throughout. The set-up might have been cheesy, but their smiles were real and you could feel the romance and excitement in the air.

I tried to ignore the lingering stares around us. Even in the dim lighting, Jason and I stood out like sore thumbs. We had Hank with us as well as an additional security guard that Hank had brought with him. The pair of them stood at least a foot over the rest of the crowd, and combined they probably out-weighed an elephant. *Very discreet.*

"What should we do first?" I asked, turning to our small group.

"Let's go check out the food," Logan said, just as Jessie spoke up.

"Can we go say hi to my friends?" she asked Jason with a timid voice.

Jason and I exchanged a wary glance. We'd have to split up. Before I could think to protest, Logan headed toward the food table, tugging me along with him. Jessie moved toward the other side of the dance floor and Jason had to think fast to keep up with her.

I shouldn't have felt a pang of sadness, I mean we were still in the same building, and we'd see each other later. But knowing that our time was so limited, that in two weeks our arrangement would end, made me sad that we'd be separated all night by a sea of teenagers.

After the food table, Logan dragged me over to where a group of boys were standing in a circle to the side of the dance floor. Before that night I didn't think it was possible to discuss video games for that long without an end in sight. *I don't care about the merits of a good cosplay outfit.* I just wanted to bash my head into the concrete pillar beside me.

I didn't want to leave Logan, so I held out, trying to keep up with the conversation while also trying not to fall asleep from how bored I was. Every few minutes a student would come up to ask me for a photo or an autograph. Normally the constant interruptions would have been annoying, but I welcomed them. You want a photo? *Great. Let's take fifteen.*

But then I spotted Jason out on the dance floor. Jessie was wearing a giant smile as he did a poor rendition of the "sprinkler". I couldn't help but laugh. The other girls on the dance floor would try to position themselves behind Jason so it looked like he was dancing with them. Their friends would snap a photo and they'd all giggle, looking down at the iPhone screen. It was funny to watch and I knew I'd have done the same thing when I was their age.

A few of them were bold enough to ask him to dance, but he never accepted, instead he stayed true to his date with Jessie. He showered her with attention, doing his best to display a stream of various dance moves. (*Some of which were truly terrible. I made a mental note to ask him why his dance moves were not on par with his bedroom moves.*)

A little while later, I got the brilliant idea to excuse myself to go to the bathroom. I figured I could take my time; maybe walk around the perimeter of the dance just to have something to do. I wanted to be a nice date to Logan, but it was clear that he was a teenage boy, and girls, even a celebrity crush, couldn't hold his attention like a good ol' video game discussion could.

I watched Jason on the dance floor as I walked through the dance. He glanced up just before I turned the corner to the bathroom and his eyes locked on mine. I smiled and waved, and he flashed a playful smile. I would have lingered there longer, but another group of girls walked up to ask Jason for a picture. *The man clearly had his hands full.*

Hank pointed me in the direction of the bathroom and I took my time once I was inside, listening to the conversations taking place around me. They were exactly what you'd expect from a deliciously trashy MTV show.

Girl A: "Shithead Tommy hasn't asked me to dance all night. Why did he even bother asking me to come if he wasn't going to pay attention to me?"

Girl B: "Yeah well, at least Tommy said you were hot. I bought a new push-up bra and Lucas hasn't even noticed. He's been up at the DJ booth, requesting dumb songs."

Girl A: "Our dates suck."

Girl B: "I know. We should have just stayed home and watched a movie."

Girl A: "Whatever. I think Jason Monroe is still here. Sally said she was going to try to kiss him."

Girl B: "Like he would kiss a high school girl. Sally's a prude anyway."

Girl A: "Do you think I should stuff more toilet paper down my bra? I feel like my boobs have gotten smaller since I got here."

Girl B: "No. God. Tommy will notice. You already have enough toilet paper in there to deflect a bullet."

Girl A: "Whatever, your boobs are like giant water balloons. Why would I take advice from you?"

I couldn't hear the rest of their conversation because I had to flush my toilet, and once they knew someone else was in the bathroom with them, the pair of them scurried out like wild banshees. I stepped out of the stall and washed my hands, inspecting my make-up in the terrible lighting that exists in high school bathrooms. *Dear god, no wonder teenage girls are insecure.* I think I could see every one of my pores.

After stalling for another ten minutes, I finally pushed the bathroom door open, knowing Logan was probably wondering where I'd gone. But before I could head back into the dance, I saw Jason standing in the hall with Hank and the other security guard. Once he saw me approaching, he stepped forward with a devilish smiled.

"I was about to send in someone to check if you were okay."

I laughed. "I needed a break from your cousin. I couldn't listen to him talk about Grand Theft Auto for one more second."

Jason laughed and shook his head. "Yeah, I should have warned you about that."

He stepped closer and held his hand out for me to take. I stared down at it, thoroughly confused. Then I glanced down the hallway to find it completely deserted. *Weren't there teenagers ready to snap a photo as soon as they saw us holding hands?* That photo would have been worth quite a lot if they sold it to the right person.

"The coast is clear," Jason said. "C'mon, let's take a walk really quick. I talked Hank into letting us have some alone time."

The idea of alone time piqued my interest. In the last 24 hours Cammie had kept me completely occupied. Before I could offer a response, Jason wrapped his hand around mine and tugged me around a corner. Most of the overhead lights were off in the side hallway, but the few left on illuminated the expansive space. Lockers flanked the walls on both sides, but every few feet they cut off to allow for a classroom door. Jason tried the handle of each door we passed, until one, in the center of the hallway was finally unlocked. He grinned back at me as he pushed it opened and then pulled me inside.

I think I'd had a fantasy just like this in high school, except it involved a young English teacher who read Shakespeare aloud to our class.

That memory was pushed aside as Jason flipped a switch, illuminating half of the science lab, and leaving the rest of it in the shadows. Black tables were spaced around the room, set up with sinks and outlets to conduct experiments.

"What a seductive location," I joked, twining my fingers with his.

He smirked. "I really have a thing for Bunsen burners."

"What are we doing here?" I asked, turning to look back out through the small window on the door. I expected to see sneaky high schoolers, vying for a spot in front of the window, but the hallway was completely empty. No one other than Hank and the other security guard even knew we'd left the dance.

Jason turned to me and cupped my face between his hands, stealing my thoughts.

"We're not doing anything," he replied before pressing a kiss to my lips. I tilted my head, trying to find something to center myself around. There was only Jason, so I gripped his suit jacket and held on for dear life. His tongue slipped past my lips and I used the lapels of his tuxedo to pull him closer.

I couldn't believe we were doing this in a school.

In a classroom.

"Jason," I breathed, trying to grab a hold of our lust even for a moment. But it was impossible. Jason pushed me back against the chalkboard and started tugging my dress up around my hips. *Oh holy hell, I was about have sex against a chalkboard.* Some teacher had written a scientific term on this board 24 hours earlier, and now I was getting boned against it. Hopefully I wouldn't walk out of the room with $E=MC^2$ printed across the back of my black dress.

"We're going to get in trouble," I warned as I worked at his tuxedo pants. They were impossible to take off, with hidden buttons and trapped doors. Or at least it felt like it to me.

"Now Ms. Heart, it's time for you to serve your detention," Jason said, unable to get the words out without smirking.

"Oh god, so gross. We are not roleplaying," I groaned.

Jason dipped his head to kiss my chin and then he slipped the spaghetti strap of my gown down off my shoulder. I shivered in response to the cool fabric sliding across my skin. *Or maybe it was the way Jason was touching me.* His hands were everywhere, they moved beneath my dress so that my head fell back against the chalkboard. The pads of his fingers slid up my inner thighs, making my stomach quiver. They inched higher and higher until his fingers found their mark and spun my world on its axis.

I could smell the chalk and the pencil shavings in the air. The weird stench of an old science experiment was impossible to ignore, but then Jason's pants were gone and his head was in the crook of my neck so that the only thing I could smell was his spiced cologne and body wash, mingling together as he pressed inside of me. It was the first time we hadn't used a condom and I couldn't fathom how excruciatingly beautiful it would feel to have him inside of me like that.

"Brook," he whispered as he paused and pulled back to look into my eyes.

I wanted to turn his face away or close my eyes, anything to prevent him from seeing what I'd been constantly trying to hide for the last two weeks. *Just let me pretend like this is nothing.*

I could lie to myself. That part was easy. It was lying to *him* that I knew I wouldn't get away with.

He pulled away slowly, drawing his hips back, and then sinking back into me again, maintaining the eye contact that was tearing me apart. He kept up that maddeningly slow pace, stealing my heart and gripping it in his hands. *Couldn't he see it all?* It was there plain as day. Everything I felt was splashed across my face like a blinking neon sign.

Except neither of us dared to say a word. I tilted my head back, stared up at the paneled ceiling and let myself come apart around him.

Maybe he didn't see it because he didn't want to.

Chapter Twenty-Two

"Are you awake?" Cammie asked, prying my eyelid open with her fingers.

"No," I lied, turning my head away from her hand. She laughed and rolled over on top of me so that her weight pushed me into the mattress. *Why don't the social rules that exist for the rest of society apply to sisters?* She started jumping up and down, dipping me into the bed. *This would not be appropriate behavior for normal people.*

"Wake up, wake up, wake up," she said, reminding me of what she used to be like on Christmas morning—a complete hellion.

"Cammie, you skinny twat, get off me."

She jutted out her bottom lip and then let her upper body fall forward onto me.

"Ow!" I yelled as her head collided with my chin.

"Sorry, but you're boring when you sleep and I'm curious about last night," she said, rolling off of me once she realized I wouldn't be going back to sleep. *Due to the freaking broken jaw she just gave me.*

"Nothing happened," I answered, staring up at my bedroom ceiling. After we left the classroom, we found our dates and headed to the limousine. The ride home was quiet and full of tension. It wasn't there on the way to the prom, but it was filling up the limousine on the way home. It was everything I could do not to roll down the window just to alleviate the pressure.

Cammie didn't question me further; instead she leaned over and rested her head next to my shoulder so that we could lay side by side in silence. After our parents died and I became Cammie's guardian, Cammie and I slept together most nights. It was easier that way. Cammie was my constant, *my rock,* and I wanted her with me all the time. Laying there in Jason's house, she still felt like my constant and I clung on to that feeling for as long as possible.

"Could you play me what you have for the duet so far?" she asked.

I nodded and sat up, but when I looked over, my guitar stand beside the bedside table was empty. I must have left my guitar in Jason's room the day before.

"Hold on, let me go get my guitar," I said, slipping out from beneath the sheets.

Cammie relaxed back onto the pillows. "Fine, but if you aren't back in five minutes. I'm going to come looking for you. And I don't like to knock, it ruins the surprise."

I rolled my eyes as I walked out of my room. I wouldn't be gone long. Jason probably wasn't even in his room anyway.

I took the third floor steps two at a time and was about to knock on the door when I heard the first strumming of a guitar. I should have walked away or knocked. I should have let him know that I was standing there, but I couldn't because a second later, I heard his deep voice start to sing, and I was completely lost.

Loving you is the sweetest sorrow
Too much today, not enough tomorrow
If this is what it's like
Then I chose wrong

I stood there for another moment, hoping he'd keep singing, but then I heard the distant sound of his cell phone ringing. I pressed my ear closer to the door. Of course I knew that what I was doing was wrong, but I was so close to really learning something real about Jason. I couldn't just walk away.

"Hi angel," he spoke softly. "No, I'm not too busy to talk. Did you sleep okay last night?"

"What are you doing?" Cammie asked, making me jump at least three feet in the air.

I spun around to face her, holding a hand to my chest as if that would calm my racing heart. She stared up at me from the second-floor landing, but I had no words. My mind was frozen as I tried to memorize the lyrics I'd just heard him sing and also process whether or not they could potentially be about me. *Loving you. Loving you. Loving you.*

But who was he on the phone with?

"Are you spying on him?" Cammie whispered, stepping closer to the stairs. My eyes widened even more.

I shook my head and shot down the stairs past her, grabbing her hand as I went.

"I'll play you what we have later. Let's go get some breakfast," I said, not bothering to turn around to see what she was thinking.

• • •

Cammie left later that afternoon.

As I stood in the doorway watching the car pull away to take her to the airport, my stomach twisted itself into knots. She'd been my buffer for the last two days. With her in Big Timber, Jason and I were on hold. But with her gone, there was one less obstacle sitting between us.

I pulled on a pair of jeans and my red boots so I could wander around the property. I paid Dotty a visit and even convinced Jasper to take a sugar cube from me. (The damn horse sniffed it for like thirty minutes before he decided it wasn't poison.) I walked through the woods around the house, breathing in the fresh pine smell and trying to work through the unsolvable equations in my head. I helped LuAnne with lunch and sat with her for an hour after, flipping through home makeover magazines and picking out my dream kitchen.

Basically, I did anything to avoid seeing Jason.

The night before, I was still deluding myself into thinking that he and I were on the same page. We were having fun. No commitments, just sex. But then, hearing him sing that song about love made me realize that I wanted that. I wanted him to write a song about me. I wanted his love for me to be greater than the complications in his life. I knew he was complicated. Everything about him spelled that out, but someone had to be able to break through that exterior, right?

So why couldn't that someone be me?

Apparently I wasn't the only one playing the avoiding game that day. When I finally worked up the courage to go upstairs, Jason wasn't there. His room was empty, the porch was empty too, and when I glanced over the railing, I saw that his Jeep was gone.

The massive house was quiet and I was left with nothing to do to get my mind off him, so I went into my room and worked through some emails and did an extra workout. My trainer would be proud to know I'd done an additional power yoga session, but even that didn't cheer me up. I just wanted to see Jason and ask him what he was thinking.

• • •

It's interesting to consider that I was a full believer in love. I'd built my career on writing songs about love because I truly believed in what they stood for. But now that life was presenting me with my very own version of a love song, I was trying my hardest to rewrite the lyrics. There were so many things standing in our way. We'd only known each other for three weeks; he wasn't ready for a relationship; there were more things we *didn't* know about each other than we *did* know; relationships between celebrities hardly ever worked out. It was easy to construct the brick wall between us, so easy that when he burst through my bedroom door at midnight, I should have held strong behind that wall—but it took one look at him standing in my doorway to completely bulldoze it down. Just like that, I was lying there defenseless once again.

"I don't want to talk about anything," he said, walking toward the bed and tearing his shirt off.

I pushed myself up off my pillow. "Neither do I."

And that was truth. I didn't want to talk to this man about the logistics of our love. *I wanted to feel our love*, to soak in it while I still could.

His pants fell as he unbuttoned them at the waist, and I pulled my nightshirt over my head.

"I don't know what's happening," I said as he crawled up onto the bed, pulling the blanket off me.

"Neither do I," he answered. We were mimicking each other's answers, and it was clear that any decisions that needed to be made wouldn't be decided that night.

I'd missed him so much in the last few days. We'd had our moment the night before in the classroom, but it was clumsy and rushed, nothing compared to the magic we'd created in the days leading up to Cammie's arrival. Now we were all alone again, just he and I, with the rest of the night ahead of us.

"Please don't tell me to leave," he said dipping down to kiss my neck, dragging his soft lips down my chest.

"No. No. Don't leave," I said, hearing the thin cracks forming in my voice.

I'd rip my heart out before I'd asked him to leave. None of this was healthy, but it had been a disease from the very start. I was completely helpless to the side effects of that disease now. I'd do what I did every time: let his body take over mine like a cancer.

His fingers laced with mine as he pushed my arms up over my head to lock them in place.

The first time we had sex that night, it was rushed and loud and desperate. *I was frantic for him*. But the second and the third time, they were slow and lazy, as if the world began and ended on that bed in Jason's guest room.

I don't remember asking him to stay in my bed after we were done, but I don't remember him wanting to go either. So for the first time, he and I didn't flee after sex. *We stayed.* At the time it hadn't felt monumental, the act of sleeping in the same bed, but when I'd awoken the next morning to find my world shifted upside down once again, I'd cling onto that idea for dear life.

Was I the one pushing us to be something more?

Had Jason led me on?

Had I turned every moment into something more than it actually was?

Chapter Twenty-Three

The next morning I woke up to find my bed empty, the noise from the kitchen jarring me awake. Usually there was coffee brewing, bacon sizzling, newspapers crinkling, but that morning, the sounds were off. There was a woman's voice, muffled by the space in between the kitchen and my room, but I knew it wasn't LuAnne's. It was too young, too soft. I also thought I could hear a child's laugh, but that didn't seem possible. But then there it was again– loud and happy, traveling through every nook and cranny of the house.

With a smile on my face at the idea of meeting new houseguests, I dressed in a loose cotton dress and wrapped a cardigan around myself, not bothering with any make-up. My blonde hair was curly from going to sleep with it damp, but I didn't mind the wild look.

Before I headed downstairs, I noticed a note on my nightstand scribbled in Jason's terrible handwriting. I laughed and shook my head as I padded over to pick it up. I recognized the lyrics he'd sung when I've first arrived at the ranch, but they were scratched out, replaced with new ones.

"Don't want you to stay
Can't tell you to go"
"Want you to stay
Wish you'd never go."
Now, hurry and wake up. - J

I bit down on my lip, debating whether to keep the note with me all day or to leave it on the side table for safekeeping. Since I couldn't trust my sweaty hands, I left it behind.

When I opened the door of my bedroom, the lively sounds from the kitchen amplified tenfold. I trotted down the stairs, craning to see who our houseguests were. When Jason spotted me on the stairs, all conversation stopped. He'd been walking out of the kitchen, maybe on his way to wake me up, but he paused when he saw me. Like a scared animal, his eyes went wide and his lips twisted into a frown.

If I had to pick, I'd say it was that look that told me something was very off.

He swallowed slowly and then started walking toward me again.

"Can we go upstairs and talk for a second?" he asked, reaching out to grab my arm from around my waist.

I shook my head. "No."

I didn't want to go upstairs; I wanted to know who was in the kitchen. Maybe before I saw his shocked expression, I would have followed him blindly, but now my curiosity was winning out. I pushed past him, and for one brief moment, he resisted, his hand on my arm, his deep brown eyes warning me to turn back.

I wasn't going to turn back.

It was far too late for that.

My breath caught when I saw the little girl whose laugh had filled the house from the moment I'd awoken. She was sitting at the kitchen table with markers spread out around her, coloring away on a piece of paper. Her red hair was long and curled into tight ringlets that bounced every time she moved. Pink plastic glasses sat on the bridge of her nose. She couldn't have been older than seven or eight, but I could see how well she colored from across the room. So close to the lines, I wanted to commend her on her work.

But then my gaze slid to the woman sitting directly beside her. Our eyes locked as I realized she was just as stunning as the little girl beside her— with the same bright red hair. She wasn't the type of stunning I was used to from my life in Hollywood. There was nothing fake about her. Her hair was pulled up into a loose ponytail and her complexion looked naturally flawless.

"Oh hello," the woman said with a tentative smile. Her gaze flitted between Jason and me as if she wasn't quite sure who could explain the situation better.

"Um, hi," I said, unable to muster actual conversation as my brain worked overtime to figure out who she as. Jason's cousin, Jason's sister, Jason's friend, Jason's long-lost twin, door-to-door sales people. Nothing fit, because deep down I already knew what I was walking in on. The phone call the day before had proved it.

The woman stood up from the table and walked to join us in the doorway of the kitchen.

"Lacy, stay in here and color for a second," the woman warned with a sweet edge to her voice.

LuAnne, who I hadn't even realized was standing at the stove, spoke up. "I'll watch her, Kim."

The woman— Kim— smiled toward LuAnne and then slid past the kitchen doorway in pursuit of the living room. Jason followed after her, but I stood frozen in place, unsure of where I belonged. I didn't want to go back into the kitchen and I sure as shit didn't want to go into the living room. Maybe if I just silently went upstairs, we could pretend that I'd never come down in the first place.

"Brooklyn?" Jason asked from the doorway to the living room. His hand gripped the wooden frame as he willed me to cooperate.

With a heavy sigh, I found myself walking past him and taking a seat on the couch across from Kim. I'd rarely gone into the living room before that day. LuAnne always kept it immaculate and I felt awkward moving the pillows around or turning on the TV. It was my least favorite room in him house because it was the least lived in. *Maybe now it would be my least favorite room for a different reason.*

"I'm Kim," the redhead said, bending over the coffee table to offer me her hand.

I stared at her dainty fingers for a moment before taking it. She had none of the guitar calluses that I was used to feeling on my own hands.

"Brooklyn," I said simply when my eyes locked on the massive rock sitting on her ring finger. It had to have been at least two carats, flawless and twinkling in the morning light from the window behind me.

My gut clenched.

"Brooklyn, this is my—"

"Wife," Kim answered with a terse smile.

Wife.

Wife.

Wife.

What the fuck? Is wife Spanish for "cousin" and no one had told me? Why the hell hadn't I paid attention in school? There had to be a translation for wife that meant something other than a married woman.

In the matter of two seconds I had a dozen emotions seep through my bloodstream. Shock, confusion, disbelief, denial, anger, guilt, jealousy, and then sadness. Such sharp sadness.

I shot up off the couch and ran to the doorway, trying to keep the tears from spilling down my cheeks. Unfortunately, they were already slipping down my chin and dripping onto my neck. I used the back of my hand to wipe them away as subtle as possible. I stayed facing away from them as I spoke.

"I just realized that I have a bunch of phone calls to return," I said with stuttered speech as I ran toward the stairs.

"Seriously, Kim?" Jason asked.

"What, Jason? That's what we are! You're still my husband."

No. No. No. *I didn't ask for this*. I shot up the stairs and shut the door to my room behind me, wishing for once that there was a lock on the door. Lock or not, once I was alone, the tears really came. My chest convulsed and I lunged forward holding my knees and crying with abandonment. There wasn't even time to process the last ten minutes in my life. I was still *feeling* it.

"Brooklyn." *Tap, tap*. "Brooklyn, let me in for a second."

"If I open that door, you won't be leaving with your body fully intact."

Jason growled. "This isn't a fucking joke, Brooklyn. Let me explain. You're being ridiculous."

I love being told I was ridiculous after finding out that the man I'd been falling for the last three weeks was married. That's like piss icing on the shit cake.

"Go to hell," I spat.

I heard his growl on the other side of the door, but after that, it was silent. I don't know how long he stayed there, because I was too busy going through various stages of grief:

1. Tearing up the cute note he'd left me that morning.

2. Trying to drown the note shreds in the bathtub.

3. Flushing the shreds down the toilet instead, when drowning had proved ineffective.

4. Sitting on the top of the toilet seat and crying.

5. Hating myself for caring enough to cry.

6. Crying more because I hated myself for crying.

7. Checking to see if the note had actually flushed, and crying harder when I realized that it was gone for good.

Hours passed or maybe it was just a few minutes. I couldn't be bothered to check the time while I was busy trying to talk myself out of murdering Jason. Either way, I didn't realize Kim had joined me in the bathroom until she was standing right in front of me as I sat against the bathtub. I'll be honest, the first thing I did was look for a weapon in her hands. I wouldn't put it past her to want to kill me if she knew I was sleeping with her husband, but she wasn't holding anything except for a box of tissues.

"Are those for me or for you?" I asked, pointing to the box.

She pushed them toward me. "I'm so sorry."

My eyes flew up to hers. "What? Why are *you* sorry? I'm the 'other woman'."

Instead of answering me, she positioned herself against the bathroom wall and then slid down to sit on the floor. "I was out of line back there. I purposely hurt your feelings when I should have told you the truth."

"You aren't Jason's wife?" I asked, hating how hopeful I sounded.

She winced. "Technically I am."

I held up my hands for a time-out. My body couldn't handle the back and forth. I needed a straight answer or I was going to lose it.

"I came to ask him to sign the divorce papers once and for all," she explained.

Her words sank in slowly, as if from a dripping faucet.

Jason was married.

Jason was still married because the divorce papers weren't signed.

Jason hadn't signed the papers.

Jason didn't want to be divorced.

"While I appreciate you trying to set me straight, I kind of just want you to leave."

Her mouth fell open at my direct approach.

"I'm sorry, that sounds terrible, but I just want to pack up my stuff and get the hell out of here. You have your own shit to work out with Jason, but he and I are over. Or we never started because let's get real, Jason is a one-man show. I was never really with him to begin with." I stood up off the ground. "So thank you for the tissues, and thank you for being so pretty. I want to hate you because of how pretty you are, but I can't because you're also nice, which sucks."

She smiled, but then bit down on her lip to conceal it.

"Ugh, and you think I'm funny," I said, raking my fingers through my hair. "Great. What the hell am I supposed to be doing right now?"

She shrugged, but kept silent, aware that I was going through some kind of existential crisis and needed to find my way out on my own. She stood up and stared at me with pity for a few seconds before moving toward the door.

"For what it's worth, I think you guys would make a really good couple."

I laughed, "I don't even know what to do with that statement, so I'm just going to tuck it away with the other weird shit I've heard today."

• • •

I'd never been so happy to have an assistant that could make anything happen than I was that afternoon. As soon as I informed Summer of my need to "get the hell out of Dodge", she booked me a private plane for 1:00 P.M. It was just the right amount of time to pack up all of my stuff and say goodbye to LuAnne, Derek, and Dotty. I had plans on slinking out when no one was looking in an effort to avoid Jason, but when LuAnne told me he'd gone into town to talk with Kim and Lacy, I took my time giving her a giant hug.

Yes, I was totally giving Montana the ol' Irish exit, and sure, maybe I should have stayed and listened to Jason say "I'm sorry for lying. I'm sorry for everything." But the fact is – I wasn't totally sure that he was. *He'd told me he didn't want complicated. He told me he didn't want a relationship*, so why would he feel the need to come groveling back to me? I would have really, really enjoyed hearing him apologize, which is why I couldn't stay on the off chance that he wasn't sorry at all.

Just thinking about that outcome made it that much easier to leave Big Timber behind. I'd really miss my time in Montana. If my downtown condo had a horse stable and a couple acres, I would have taken Dotty back with me, but alas, I had to leave her behind with a handful of sugar cubes to remember me by.

I would have cried as I stuffed my guitar case into the trunk of the car waiting on the gravel drive, but I had no tears left. I looked back to where LuAnne and Derek were standing up on the porch steps. Derek was just as sweaty as the day I'd met him, but he had his cowboy hat resting over his heart and a solemn expression masking his features. A part of me wanted to think that Jason didn't deserve these people, that they were too good for someone like him. *A liar.*

But I knew better.

As the car pulled away from the house, I thought about the fact that Jason and I still had the last part of our duet left to finish that morning. We'd been procrastinating the last few days, putting off the inevitable because we knew as soon as we'd finished, I'd have to leave for LA.

But the ending was always there, waiting for me to discover it. I'd written it down onto a torn piece of paper and slipped it beneath the door to Jason's room before I left for good.

Loving you would be as easy as taking a breath
But to give you up, that's a dance with death

We were over from the start
You always kept your distance
You never said you'd give your heart

So now it's time for this to end
It shouldn't be hard to say goodbye
After all, a friend is just a friend

Chapter Twenty-Four

I touched down in LA to find five missed calls and three text messages from Jason.

Jason: Answer your phone, Brooklyn.

Jason: I went to talk to Kim because I didn't know you'd get on a fucking plane and leave as soon as I left.

Jason: I just read the last of your lyrics. Don't bother calling me back.

"He thinks I want to call him back?!" I shouted before slicing through the apple sitting on my kitchen counter. Cammie had picked me up from the airport and I'd filled her in as much as possible. Most of it was just a string of expletives, but she'd managed to piece together the story: The motherfucking-asshole-whore had a wife.

We'd gone back to my condo and I'd had every intention of calming down, but then I read his final text message and I was back to square one.

The knife slid through the apple with ease and then I pulled it back and kept right on cutting until I'd all but minced it into nothingness.

"How about I take over cutting the apple? You're going to hurt yourself, or even worse, you might hurt me," Cammie smiled, trying to defuse the situation.

"Oh, Cammie, don't be ridiculous!" I said before slamming the blade back down onto the chopping board. It was a millimeter away from chopping my thumb off, a fact that Cammie also noticed. She pinched my arm until I dropped the blade and then I slunk down to the cold kitchen floor.

"Oh, no. No. You don't get to just lay down on the tile like all of your bones turned to Jell-O," she said, gently kicking my side.

"Maybe I should just keep laying here, Cam," I said, letting the cold tile sink into my skin. "Maybe I'm just so sad that I'm going to lay on this kitchen floor for the rest of my life. Boneless."

"Oh my god, have I ever told you how much of a drama queen you are? You could have been a southern debutante in your past life."

I kicked in the back of her knee so that her leg buckled and she fell down onto the tile next to me. Misery loves company. Her elbow stabbed my stomach and my knee went into her back as the two of us groaned and readjusted so that we could both fit in between the kitchen island and the kitchen counter.

"This is gross. When's the last time you cleaned these floors?"

"I don't know, sometime before the BJ era," I answered.

She took a deep breath. "I'm about 50% sure that you're not talking about giving guys blow jobs all over your kitchen floor, but I'm going to need confirmation on what that acronym stands for."

"Before Jason," I sighed melodramatically.

With a groan, she pinched my side. "You're being ridiculous."

I shrugged.

"Now what?" she said, rolling her head to the side so she could get a better look at me.

I smiled the first smile since waking up that morning.

"Now, we drink," I said, shooting up to my feet and running to my refrigerator. Being in the music industry meant that I had copious amounts of high-quality alcohol. It was the gift that kept on giving. When I pulled the refrigerator door open, the first thing I saw was a nice big bottle of champagne sitting on the bottom shelf.

"Cammie, grab some glasses so we can have some—" I paused so I could turn the bottle around and read the label, "Bollinger Blanc De Noirs Vieilles Vignes Francaises."

When I looked up, Cammie was staring at me with a blank stare. "Speak English, whore."

"Don't call me a whore even though that's exactly what I am," I said, feeling the tears burning my eyelids. "I'm literally the definition of a whore. No, wait. I'm worse—I didn't even get any money out of the deal." I kept rambling as I ripped the paper off of the top of the champagne bottle and started working at untwisting the cork. I'd popped two or three corks in my life, so I figured I had it down pat.

I did *not* have it down pat. I held the green bottle to my stomach and pointed the cork away from me, but it wouldn't come out, even as I nudged it gently. I looked down at it and started to pull again, but Cammie reached out and pulled my hand away.

"Don't open it in the direction of your eyes!"

I sighed, "Fine. Give me that knife and I'll chop off the end of the bottle like a pirate," I said, holding my hand out in annoyance.

Oddly enough, Cammie wouldn't let me do that either, so we went across the hall, to my neighbor's condo and knocked on the door so we could ask the older man who lived there if he could open the bottle of champagne for us.

Except we never got the chance to hand it over to him because when he opened the door he was wearing a banana hammock and a ski mask. *Only* a banana hammock and a ski mask.

I screamed because he looked like a burglar. The Banana Hammock Burglar. But apparently, it was all a giant misunderstanding. He was hosting "an orgy of sorts" and thought we were his guests that had been running late. Once we assured him we were not, and would never be, attendees at his orgy, he popped the champagne for us and we went on our merry way.

When we closed the door to my condo, I completely lost it. I started crying so hard that I couldn't get coherent words out. Cammie kept asking me what I was saying and I kept repeating it, annoyed that she couldn't interpret my speech.

Finally, I dropped my hands and looked up at her as I spoke. "I'm a whore, I'll never have a proper orgasm again, and now I live across the hall from an old people orgy fest. Why can't this day just end already?"

I didn't realize it at the time, but I was about to drink that bottle of champagne with Cammie and promptly pass out on the couch in the living room in a pool of my own drool. It wasn't the best way to end the worst day of my life, but I was happy to wake up the next day in my own condo with candy wrappers and tissues stuck in my hair.

Until I heard pounding on my front door, followed by Jason's deep voice.

"Open the door, Brooklyn," he shouted, continuing to pound away.

Shit.

Chapter Twenty-Five

Jason was here. Jason was in LA. Oh, hell no. How dare he follow me back to LA as if he'd planned to make some grand, romantic gesture? I'm a simple girl. The only romantic gesture I need is TO KNOW WHETHER OR NOT A MAN IS MARRIED.

I pushed up off the couch and checked my reflection in the hallway mirror. Oh dear god, a small family of raccoons had infested my hair and was now planning on making it their permanent home. I had a jolly rancher stuck to my cheek, which seemed strange until I remembered a hazy memory of daring Cammie to launch a jolly rancher from across the room to see if I could catch it in my mouth. We'd tried like fifty times, and apparently I hadn't cleaned them all up by the time I'd passed out on the couch, which is why the melted sugar was imprinted on my cheek.

I peeled it off my face, but it left a layer of residue that I couldn't get off in time before I reached the door. Since I couldn't do anything else with the Jolly Rancher, I popped it into my mouth and opened the door. (This was a really low point in my life, so if you could reserve your judgment about that, I'd appreciate it. And it was a blue raspberry one, *as if you'd waste it either.*)

When I swung open my front door, Jason was leaning against the doorframe with his head down, staring at the floor. As soon as the door opened, his gaze shot up to me and he pushed through the doorway.

"Oh sure, welcome to my condo, asshole," I said, moving out of his way and closing the door behind him. "Would you like an ice cold bottle of fuck-off, or how about a get-the-fuck-out martini?"

I hadn't checked, but I assumed that Cammie had fallen asleep somewhere in the condo the night before, and hopefully she was smart enough not to come out and join us during the fight that was about to ensue.

I watched him stalk toward the kitchen and then spin around with his back to my marble island. He was seething, his chest rising and falling with anger, but I wasn't going to give in. The bastard could stare at me all he wanted.

"You left without hearing the real explanation and now you think you've got it all figured out."

He'd dressed it up with fancy wording, but he truly meant the age-old excuse: "It's not what it looks like."

I rolled my eyes and folded my hands over my chest, only then realizing that I was in fact not wearing a bra. My eyes darted to the couch and I saw it resting on top of a champagne bottle. Clearly, I hadn't been keen on wearing it to bed.

Great, so I had to argue bra-less with Jolly Rancher gunk on my face.

"It doesn't matter," I answered because I knew it would hurt him. I wasn't done building my anger from the day before. I wasn't ready to think rationally or let him sweet talk his way back into my life. I just wanted to hide behind bitchy comments until he was too angry to stay any longer.

"Talk to me."

Oh, fuck that.

"We don't talk, remember? That wasn't part of our set-up." I pointed back and forth between our bodies for emphasis. "We were a series of one-night-stands. Over and over again. So let's not pretend there's anything more. You wouldn't explain a wife to a one-night-stand, so don't explain it to me."

"That's bullshit and you know it."

I laughed. I didn't know anything. Not a single thing. I thought I'd been chipping away at a guarded man, slowly weaving myself into his life until he couldn't *not* be with me. Instead, I was having sex with a married man, like a dime store hooker.

When I'd heard him singing on the third floor, I thought his song had been for me. But that song was for his wife.

They were never for me.

This entire time I'd been a delusional idiot. I'd been staring at an optical illusion. Once I saw the real image, *the image I was supposed to see*, I could never go back to the picture I saw before. My mind already knew what was real and what was fake. That knowledge made the tears start to form again, which was *not* happening in front of Jason.

"I thought you told me you could handle our situation. You were the one to push it, even when I told you I was complicated."

"I know!" I yelled, unable to put the lid on my emotions. "Don't you think I know that?"

I'd had enough self-loathing circulating through my system; he didn't need to continue to point that fact out to me.

"So then why are you backing down now?" he asked, taking a step away from the island.

"Why am I backing down?" I asked, flailing me arms out to my sides. "Because you're married! Which puts me in the home-wrecker category. Do you realize that? Do you realize that by not telling me the truth, you've forced me to become the other woman without even realizing I was doing it? I'm not a bad person. I don't sleep with married men."

He shoved his hands through his dark hair, gripping onto the ends for a moment as he squeezed his eyes closed.

"Yes - I'm technically married. But not because I'm in love with Kim. I was never in love with Kim."

I laughed, but it came out sounding like nails on a chalkboard. "That means nothing to me. I bet half of married men would say that at any given time."

His hands finally dropped from his hair and he cleared the distance between us in a matter of seconds. "That's not what I mean, Brooklyn. Kim is with another man. That ring on her finger is from another man."

What the hell kind of crazy shit had I walked into?

"Lacy isn't my daughter. Kim had her before we met, but I still raised her for the five years that we were married. I tried to adopt her but Kim kept putting up road blocks."

I backed up against the counter and crossed my arms, prepared to listen to whatever he had to say.

"When Kim filed for divorce, I had no claim to Lacy. Kim could take her and I'd never get visitation. She's not my child, I know that, but it felt like in one fell swoop I was losing my entire family and I couldn't do a damn thing about it.

"So when you left Montana yesterday without even waiting for an explanation, it reminded me of why I purposely wanted to keep things simple with you in the first place."

"Why didn't you just tell me about all of this?" I asked him.

"I didn't want to. I wanted to keep you separate from them. You were supposed to help me write a song and then leave," he said, avoiding the question all together.

His words shouldn't have had the ability to hurt me anymore. I clearly deserved his anger, but I couldn't just stand there and take it.

"That's exactly what I did," I argued. "I left when the song was finished."

"That's it?" Jason asked, narrowing his eyes on me.

I wanted to yell, *"No, that's not it."* Instead, I forced a sharp nod. "That's it."

I didn't ask for this. At twenty-seven, I didn't need complicated. I needed simple and easy. I needed someone who was ready to settle down.

I took a deep breath. "I'm really sorry about everything you're going through Jason, but I just need some space. A breather," I said, feeling confident in my decision.

"Say what you really mean, Brooklyn," he said, stepping directly in front of me so that I had to crane my neck back to look into his eyes.

"I am."

He shook his head. "Say the truth."

"I don't have to," I said, feeling the first tear slide down my cheek. "I wrote it down in the lyrics."

His eyes pinched closed as he absorbed my words and how final they felt. I studied his features, so contorted in anger and sadness that it was hard to make out just how beautiful they were. When his eyes opened again, he didn't say a word. Our eyes locked for three seconds. Three long seconds. *Three... Two... One.* And then he was gone. He was gone, and my door was slammed shut so hard that the hinges rattled, and I was left to crumble to the floor.

I stabbed the heel of my palms into my eyes and cried, letting loose the emotion that I'd felt the entire time I'd been with Jason, but was never allowed to show. I was supposed to be the cool, confident girl that could have the sex without the commitment, have the orgasms without the relationship. In reality, I was as much of a fraud as Jason was.

"Wow. Did I just hear you break up with Jason Monroe?" Cammie asked from across the apartment.

I laughed at how wrong she was. "No. That was the end of our collaboration," I clarified, trying to soak up my tears with the back of my hands before pressing up to my feet.

"Wow. No wonder you're a solo artist then," Cammie said, tilting her head to the side and studying me with a wary glance.

I rolled my eyes and did my best to pretend that everything was fine. I'd lived a long life without love and now I would just go back to that. Simple as pie.

"Where'd you put that bag of Jolly Ranchers?" I asked.

She tried to hide her smile. "You took the bag over to your neighbor across to hall and told him he could use them in his orgy because you were done with them."

Oh shit. "No, I did not."

255

She nodded solemnly. "You definitely did."

I clapped my hand over my eyes. "Great. I have to move now."

• • •

The next morning a courier arrived and slapped me with a document from Jason's legal team that detailed certain facts that I was and was not allowed to say in public or to the press. Our relationship as a whole was off-limits. During press for the Grammy performance, I was advised to keep the conversation platonic. No mention of Lacy or Kim would be allowed to go to print. If I slipped up, there would be a lawsuit.

I didn't have to sign. If he wanted all of that private, he should have explained everything beforehand and had me sign at the beginning.

Still, that two-page document took my broken heart and tore it apart all over again. I was merely a loose end that needed to be tied up.

After two hours of stewing over it, I signed the papers and mentally added a "fuck you" to the end of my signature.

Chapter Twenty-Six

Yes, I regretted letting Jason leave my condo that day.

Yes, I knew that the correct decision wasn't always black or white.

Yes, I looked down at my phone every morning and wondered if I should give him a call.

No, I never did.

Put on my clothes, they're the same as before
Count to two, and then to four
Each day I know is new
but still you've left me, turned my whole world blue

You can stay hidden forever
No one can pull you out
I told myself never say never
But now I'm starting to have doubt

I told you where to find me
I told you where I'd be

You left me there, waiting
Waiting with a plea

You can stay hidden forever
No one can pull you out
I told myself never say never
But now I'm starting to have doubt

So won't you find me
This is my final plea
Because for you, I'll wait
But please, don't be too late

The music paused, the red recording light flipped off. I tugged the thick headphones down off my head. The vocal booth was small, but after recording a half dozen albums inside the four walls, it'd become a second home of sorts.

My team was sitting on the other side of the thin glass: Summer, my agent, and the studio director, Tom. He always helped mix my music and I didn't trust anyone else behind the studio dials.

"I love it. It's been a while since you've done a break-up song," Tom said, pressing replay on the song I'd just sung into the condenser microphone. It was hard to listen to the lyrics. They were still raw, the sadness was so easy to decipher in my voice. I hoped they just thought I was acting for the sake of the song. It wouldn't work if I didn't sound tormented by loss, so what did it matter to them if that loss was real or not. *Just as long as I sold records, right?*

"It's gold, Brooklyn. I've gotta run. Don't forget that your rehearsals for the Grammy performance start tomorrow," my agent said before answering a call and stepping out of the studio.

Summer was the only one who stayed silent and I feared it was because she knew the truth about where I'd found the inspiration for the song. She nodded at me with a solemn smile and then stared back down at her phone, probably reworking my schedule. I was behind on a lot of commitments and on top of that, I'd need to start recording my next studio album. The song I'd recorded a moment earlier would be the first track on the CD and I feared most of the other songs would have a similar feel.

They say you should write what you know. So, that was my plan.

• • •

I had one week until the Grammys and every spare moment in those seven days was planned out to a "T". I had three rehearsals, Cammie's graduation, dress fittings, workouts, voice lessons, and countless interviews.

Yet somehow there was still ample amount of time to think about Jason. He'd made a change to the beginning of our duet. I would have protested it that late in the game, except the changes were good. Really good. His assistant had sent them over the day before and I'd sat there reading them and trying to decipher the secret meaning of every word as if they were pieces of Jason's soul. Sadly, after an hour of staring at a computer screen, I came to the conclusion that they were just words.

• • •

The first day of rehearsals for an award show is always a frenzy of activity. The sheer manpower that goes into putting on an event of that magnitude is almost equal to the number of guests who would actually be in attendance.

I stayed in my dressing room after I'd arrived; enjoying the peace and quiet once my voice coach had left. I knew I was due on stage in a few minutes for my rehearsal, but I couldn't help scribbling lyrics down in my notebook. In the last few days it'd been permanently attached my hand, housing the words that were tumbling forth without much effort at all.

We were never really friends
Always something more
Maybe if I'd seen it before
I could have kept you from walking,
Kept you from walking out that door

A gentle knock on my dressing room door pulled my attention from my notebook.

"Brooklyn, we'll be ready for you onstage in fifteen," a stagehand announced on the other side of my door.

"Thanks!" I called back, glancing down at the lyrics one more time before stuffing the notebook back into my bag. I was still trying to cram it all the way in when my dressing room door opened.

"I thought I still had fifteen minutes," I protested, before looking up and coming face to face with a man who was most definitely not a stagehand.

I hadn't seen Jason since he'd slammed the door on his way out of my condo a few days before, but there he was, looking too handsome to ignore. His features were lit by the shadows of my dim dressing room and I paused on my way to sit-up, just taking him in.

"Sorry. I should have knocked," he said, but he didn't turn to leave, so clearly he wasn't that sorry.

I crossed my arms and stood up off the couch, steeling myself for whatever he was about to say.

"We have fifteen minutes until we need to be on stage," I pointed out.

He nodded. "I wanted to talk to you before we went up there."

"Okay," I answered, standing even straighter. "Talk."

"I'm sorry for not telling you about Kim."

I had wanted an apology so badly. I had wanted him to acknowledge his wrongdoing, but not before we were about to be on stage. Not when I was about to have to spend the next few hours singing with him. So I just nodded, once.

"Is that all?" I asked, moving toward the vanity to grab a clip for my hair. It usually got warm on stage and I knew we'd be up there for a few hours. Also, I really needed an excuse to turn away him.

"I shouldn't have kept everything from you, but you should have been honest with me, too," he said.

My head snapped in his direction, but he didn't back down.

"Honest about how you felt about us," he continued. "You should have waited and listened instead of jumping on the first plane out of Montana."

I laughed, completely taken aback by his comment.

"Yeah, maybe I should have. Now can you please get out of my dressing room?" I gritted my teeth together to keep from tearing up.

"I'm sorry about that stuff from my legal team. None of it was sent with my consent," he said, walking toward the door and propping it open for a moment.

I shook my head. "Don't worry about it. My camp would have done the same thing."

He smiled gently and looked down at his feet. "Yeah. Cammie sent me a fruit basket with a note that said, 'One of these has been poisoned. Enjoy.'"

My mouth dropped and his features softened just barely. I could see a piece of the carefree Jason I'd come to love at his ranch.

"She always did try to fight my battles for me."

His jaw clenched. "I don't think you need anyone helping you. You're using my past to push me away all on your own. If you want us to be over, that's your decision, but I didn't take you for someone who gave up so easily."

I shrugged, staring down at the carpeted ground, searching for an explanation that wouldn't come.

He left without another word.

I wanted to shout at him. How dare he push the blame onto me in this situation? He was the one who didn't want "complicated". He was the married one.

A stagehand came to get me a few minutes later, after I'd wiped the stray tears from my eyes. I followed him blindly, trying to collect my thoughts so that I could actually concentrate during the rehearsal.

I saw Jason when I was halfway up the stairs backstage. He was already on his mark, adjusting the monitor in his ear so that he'd be able to hear himself practicing. I looked down at my own monitor, adjusting the wireless receiver in the back pocket of my jeans.

There were a couple dozen people sitting in the audience at the Staples center. The show's producers, assistants, stagehands, costume designers, sound engineers, set designers. They were all there to watch rehearsals, which meant they'd be the first group of people to watch Jason and I sing together. *Lovely.*

"How's it going?" the choreographer asked us as I stepped up to the gray 'X' taped onto the stage about two feet away from Jason. My microphone was set up in front of the mark, and my guitar was resting on a stand next to it. With everything else going on, getting to use my own guitar felt like having a security blanket.

I shot Jason a side-glance. "Been better," I replied, aware that our conversation was easy to hear by everyone in the audience.

"I think I'd have to agree," Jason said, gritting his teeth and staring down at his guitar in thought.

The poor choreographer had no clue what to say to our responses. "Alright then, let's run through the song once. I'll get a feel for the sound, and then we can adjust things as we go. This is going to be a stripped-down performance. The two of you together is flashy enough so we won't need to add much else."

We nodded and started strumming on our instruments to warm up and test our sound monitors. I took a few breaths, relaxing my fingers over the fretboard.

The choreographer moved to the back of the stage and the house lights dimmed as the lighting crew focused a spotlight on Jason and me. I'd warmed up in my dressing room with my voice coach, but being out there was a different ball game. Even at Jason's ranch, I'd never given it my all. We were always strumming in his room, singing quietly and playing softly.

It was finally time to put our hearts into it.

• • •

Later that night, LuAnne called me. I was in the middle of staring aimlessly into my refrigerator, hoping that dinner would magically make itself, when her name lit up my phone screen.

"Lu? Is that you?" I asked, like an eighty-year-old. *Side note: why do we still not trust caller ID?*

"Brooklyn! How are you? Did I catch you at a good time?"

Her voice was so good to hear— it was almost as good as having her there in person. *Almost.*

"Yes. Yes, what's up? Is everything okay?" I'd given her my number before leaving Montana, but I hadn't expected her to call to catch up so soon.

"Everything is great," she said. I listened to her feet shuffle across the floor before she spoke up again. "I've just been thinking about a few things, and I'm calling because I doubt Jason is going to give you the full story about his past. He's so weird about things, never likes to admit that he's a good man deep down. If his mama were still alive, she'd be calling you herself, so I'll have to do it for her."

I frowned, trying to keep up. "What are you talking about LuAnne?"

She sighed. "Just give me five minutes and I'll explain it."

I took a seat on my sofa, happy that for once Cammie wasn't at my condo. I settled in and LuAnne started her story, filling in pieces of Jason's life that he may not have ever told me himself.

"Jason and Kim were good friends growing up. They were both quiet, smart kids in a small town so it wasn't a surprise that they got along well. Their senior year, Kim got pregnant by some boy from out of town. I don't know all the details, but I do know that she went to Jason before she told anyone else about it. Apparently she was on her own with the baby. Big Timber isn't the most progressive town and her parents were old fashioned. As you can probably guess, Jason wanted to help Kim. He loved her as a friend, so he did the right thing.

"As far as the town knew, that baby belonged to Jason. They got married the summer after their senior year."

"*That's* why he married Kim?"

"Yep."

"So this was all way before his career took off?" I asked, trying to get the timeline straight in my head.

"Years before."

My mouth hung open before I thought to ask a question. "What about the media? Why didn't they ever find out he was married?"

"Their marriage license is stuck in some file down in the Big Timber courthouse. I can't remember the last time our town took kindly to media snooping around about Jason, especially after he got big."

"Didn't he wear a wedding ring?" I asked.

She sighed. "The second Jason went on tour, their rings went off. Jason didn't want Kim and Lacy shoved into the spotlight, and Kim wanted the freedom that came with a bare ring finger."

LuAnne stayed silent as I tried to process the story.

"I can't believe Jason did all of that," I said, still

processing his past.

"Exactly," she said. "So maybe you should go easy on the guy."

I laughed, taken aback by her brazenness. "I will. Thanks for telling me all that, LuAnne."

"You're welcome. Don't call me back until you two have made up. I want some babies at this ranch."

My mouth dropped for the one-hundredth time since answering her phone call.

Chapter Twenty-Seven

"So you and Jason are going to be friends again? Just like that?" Cammie asked as we sat in the limousine on the way to her college graduation. She looked stunning in a white sheath dress. Her dark brown hair was naturally wavy and sat beneath her graduation cap in an adorably dorky kind of way. Her navy graduation gown fell across her lap and she kept absentmindedly running her hand down the fabric. I knew she wouldn't admit it, but that gown symbolized a lot of hard work for her.

"No. We aren't friends."

She narrowed her gaze on me. "The lady doth protest too much."

"Huh?"

"You said no like someone who's lying about saying no."

I gave her a pointed stare. "You watched ONE episode of Criminal Minds and now you think you can read people like a detective."

R.S. Grey

She shrugged and checked out her fingernails in a dramatic fashion. "I think I can. It's a gift. For instance, I know that you still like Jason, dare I say, you *even* love him. And he isn't a complete idiot, so he loves you, too." She looked up at me. "There, how did I do?"

I looked away, trying to concentrate on the scenery outside of the limousine window. "Terrible. You would make a horrible detective."

When we pulled up outside of her university's stadium she moved toward the door of the limousine. But before she got out, she looked back at me and winked.

"Just so you know, you're a cute liar."

I flipped her the bird but she was climbing out and didn't see it. Instead, a thin Asian man, with a giant camera hanging around his neck, peered into the limousine at that exact moment, placing himself on the receiving end of my crude gesture.

"Oh god, I'm sorry," I said, trying to clear up the situation, but the driver was already shutting the door. Whelp, there goes my Asian male fan base. All *one* of them.

The logistics of the graduation were complicated. It wouldn't work for me to sit in the audience, so the school set up a private suite on the mezzanine level of the stadium. Hank was very happy with the security situation, but I was pissed that I couldn't do my original plan for when Cammie walked across the stage. *Hint: it involved ten foghorns and a dozen male strippers.*

At first, I was all-alone. Hank was manning the doors and putting on his usual stoic facade. But then Summer, and one of my cousins, Patricia, arrived. We had a tiny

268

family, made smaller with our parents gone, so I was glad that Patricia had taken the time to travel from New York and support Cammie.

The private suite had chilled champagne and food lining one of the walls. About five minutes into the first graduation speech I decided the entire event would be much better with alcohol, so I set out on a mission to open the champagne bottle.

Just as I reached the bucket of ice, the door to the suite opened and Grayson Cole walked in looking like a walking ad for Armani in a tailored navy suit and tie. His brown hair was slicked back and his eyes were as piercing and sharp as ever.

"No way!" I said, forgetting the champagne all together. "Grayson!" I ran over to give him a hug, but even in my heels, he had to bend to wrap a friendly arm around my shoulders. "What are you doing here?"

When I pulled away to look up at him, he didn't seem to know the answer to that question any more than I did.

"I had my assistant call Summer," he said.

Yeah, that wasn't the answer to my question. *What in the world was he doing at Cammie's graduation?*

He took my confused smile as a cue to continue to explain his presence. "I wanted to check out the new crop of up and coming architects," he shrugged, slipping his hands into his suit pockets. *Riiiight* because that made so much sense.

Regardless of his true intentions, I was happy to see my old friend. He looked devastatingly handsome, a fact which I knew Summer and Patricia were equally as happy about. If nothing else, we'd have some eye candy for the next few hours of the ceremony.

Grayson took over the champagne duties, popping the cork like a seasoned pro and then pouring us each a small glass.

"How was Montana?" he asked as we moved to stand near the glass window so that we could look down at the graduates. I had no clue where Cammie was; she'd refused my advice to bedazzle a penis on top of her cap so that I could spot her easily. Clearly, she should have listened to me.

"Montana was…"

The correct adjective seemed to elude me. Good, bad, sexy, terrible. None of them fit.

"…pretty much what you'd expect it to be," I answered, giving him a small smile.

He nodded as if understanding, but he didn't attempt to garner any more details. Grayson was good about that. He was a surface type of guy, even with old friends, but that's how he preferred it, so I never tried to dig deeper. Sometimes you just have to give people their space.

The one subject I wasn't willing to budge on though, was Cammie. I hadn't brought her up to him in a few weeks and I didn't know if they'd ended up contacting one other. The fact that he was at her graduation spoke volumes. I just needed to figure out if he was there for her. I smiled at the thought.

"Cheers," I said, tipping my champagne glass toward him just as the door to the suite opened again. *Wow, this was shaping up to be quite a party.* Next thing I knew, Hank would be doing a strip tease for us all.

Except when I turned toward the door, it wasn't another friend joining us.

Or at least I'd told Cammie he wasn't a friend.

Jason walked into the suite like a man on a mission, sucking out any spare oxygen from the space so that I was left holding my breath. He shoved his hand through his hair as he scanned the five of us. When his eyes locked on me, he took a deep breath and let his hands fall to his sides.

"Hi," he said, stepping inside the suite so that Hank could close the door behind him.

I was completely frozen in shock. My cousin, Patricia, was humming with nervous energy and either there was a mouse in the suite or she was making some kind of squeaking noise with her mouth.

"Holy shit. You're Jason Monroe. My friends are not going to believe this," she said, pulling out her phone. Jason blinked at her for a second and then turned back to me, clearly unfazed by her excitement. He wasn't nearly as impeccably dressed as Grayson. Wearing dark jeans and a leather jacket, he didn't even look like he was attending a graduation, yet there he was.

"You made it," Summer said with a smile.

"Yes. Thanks for the info," Jason said, dipping his head in gratitude.

Dammit, Summer.

"Jeez who else did you contact about Cammie's graduation? Is the President about to walk through the door with Michelle on his arm?"

Summer laughed. "No, but the Pope sends his regards," she said, sipping her champagne and turning back toward the window like she wasn't to blame for the fact that Jason was now standing in the suite with us.

Grayson, the ever gracious business man, stepped forward to introduce himself to Jason, and when their hands touched I thought my brain would short circuit from the sheer amount of hotness in that one handshake. I'm surprised their hands didn't fuse together.

After everyone knew everyone, and my cousin had taken half a dozen pictures with Jason, he turned to me with soft features.

"Could I talk to you outside for a second?" he asked, pointing to the door.

I stared at the suite door, trying to gather my wits. If I followed him outside, no one would be there to prevent me from jumping his bones. *But* if I followed him outside, I could jump his bones in private.

Confident in my decision, I headed to the door, conscious of everyone's eyes on us as we left the suite.

"So, you're at my sister's graduation," I said, crossing my arms and leaning back against the wall once we were alone in the hallway. He looked both ways and then tugged me further away from the suite, presumably so our conversation couldn't be overheard.

"Yes, I am," he answered simply.

"Why?"

He dropped my arm and fell back against the wall across from me. The added space helped clear my head.

"I know LuAnne called and told you the full story about my past," he said.

I frowned. "Are you mad?"

He shook his head. "I'm relieved you know everything now."

"Is that why you came here?"

He dragged his teeth along his bottom lip, forming a reply. "I realized that your lyrics were true— the part about us being over from the start. And that's my fault."

I grunted in disbelief. "Go on."

He rolled his eyes at my sass but I couldn't help it. "I didn't want to be your friend. I didn't want to collaborate with you, but I didn't have a choice."

"Wow. How romantic," I said.

He groaned and dragged his hands through his hair again. I was going to cause him to bald prematurely from all of the stress.

"No, just listen. I didn't need a woman in my life. I was still trying to sort out my past. But if I'd pulled my head out of my ass for a minute, I would have seen the truth."

I folded my hands behind my back and met his gaze. "What's the truth?"

"We should have been friends from the start. Real friends."

His earnest expression, and the fear of rejection in his dark eyes, softened my resolve.

"You're really just here to make sure that Cammie doesn't send you anymore poisoned fruit," I said, smirking.

He smirked back. "True. That's mostly the reason."

We were stitching together a bridge, attempting to repair a relationship that was nonexistent to begin with.

I stuck my hand out between us. His dark gaze fell, studying my proverbial white flag for a moment before he peered back up at me. His features were relaxed then, his grin the most beguiling part of his appearance. When he took my hand, his finger struck my pulse point and I inhaled a sharp breath.

"I'm sorry about running and I'm sorry about misjudging the situation."

He nodded, with a small smirk.

"Friends?" I asked, trying to control the excitement in my voice.

Oh, c'mon, who was I kidding with the "friends" bullshit? I wanted to open the suite door to our left and push him inside so I could have my wicked way with him. But that's what the old Brooklyn would have done. The new Brooklyn, who was cool, calm, collected, and didn't need carbs or caffeine (and apparently only used words that started with a "c") could just shake his hand and pretend to be unaffected.

"Friends," he agreed before dropping my hand.

"Just to clear it up, do friends have sex?"

He laughed, "No. I don't think they do."

Damn.

"What about just oral? Like a 'how ya doin' blow job? That's okay, right?"

He laughed and shook his head, pushing me toward our suite with his hand on my lower back.

"Do you do that sort of thing for Grayson?" he asked, watching me out of the corner of his eye.

I laughed. "Oh, nice, I would have brought Grayson around earlier if I knew he'd make you jealous."

He shook his head a little too adamantly. "Nah, friends don't get jealous of friends."

I patted his chest just as we got back to the suite. "Keep thinking that, buddy," I teased. Before I could pull my hand away, he caught it in his and pressed it harder to his chest so that I could feel the rhythm of his heart beneath my palm. *Okayyyy then, this... this was seriously not something I could do with someone who was just a friend.*

"After you, *buddy*," he drawled with way too much seduction. *Was buddy a euphemism for something?* It definitely sounded like it.

Before I could delve deeper into that question, Hank pulled the suite door open for us and Jason released my hand.

• • •

"You did it!" I yelled as soon as Cammie slid into the limousine. We'd all been sitting inside, waiting for her to join us so we could make our reservation for lunch. I'd extended an invitation to both Jason and Grayson (hah, that has a nice ring to it), but Grayson insisted that he wanted to drive separately and meet us at the restaurant. I swear the man was more hormonal than a pregnant woman in her first trimester.

Cammie held her arms up and cheered as she scooted along the black leather. "No more studio. No more impossible projects and no more annoying professors!" she sang. Then she glanced to the end of the limousine where Jason was sitting, and her smile fell.

"Damn. Looks like my fruit basket didn't work. You're supposed to be dead," she said, glaring at him. "I guess you didn't try the grapefruit."

Chapter Twenty-Eight

I'll admit, Cammie wasn't the most gracious person in the world, but usually she didn't verbalize her death threats. Clearly, I'd screwed up with her somewhere along the way.

Jason chuckled and held out a graduation card for her to take. She eyed it like it was a snake about to bite her, but then she reluctantly accepted it. Of course, she didn't bother to open it.

"I guess they'll just let anyone into these things," she glared. "I thought I told Hank to kill on sight—"

"Cammie! Be nice," I warned as the limousine pulled away from the stadium.

We had fifteen minutes to make it back downtown for our reservation at a trendy French bistro. (Fifteen minutes to persuade Cammie to lay off Jason.) I'd reserved a back room and had hired a party planner to make it extra special for Cammie since she insisted she didn't want a graduation party.

"I am being nice. This is my nice face, see?" She

proceeded to force her lips apart in the most awkward smile I'd ever seen.

"I've raised an animal," I said, tossing my hands into the air in defeat.

"A cute one," Summer said, winking at Cammie.

"You should read your card," Jason said, pointing to where Cammie had dropped the small cream envelope onto the leather seat next to her.

"Maybe you should read my lips: N-O. Not after what you did to my sister."

Oh, great. *World, welcome to my drama. Here, have a front row seat.*

"Cammie, seriously, everything is fine," I said, trying to meet her eye so that I could reassure her. I couldn't blame her for wanting to be protective of me, but I already had Hank. I didn't need Cammie, too.

"Fine," she said, grabbing the envelope and tearing the envelope open with her finger. We all sat there watching her unfold the card. I wasn't close enough to make out what the front said, but it looked simple enough. It took her a little while to read, but I didn't pry. When she was done, she licked her bottom lip and nodded while she stuffed the card back into the envelope.

"You are one charming suckwad, Monroe, I'll give you that," she said, giving him a sly smile.

I didn't even bother chastising her because Jason cracked up and shook his head. Whatever was inside that envelope had hopefully changed Cammie's opinion of Jason, and I had to use every ounce of willpower not to reach across the seat and rip it out of her hand so that I could read it too.

"We're here," Summer said, clapping her hands and bringing everyone's attention toward the bistro coming up on our right. It was a hidden gem in the city. The front of the restaurant was painted black with a glossy sheen. Gold filigree spanned the windows, creating works of art that dotted the exterior. Grayson was standing against the side of the building with his head down as he scrolled through his phone. The moment she saw him, Cammie froze.

"What the hell is Grayson doing here?" she asked, the color visibly draining from her face.

She hadn't even had that bad of a reaction when she'd seen Jason.

"He came to your graduation, so I invited him to lunch," I explained, studying her.

The limousine driver parked near the entrance of the restaurant and we all stepped out onto the sidewalk. Cammie moved to take her cap and gown off, but I held up my camera.

"Leave it on for two photos and then you can take it off," I pleaded. I really wanted a cheesy photo of her to frame for my fireplace.

She sighed and stepped outside, all evidence of her sassiness left behind in the limousine. When I posed her against the glossy backdrop of the restaurant she didn't even fight it. She plastered on a smile and let me snap away — all without acknowledging Grayson's presence.

I peered over to watch him out of the corner of my eye, but he wouldn't look away from Cammie. He was studying her with a furrowed brow, his lips tugged into a thin line that wasn't *exactly* a frown. *Okay, it was pretty close to a frown.*

"Okay, are we done?" Cammie asked with an unusually timid tone. No one made Cammie shy, no one except Grayson apparently.

"Yes. I got some good ones," I said, scrolling back

through the last few photos.

"Finally! I'm starving!" Summer said, moving to hold the door open for everyone. Grayson hung back, teetering on the curb with his hands shoved in his suit pockets.

"Cameron, may I speak with you for a moment?" he asked with an air of polite indifference that I wasn't used to. My gaze snapped to Cammie as she swallowed slowly and nodded.

"You guys can go inside," she said, her dark eyes wary and unsure.

I had no clue what he wanted to talk to her about, but if it got rid of the tension between them, I was all for it. I ushered everyone in and resisted the urge to watch Cammie and Grayson talk through the bistro's window.

Jason slid his palm to my lower back as we wove through the restaurant.

"I think Grayson might be even more brooding than you are," I joked, glancing over my shoulder at him.

He smirked at my assessment. "I'm not brooding. I'm quiet."

I chuckled. "Same thing. When you're hot and quiet, women think you're brooding."

His eyebrow perked up. "You think I'm hot?"

"Yup," I answered confidently. "Like look at that toddler- she's so hot."

He laughed. "I think you're confused about what that word means."

A small archway opened up into the back room where the party planner was finishing up lighting the remaining candles. She'd completely transformed the room with multiple floral arrangements in the center of a white linen table. A small but decadent cake sat on the side table that also held a buffet of food perfect for a late brunch.

A framed photo of Cammie sat near the end of the table. She was sitting between our parents on the beach, her grin marked with missing teeth. She'd been dealt an interesting hand in life, having lost our parents at a much younger age than I did, but looking at her now, it was hard to believe she wasn't always so responsible and put-together. Sure, she had a sharp mouth and sometimes she could really benefit from a filter, but I was so proud of the woman she'd become.

I'd just turned from looking at the photo when she walked beneath the archway to join us. Grayson wasn't behind her.

I frowned. "Did you kill him?"

When my joke didn't spark a laugh, I knew something was up. Her eyes were focused on the table before her, her thoughts seemed a million miles away.

"What did Grayson want?" I asked, rounding the table toward her. *Had he hurt her feelings?* She looked like she'd just been slapped.

"He wants me to come in for an interview at his firm."

My mouth fell open. That was the absolute last thing I thought she was going to say.

"That's great, Cammie!"

She nodded numbly. *What the hell had he done? Given her a lobotomy?*

"Isn't that good?" I asked, bending down to meet her eyes.

She shook her head, not to say no, but as if to clear her thoughts. "Yes. Yeah, it's good. Let's eat," she said, taking a deep breath and looking up to the buffet table.

Jason and I exchanged a glance, but he shrugged. Whatever was going on with her, she clearly didn't want to discuss it right then, and I'd let her get away with it. It was her day.

Over plates brimming with delicious food, I recounted stories of baby Cammie and teenage Cammie — oddly, many of the story lines were similar. She was a willful person, no matter the age.

When it was time for dessert, a waitress came around and cleared our plates away. I took the opportunity to turn to Cammie while everyone was preoccupied.

"So when do you think your interview will be?" I asked quietly, ensuring our conversation was private.

She shrugged, playing with her fork. "He said he'd be out of town on a project for two weeks, but that his assistant would give me a call."

"Will you end up going through with it?" I asked.

She dropped her fork and the metal clanked softly onto the ceramic plate. "Of course. I'd be stupid to turn down an interview with his firm."

Her dark eyes slid to me and I saw so much emotion buried beneath her gaze.

"Well, I'm sure you'll do great," I assured her, squeezing her hand.

• • •

The days after Cammie's graduation were packed with meetings, dress fittings, rehearsals, and appointments. My trainer had me working out twice a day (which I tried to argue was a form of capital punishment, but he wouldn't hear of it). As soon as I'd finish one thing on the agenda, Summer would be waiting by the door, ready to whisk me away to my next task. Grammys week never got any easier, and being one of the performers only made matters worse.

When I woke up two days before the award show with a giant pimple on my face, you would have thought World War III had just been declared.

"Dear GOD, someone just kill me now — I can't walk the red carpet like this."

Looking back, the pimple was probably the least of my worries, but it was physical, tangible, and so I focused on that and not that the fact that my life was crumbling around me. *(<- See how dramatic I can be when my trainer forces me to work out twice a day and my nutritionist cuts my carbs in half?)*

"You need to calm down, Brooklyn. You can't even see it and it'll go down by Sunday," Summer said, ushering me through the door of the Roberto Cavalli show room where I was having my final dress fitting. *And when I say "dress" I really mean "dresses".* I had three wardrobe changes in all: The red carpet look which was a white poufy thing, the performance look which was a tight red dress that dipped far too low and showed off lots of leg, and then the after-party look which was a just as tight as the red dress, but black with smooth silky fabric that would be easier to dance in.

"Whatever you say. You'll be the one talking me off the ledge Sunday morning when the make-up artist is having to fill in my pores with cement to get a clean work surface."

"You're not even making sense anymore," she said, shaking her head and pushing me toward the raised platform in the center of the show room. Mirrors surrounded the platform on three sides so I'd be able to see my gowns from every angle.

"Oh, before we get started, the label has asked me how you and Jason will arrive at the venue on Sunday,"

Summer said.

"Separately," I answered. "I'm not taking a date, unless Cammie counts."

"She does, but she won't fill out a tux nearly as well," she said with a smirk.

"Perfect — it's settled. Next item on the list."

"Are you two dating?" she asked as if she were scrolling through items on a check list.

"Summer," I warned, meeting her eyes in one of the mirrors before me.

She shrugged. "Thought I'd try and see if you would answer truthfully."

"He and I are friends. I *think*, we're friends at least."

"Right, and I'm secretly in the FBI," she said with an eye roll.

"I'm serious. Yesterday at rehearsals, we joked around and talked. It was normal and just what friends would do."

"Have you or have you not had sex with him?" she asked.

I propped my hands on my hips. "I can't recall."

"And what about his *marriage*?"

I rolled my eyes. "He's signed the divorce papers and she's engaged to another guy for god's sake. He was trying to get some kind of custody of Lacy, but it's looking like that's not possible."

"Oh no, really?"

I nodded, sad at how complicated the situation was for him. Just then, one of the design assistants stepped into the show room in tight leather pants and an off the shoulder black sweater. Her spiked heels clapped against the stained concrete floors as she stepped closer.

"So sorry to keep you waiting. Let's get started," she

said, eyeing me up and down. She glared a beat too long on the pimple. Motherfucker, it was huge. *I knew it.*

"Your final rehearsal is tomorrow?" the assistant asked with a constipated smile.

"Yes," I answered, trying to ignore the clenching of my stomach. With everything going on, my nerves had been pushed to the back burner, but every time someone brought up the impending award show, the feelings came rushing back in.

"Well, let's hope you can pull it off," the woman said, clapping her hands twice to beckon a second assistant who rolled out a garment rack from the back room. My three dresses hung from the metal bar, each more beautiful than the last.

I stared at myself in the mirror, trying to see the confident woman that I knew was there somewhere. The truth was, it wasn't the Grammy performance that I was nervous about— it was what happened after, when Jason and I no longer had a reason to hang out together at rehearsals. I knew I'd either have to come clean and tell him the truth: *Surprise, I don't want to be your friend, you ridiculously sexy man. I want to date you and have your babies.* Or I'd have to just play dumb and continue to live a lie. I'd have to watch him go back to Montana or wherever else he was heading once the Grammys were over, and I'd have to live with the fact that I never told him the truth about my feelings for him.

Oh yeah, and I had this *little* performance in front of a million people to do in two days. *No biggie, right?*

Chapter Twenty-Nine

Things to know concerning Grammy prep:

1. You don't eat for like 24 hours beforehand. I'm serious. People who tell you that they actually eat before stepping onto the red carpet in a couture gown are a bunch of freaking liars.

2. Getting ready for the big day is a marathon, not a sprint. Except if you're me, and then your trainer does in fact make you sprint everyday leading up to the actual event.

3. My body had been massaged, plucked, prodded, and facial-ed.

4. I hadn't had a decent night's sleep in over a week

The night before the Grammys, I was tossing and turning as my mind worked over every single scenario that could possibly play out during the show the next day. *What if the lights cut out? What if my microphone broke? What if*

I forget my lyrics during the song? What if a bear was set loose inside the Staples Center?

As you can see, I was starting to plan for *all* plausible outcomes.

Which is why I didn't hesitate to roll over and check my phone when I heard it vibrating on top of my nightstand. I hadn't been asleep anyway.

Jason's name flashed across the screen, but I couldn't fathom why he'd be calling me at midnight.

"Hello?" I asked, holding the phone up to my ear.

"Did I wake you?" he asked.

"Nope. I was just thinking about the best way to defend myself with a mic stand if a bear was on stage with us tomorrow night."

He chuckled. "Huh, I hadn't thought about that," he admitted. "Come let me in."

I sat up and glanced around my room, trying to comprehend what he meant.

"Let you in... my condo?" I finished, utterly confused.

"Yes, and hurry, the pizza box is burning my hand," he said, as if his request was perfectly normal.

I shoved my blankets off my bed and continued to hold the phone up to my ear as I walked through my silent condo. All the lights were off since I should have been asleep three hours before. I flipped the light on in my kitchen and went to the front door.

When I swung it open, Jason was standing there with a boyish smile and the most delicious pizza I'd ever had the pleasure of smelling.

"Well, hello there," I smiled, pushing the door open wide enough for him to step inside. Then, I promptly stole the box of pizza out of his hands. When I pried it open, my eyes feasted upon cheesy, pepperoni goodness. "Oh sweet, baby Jesus. This smells like crack."

Jason rolled his eyes and stepped into the kitchen to retrieve two plates as if he joined me for a midnight snack in my condo all the time.

"This is technically off limits," I said, eyeing the pizza like it had the ability to kill me. Which is theory, it did. But let me tell you, as Jason pulled out that piece of pizza and held it up for me to take my first bite, it tasted *pretty damn good*. I ate two slices and enjoyed every moment of it. If I had a little flab on my stomach on the red carpet the next day, I'd just let the paparazzi spin it into a baby speculation story— *that'd keep them occupied for a while.*

"So I'm guessing pizza was a good choice?" he asked with a cocky smile.

I picked up a stray pepperoni from my plate and popped it into my mouth. "Oh yeah."

He nodded before taking the pizza box to my refrigerator. He could hardly fit it inside among all the fruit and vegetables that my nutritionist had loaded me up with earlier in the week. *I swear if I die soon, the cause would be death by vegetables.*

"How'd you know I'd be awake?" I asked once he'd shut the refrigerator door and turned back to face me. Now that the pizza wasn't distracting me, I took in his appearance. He had on a worn black t-shirt and sweat pants. His arms were sculpted, but not obscenely so. Even still, I had a hard time focusing on my attention anywhere else.

"It was a wild guess," he said simply, meeting my eyes with a grin of his own.

"I technically have to be up in a few hours to start getting ready for the press and everything. Tomorrow is going to be a long day."

He leaned forward and propped his hands up on the kitchen counter so that he could support his upper body.

"Well, I guess I should probably go then," he said, though he didn't bother actually moving his body. Clearly, he didn't mean what he was saying.

"Guess so," I replied with a slow smile that built upon itself the longer he watched me from across the island.

"It's pretty late," he said, although he wasn't looking at his watch. His dark eyes were pinned on me.

I could have told him to leave, but instead I shrugged. "You could stay here if you want, you know, just to make it easier for you."

He glanced around my kitchen as if I had asked him to literally sleep on the counter.

"I mean, I have a comfortable couch," I said, pointing to my living room.

His eyebrow arched and he finally pushed himself off of the kitchen island. "I'm not sleeping on the couch."

I rolled my eyes. "Oh please, get over yourself. You're not too good for the couch just because you're a fancy pants singer."

I'm sure I would have kept on rambling had he not stalked around the island and forced my silence with his lips. Oh, *ohhhh*. He wasn't going to be sleeping on the couch because he wanted to sleep in my bed.

It'd been over a week since I'd felt his lips on mine, but my body hadn't forgotten what heaven felt like. His lips were just as tender and firm as I remembered, and the way he caged me against the island turned any protests into soft, encouraging moans. My hands glided up over his t-shirt, over every dip and curve of his hard chest. If he didn't do something fast, I'd be having quite a blissful moment on the stool in the kitchen.

"Couch or bed?" I asked, trying to shove myself off the barstool. He didn't answer, and he didn't let me up. His arms bent and his head dipped down to steal another kiss. The stool wobbled beneath my shifting weight, but I clenched onto his arms and he held me up. One of his hands worked at my shirt and a chill ran down my spine. Holy, we were going to do it right here, on this stool like a bunch of heathens. *Bring it on.*

I fumbled with his belt buckle and then tugged his pants down just far enough to get to his boxers.

"Stand up," he instructed, gripping my biceps to lift me off of the stool. I'd barely found my footing when he tugged my pajama shorts and panties off. The draft from the air conditioner hit the crest of my thighs and goose bumps pricked the back of my neck. I stepped out of my clothing as he tore off my tank top, and suddenly, I was naked. Naked, with my dishes in the sink and my stray cutting board silently judging me from afar.

"Tell me if it's uncomfortable," he said, guiding me back to the stool.

I'd have to be sitting on a bed of hot coals to tell him to stop. And even then, I'd probably just go for the ass burn. My head fell back and my eyes fluttered closed as Jason's fingers skirted along my skin. He was igniting my blood, trying to coax out our passion, but I'd been ready for that moment since I'd found him on the other side of my door.

"Did you hear me?" he asked, nuzzling the skin beneath my ear and then gently biting down on my earlobe.

Holy mother of—

"Yesssss," I dragged, answering him as best as I could just as his fingers skimmed to the center of my thighs.

That was the last moment in which I was capable of human speech. For the next hour, I communicated in a language only shared by whales and other large marine animals. Mostly just really long moans and sharp cries. *Classy, I know.*

The edge of the kitchen island pressed into my back, the marble cold and hard, but Jason's skin was so warm. I clung onto him as he pulled out and sank into me over and over again. There were a few times when the stool threatened to tip over, but Jason kept us upright, shielding my body against the kitchen island with his chest and arms.

I dug my nails into his back as he gripped the back of my thighs with a sense of entitlement, ownership.

I *wanted* to feel that from him.

And that's when I realized what I was doing.

I was getting lost in him again. Completely lost in his eyes, and arms, and confident mouth on my body. I didn't realize until it was over and I was left coming down from my second mind-blowing orgasm that I'd given him exactly what he wanted. *Again.*

Me with no strings attached.

And even worse, I realized it'd been, dare I say... a booty call.

Arriving at a late hour without notice - check.

Having sex - check.

No expectation of a relationship after - check.

Crap.

As a twenty-seven year old woman with a good personality and decent tits (when I wore the right push-up bra), I needed to grow a freaking backbone. Yet, there I was, letting Jason take whatever he wanted without any regard for *what I wanted.*

"You look like you're lost in another world," Jason noted as he tugged his pants back into place.

Any excitement that had just been circulating through the kitchen had been stamped out like a light. I couldn't even look him in the eye as he handed me back my tank top from the floor.

"I think I am," I replied when I realized he was still waiting for a response.

He used his finger to nudge my chin up so that I was forced to stare in his eyes, but it was too hard. I clamped my eyes shut and fumbled for the first excuse I could think of.

"I think that pizza made me sick," I complained, pressing my hand to my stomach for emphasis. When I opened my eyes again, he was frowning and his eyes were dark, empathetic.

"Can I get you something? An antacid? Water?"

Stop. Stop being so easy to love. *You aren't love. You're sex and pleasure and all the easy things in life.*

"No," I shook my head, pulling out of his reach. "I think I should just try to get some sleep before tomorrow."

He pulled his hand through his hair, causing the short strands to stand on end. His brows knitted together and for a second, I thought maybe he didn't want to leave.

"Why don't you go lay down and I'll let myself out when you've gone to sleep?"

I wanted to shove him out of the front door. I thought we could be friends, but that was me agreeing to whatever he wanted to give me. It was pathetic. I didn't need table scraps. I needed to break the cycle.

I nodded in lieu of a verbal reply considering tears were already dangerously close to falling and I would *not* cry about this situation for one more moment.

"Brooklyn," he called as I walked toward my bedroom. I looked over my shoulder to see him encased in the light from the kitchen. He looked down to the floor and then back up to me. "Let me know if you need anything."

I nodded and kept walking toward my room, happy to be alone once the door closed behind me.

I had one last day with him and then I wouldn't have to pretend anymore. There would be no more wishful thinking, no more late-night sex sessions. I had to quit the habit or I'd never be able to move on.

So we'd sing our duet and then the day after that, I'd start fresh and start working on my new album.

Without Jason.

Chapter Thirty

It took a lot of caffeine to get me going the next morning. Summer brought me a latte with an extra shot of espresso, but by noon, I was still in danger of crashing. I'd tossed and turned after Jason had left the night before, and when I woke up the next morning there was a note sitting on the kitchen counter that threw my brain for a loop:

Give me until tomorrow night. - J

"Fuckkk youuuu," I said, tearing the note in two. I'd watched enough movies and I'd yelled at the screen enough times to know when the pitiful character is supposed to move on and stop going back time after time. Let me lay out a few examples for you: *He's Just Not That Into You*, *Jaws*, *Jurassic Park*, *Titanic*. Okay, so maybe only one of those is actually a good example of what I thought I was living through, but still.

"Are you ready?" Cammie asked, stepping out of my bedroom in a strapless Oscar de la Renta gown. The red fabric looked killer with her tan skin and dark hair. She was my date for the evening, and she would definitely be showing me up.

"Almost," I said, pointing to the hair stylist who was still working to make my curls as perfect as possible. He'd used about three bottles of hairspray and I was currently sitting in a cloud of perfume, make-up, and hair product that threatened to suffocate me. "You look amazeballs."

She spun in a circle and laughed. "Why, thank you. Summer said we have to leave by 5:30 P.M. to make it in time for the red carpet."

"Done! Let's get your dress on now," the hair stylist said, spinning the chair around so that I could look in the mirror. I hardly recognized myself, which was usually the case by the time the red carpet looks were completed. My hair was loose and curled to perfection. My eyes were dark and dramatic and my lips were painted a bright red and would match my second dress for the night, my performance dress.

The bodice of my first dress made it almost impossible to breathe and as we rode in the limousine toward the Staples Center, I feared that my lungs were in danger of collapsing.

"If I pass out on the red carpet, you'll have to carry me past all the photographers," I warned Cammie.

"Sounds good," she nodded. "I knew what I was getting into when I signed up to be your date."

I winked. "You better put out at the end of the night."

"If by 'put out' you mean order us Chinese food while we nurse our aching feet, it's on."

I laughed and relaxed as much as possible against the limousine's seat. The traffic wasn't terrible getting to the Staples Center, but there was a line of cars waiting to drop off various celebrities and musicians so they could have their turn on the red carpet. They had to time it well so that there was a constant stream of celebrities walking the carpet. When it was finally my turn, I let Cammie out first so that she could shield me from the paparazzi. I always feared stumbling while they snapped away, capturing my face as it hit the pavement. As such, I took my sweet time standing up on my four-inch heels.

Cammie and I walked hand-in-hand toward the center of the carpet where the media were stationed like soldiers on a battlefield. Various news channels were lined up in the front for interviews while the photographers were positioned on a platform behind them so they could continue to snap photos.

Once my cheeks were in danger of falling off from smiling so hard, I made my way toward an "E News!" camera for my first interview.

"You look absolutely stunning," Gina—the red-carpet correspondent— said, holding my hand up so I could spin in a circle for the camera.

"Thank you, thank you. I have to be honest though, I had pizza at midnight last night," I joked, turning to the side.

Gina gasped playfully. "That's okay. I had a whole bag of Twizzlers while I was getting ready," she laughed, and then jumped into the first round of questions. It was all simple and fun. She asked questions about my upcoming album, about my tour dates, but then in the middle of the interview, I felt a hand hit my lower back, just above the tight material of my gown. When I spun around, the first thing to hit me was his scent. Jason's cologne was stronger than the haze of beauty products surrounding me and I had to fight not to sway on my heels. It wasn't that he was doused in it; rather it was the way my emotions reacted to his scent. Without meaning to, I'd come to associate it with pleasure and happiness.

He looked similar to how I'd seen him when he dressed up for the high school prom, but his tuxedo was designer and impeccably fitted. His cufflinks were in place and his shoes were shined. His hair was styled professionally, a fact I'm sure he hated, but it framed his handsome features for everyone to see.

Gina squealed into the microphone when she saw that he was electing to join us for the remainder of the interview.

She turned to the camera with a bright smile. "Jason Monroe is here to join us as well! We get an *exclusive* first interview with the pair who will be part of the most anticipated performance of the night," Gina spoke before turning back to us. "Are you guys ready for it?"

I could have come up with an answer for her question if Jason's hand hadn't been turning slow circles on my back. C'mon, seriously. *I don't need to get turned on in front of a news camera.*

"We are. We've been practicing for the last few weeks," Jason said, edging closer to me. The paparazzi were having a field day with the pose, snapping away from the second level like their lives depended on it.

"Could you give us a sneak peak of the performance? Maybe some insider info," Gina asked with a bright smile. She was trying to do her job, but I just wanted the interview to end so that I could step away from Jason and finish walking the red carpet.

"I think you'll appreciate the ending," Jason said, looking from Gina to me. *Ending?* We'd rehearsed this song one million times on that stage and I couldn't think of any special ending. The choreographer had stayed true to her word. Our performance would be simple and understated, none of the special effects and costume changes that would accompany Lady Gaga's performance later on in the night. Now *that* would have a crazy ending.

"I can't wait. Thank you guys for joining us. Could you look into the camera and say, "You're watching 'E News'?"

● ● ●

Just because I was performing, didn't mean I could skip the actual event and just hangout back stage. No, I had to sit in the front row with Cammie on one side and Jay-Z and Beyoncé on the other. That's right, I was sitting with hip-hop royalty while I watched award after award get announced on stage. I was nominated for two: *Best Pop Solo Performance* and *Album of the Year*. Both of which would be announced after my performance, which was good. I couldn't concentrate on a single thing knowing I was minutes away from getting ushered back-stage for a dress change and a final warm up.

"You're almost up. Are you nervous?" Cammie whispered, leaning in so no one could overhear her.

I gave her a pointed stare. "I want to vomit everywhere."

She squeezed my hand tight. "Yeah, let's try and avoid that if possible."

The show cut to commercial break and a stagehand

signaled for me to move backstage just like we'd rehearsed. My heart hammered against my chest as I let go of Cammie's hand and stood, holding my dress up so that I could walk easier. I glanced back to find Jason, but he was heading toward the opposite side of the stage, moving with a purpose. My stomach dropped. I really wanted to talk to him before we performed— just to have him tell me that we'd be okay.

I breathed deep and let the stagehands guide me backstage, directly into the behind-the-scenes mayhem.

"Ms. Heart," a young girl with a headset spoke. "You have ten minutes before your performance. Wardrobe needs you now."

The next few minutes passed in a blur. People moved around me, tugging off fabric and dressing me in more. The tight red dress was far easier to breath and move in, so I welcomed the change even if my boobs were on display. *No really, the girls were OUT.* A make-up artist went to town touching up my lipstick and face, while a hair team attacked my head.

I sat with my hands folded on my lap and my eyes closed, repeating the phrase, "just breathe, just breathe."

Our lyrics played in my head over and over again as I tried to calm my nerves and get into the zone.

"Three minutes!" a stagehand yelled as an assistant buckled my high-heels into place.

I kept my eyes closed, trying to separate myself from the mayhem around me.

"Two minutes!"

The crew led me to the side-stage where a sound assistant was standing with my guitar in hand.

"Everything is plugged in. Don't trip on the cord as you

walk out there," he instructed while another person simultaneously fitted the sound monitor into my ear.

Deep breaths were my saving grace.

"30 seconds!"

I inhaled deeply and glanced across the stage. Jason's sharp features were visible just behind the curtain. As soon as the lights dimmed and the curtain fell we'd walk out and take our places. His eyes locked with mine and he nodded once, giving me a piece of confidence that I dearly needed.

"Showtime," the stagehand yelled, gently nudging me up the stage stairs.

My heels hit the stage and I walked to my mark, the light gray "x" sitting in the very center of the dark wood floor. My hands shook and I tried to will my breathing to settle. Once we met in the middle of the stage, I glanced up at Jason. He looked so sure of himself, confident enough for the both of us.

"Breathe, Princess," he whispered as he reached for my hand, gripping it tightly and offering me a piece of reassurance just as the heavy curtain started to lift and the house lights dimmed.

I knew Cammie was sitting out in the audience watching me. I knew millions of people were tuning in for our performance, anxious to see our first duet. My breaths were quick and uneven, my heart was racing, my stomach was knotted in a tight ball, but my hands— *they knew what to do.*

The moment I settled my guitar into place and my fingers fell over the chords, everything became clear and simple.

Five…

Four...
Three...
Two...

I strummed the opening chords as Jason tapped his foot to the beat. The duet began with a short solo, the crowd focused on my fingers as they danced across the fretboard. Then Jason gripped the microphone with both hands, closed his eyes, and sang the first lines, stealing the attention, and the hearts, of everyone watching.

> *Something about you caught me by surprise*
> *Though I always knew you'd be my demise*
> *I didn't want you to love me*
> *Didn't want you thinking of me*

> *So I kept my distance*
> *Tried to ignore your existence*
> *I was blinded by my pride*
> *With you, the Jekyll to my Hyde*

> *But that's where you found me*
> *Baby, that's where you unwound me*

I joined him for the chorus, our voices blending together. Jason's voice was deeper than mine, but he had notes of a natural tenor. His range was a little less expansive, but it was obvious why our label had wanted us to collaborate. It took hardly any effort on our part to combine our pitches into a perfect harmony.

> *Loving you would be as easy as taking a breath*
> *But to look at you, that's a dance with death*
> *I'd risk it all,*

For you I would
You'd make me fall,
And fall I would

Loving you would be as easy as taking a breath
But to be by you, that's a dance with death

I turned to Jason as I sang the next lyrics. Our eyes locked as I poured passion into the words. The audience was there, but they weren't the ones I was singing to anymore.

I thought once was enough
You turned to me and called my bluff,
Maybe I should have walked away
but I couldn't resist, I needed replay after replay

Loving you would be as easy as taking a breath
But to give you up, that's a dance with death

We were over from the start
I never said I'd give my heart
So now it's time for this to end
After all, a friend is just a friend

Loving you would be as easy as taking a breath
But to give you up, that's a dance with death

So now it's time for this to end
After all, a friend is just a friend

Chapter Thirty-One

The music faded out as the crowd began to cheer. Claps and whistles rang out across the stadium and I pulled the monitor out of my ear so that I could hear them all. I knew they'd cut to a commercial break because that's how we'd rehearsed it, so I relaxed and took my first relieved breath of the day.

We'd done it.

We'd sung our duet, and sadly, I knew I'd never be able to sing alone again, not knowing how much better it could be with Jason by my side.

I turned to look at him, to share a glance that only we could understand, but when I did, I saw that he was still holding his guitar, with his monitor in place and his pick between his fingers.

I hadn't noticed him continuing to strum his guitar at first. It was impossible to hear over the noise of the stadium, but then the calls and the whistles died down. The crowd realized, just as I did, that Jason's song wasn't over.

I frowned, running through the scenarios in my head. *Had I cut our duet off short? Was I messing up part of the choreography?* Then I listened to the chords he was playing and I knew that I hadn't messed up. I'd never heard the song before.

I took a tentative step toward him, unsure of how to inconspicuously ask him what he was doing without everyone realizing that I was clueless. He smiled and turned so that he and his guitar were facing me, only me. He continued to strum the opening chords of his song, a light melody filling the air around us. It was beautiful guitar work, soft and gentle like a lullaby, but with the aid of the amps it spread across the stadium, silencing the crowd.

I could feel them enamored right along with me, but when Jason began to sing, the entire audience melted away. Without thinking, my hands shot to my mouth and I stood there, completely taken aback by the surprise ending he'd been planning along.

He wrote me a song.

You crawled beneath my skin
I pushed you away,
But still you clawed back in

Before you, I could be alone
Now I can't stand the thought of you out there
Out there on your own

Before you, my world was black and white,
So simple, oh so simple
But now I'm missing my guiding light

So please come back Brooklyn, come back to me
Cause can't you see, you've brought me to my knees
I'm not good without you by my side
And this life's stuck in neutral
If you're not along for the ride

Before you I thought I had a favorite borough
Staten Island, Queens
Seems I wasn't quite so thorough

Those are far too plain
Nothing near as good lookin'
No, nothing near as good lookin'
As you, my dear Brooklyn

So please come back Brooklyn, come back to me
Cause can't you see, you've brought me to my knees
I'm not good without you by my side
And this life's stuck in neutral
If you're not along for the ride

Maybe I could go on without you
I could leave this town and start anew

But that'd be a lonely walk
With your smile weighing on me like a cinder block

So please come back Brooklyn, come back to me
Cause can't you see, you've brought me to my knees
I'm not good without you by my side
And this life's stuck in neutral
If you're not along for the ride

So won't you come back to me,
My dear Brooklyn
Come back to me

His fingers slowed, his voice quieted and I was left standing there with his lyrics playing back through my mind. They wound around my heart until I was left with the realization that Jason had just thrust his soul out onto the stage for the whole world to see.

Unlike when we'd finished the first song, the crowd didn't stand up and cheer. The stadium was absolutely silent save for whispers that grew as I stood with my hand covering my mouth and tears streaming down my cheeks.

"I can't believe you," I said, though no one could hear me. The words were a whisper against my palm.

Each second stretched into eternity as I watched him swing his guitar around so it could rest against his back. It took him two steps to reach me and then I was in his arms, gripping onto his shirt and crying even more. I'm sure the Grammy producers were attempting to pull us off stage, but they'd just have to hold their horses because I was not letting him go anytime soon.

"I'm so sorry for everything," he whispered into my ear, as if he still had a single thing to apologize for. *Hello*, the man had just serenaded me in front of a live audience and he'd sung about Brooklyn being his favorite borough. I mean, *c'mon.*

"I love you," I promised him, pulling my head back and realizing that the entire audience of the Staple Center was on their feet. They'd loved Jason's song as much as I had.

Just before the heavy black curtain fell, we held up our hands up between us and bent forward for a dramatic bow. *I swore I could see Cammie whooping it up next to Jay-Z.*

When we walked off stage, I didn't let Jason leave my side. We had post-performance interviews and the rest of the show to get through, but I didn't care.

"I cannot believe you did that!" I exclaimed once I'd gotten him alone back in my dressing room.

He smiled and shook his head. "I'm surprised you didn't catch on earlier. They always made me stay later than you at rehearsals."

I laughed. "I always just thought you needed extra practice!"

He scooped me into his arms. "Me? Extra practice? Never."

So that meant that for at least a week, he could have let me know that he wanted to be something more than friends. He could have saved me the misery of last night and the nights before that as well.

"So what does this mean?" I asked, letting him hold me as the show's producers started knocking on my door, no doubt trying to get us back in position for the award show. The categories we'd been nominated for would be coming up soon.

"It means I love you. It means I want to give us a real chance at being together."

The knocking outside grew louder and then they started shouting our names along with a few choice expletives. We just kept right on ignoring them.

"So you'll be staying in LA?"

He smiled. "Yes, but we'll still take trips to Montana. The gang already misses you. Dotty refuses to take sugar cubes from anyone since you left."

I smiled. "On one condition," I said, twining my fingers together behind his neck.

"What's that?" he asked with an arched brow. He knew I was putty in his arms.

"We collaborate again."

He smiled, his brown eyes crinkling in the corners just before he bent down to kiss me.

"You want to do another duet?" he asked skimming his lips against mine.

"I'm thinking a whole album."

He groaned, working his lips up to my ear until I was shivering in his arms. "Let's take it one song at a time."

"Perfect. That'll be the name of our first song," I joked.

The pounding on the door threatened to break the door off its hinges.

"Brooklyn Heart, get your ass out here right now! You just won Best Solo Artist of the year!" Summer yelled through the dressing room door.

"Oh shit," I gasped, jumping out of his arms and ripping the dressing room door open. There were two stagehands, Summer, and a show producer standing there with wide eyes.

I sighed and propped my hands on my hips as if I'd been ready for days.

"Outta my way people! I have an award to accept."

I tugged Jason along as I made my way through backstage. Hopefully the producers wouldn't mind if he escorted me back on stage. I had a feeling this would be the last award I'd be winning as a solo artist and I wanted him standing by my side during the speech.

It was later, after I'd accepted my award with a bright smile and shaky hands; after Jason and I had taken our seats once again; after Cammie clutched my hand as they announced the nominees for Album of the Year, and after Jason's name was announced once the thick envelope had been torn open.

That's when he took the stage with the crowd cheering him on. I stood up and whistled as best as I could (which is to say, not at all). His dark eyes locked with mine as he accepted the award and then he looked up to the faces in the crowd and took a deep, calming breath.

Names rolled off his tongue as he thanked the label, his manager, agent, friends, and colleagues. And then his gaze fell on me and my stomach clenched in anticipation for what he would say.

"I was once asked which I would pick if given a choice between experiencing love firsthand or writing about fictional love in my songs. At the time I'd chosen what seemed like the logical choice: to write. It's what I'd done my whole life, it's something I do every day." His gaze never left mine as he held his Grammy in both hands. His dark eyes burned through me and I gripped the velvet seat beneath me for support. "But I was wrong. You can write one million songs about one million types of love, but none of those can compare to feeling it firsthand." He lifted the Grammy up in the air and looked out into the expanse of people. "So this award is for the dreamers, and the romantics, that they may follow their hearts and not their heads, and seek to find a nonfiction love song of their own."

Chapter Thirty-Two

Epilogue

"So you're going to be my brother in law now?" Cammie asked as soon as Jason and I had joined her for breakfast. It'd been a week since the Grammys, and Jason and I had spent our days in bed alternating between writing and having sex. I have to say, it was a pretty great system and we'd already finished the first song for our next album. (A fact that our record label was ecstatic over.) After nearly wearing a hole in my mattress, we'd managed to extricate ourselves from my condo so that we could meet Cammie for breakfast.

The bistro in downtown LA was bustling with families enjoying their meals. I glanced around the space, smiling at the lively atmosphere as our mugs were filled with steaming coffee.

"Cammie, Jason and I have technically only been dating for one week. We aren't getting married," I told her once the waiter had walked away.

She leaned back in her chair and stared between the two of us with a wide smile. "I give it a month."

Jason chuckled, but didn't disagree. *Dear god, would I be engaged in a month?*

No.

Nope.

Maybe.

"Let's order some food!" I exclaimed, a tad too loud for it to seem natural.

"What do you guys have planned after this?" Cammie asked, pouring some cream into her coffee.

I slid my gaze to Jason who was wearing a small smile, probably because of that new move I'd attempted in bed that morning… or maybe it was because Cammie was finally done threatening his life with poisoned fruit.

"We're going to go pick up Lacy and take her to the children's museum. She's been begging to see one of the new exhibits," he said with a proud smile.

"Sounds *very* exciting," Cammie mocked.

I kicked her under the table. "It'll be fun."

"How does that arrangement work? You don't have shared custody do you?" she asked.

Jason shook his head. "Nah, I don't have set times with her, but since Kim and her husband live thirty minutes away, they've agreed to let Brook and I take her out twice a month." He shifted to look at me with a soft smile. "I never wanted to take her away from Kim, I just wanted to make sure I could still be a part of her life as she grew up."

"I see." Cammie nodded. "If you guys want her to really like you, you should probably give her lots of candy. That's more fun than a museum."

I gave her a death stare over the rim of my coffee mug.

"Alright, fine, stick to the museum plan, but maybe supplement it with some ice cream after."

Jason laughed. "I think we can manage that," he said, squeezing my hand gently.

Cammie's phone chimed on the table and she reached for it before I could grab it first.

"What about our no phone at the table rule?" I joked.

She didn't answer me, instead, the relaxed smile she'd been wearing a moment before started to slip as she read through whatever email or text she'd just received.

"What's up?" I asked, leaning forward to see what she was reading.

I managed to catch a glimpse of the Cole Designs logo at the top of the email before she pulled the phone away.

"Nothing," she lied. "Just a confirmation email concerning my interview time with Grayson next week."

Jason and I exchanged a glance.

"How are you feeling about it?" I asked gently, hoping she'd finally offer me the truth. I knew she was nervous about the impending interview. I knew it had the ability to shape her career, but she was adamant about keeping a brave face.

"I am feeling like I suddenly have no appetite," she said, pushing the cup of orange juice away.

"You'll be great, Cammie. Don't psych yourself out this early."

Jason nodded. "I can go over interview questions with you if you want."

She smiled up at him. "If you do, you're going to need to put on a tailored suit, style your hair, and become a full-on asshole. That way, you can really prepare me for Grayson Cole."

"Cammie! He's not that bad."

She flashed me a pointed stare. "You're right. He's worse. He's treated me terribly over the last few years."

"How?" I asked, wanting her side of the story.

"Mostly like I don't even exist. He came to one of my intro classes for architecture a few years back and after his lecture was over, I went up to the front of the room to say hi to him. He completely ignored me. I *know* he saw me, but he didn't nod or anything. He walked right past me, talking with another student from my class." She shrugged. "That was the day I finally decided that he and I would never be friends."

I frowned and held up my orange juice glass for a toast, trying to lighten the mood. I'm sure there was a perfectly good explanation for why Grayson ignored her that day, but I couldn't dispute the fact that the two of them had some serious tension to work out.

"Well, here's to Cammie, who will have an amazing interview next week, and who will undoubtedly land the job of her dreams," I said with a wide smile.

She lifted her glass to clink it against mine and added on a second part to the toast with a wicked gleam in her eyes.

"And who will put Grayson Cole in his place if it's the last thing she does."

R.S. Grey

The End

Acknowledgements

(I put this in every book, because it's SO important.) To every reader that takes a chance on an indie author, thank you so much. It means the world to me that you took a chance on this book.

To my family for all of their unconditional support. Especially Lance, who gave me a year "to see if this writing thing could work out" and never once pressured me to go after a more reasonable dream.

Mom, I'm listing you here because you always deserved to be thanked. You keep me sane on most days, and for that, I am grateful.

Lance, you get a second mention. Thank you for reading and add your own humor to this book. You make my jokes 10x funnier.

To Jenni Moen and Janosie (Josie) Bordeaux for being my two favorite author friends in the world. Thank you for being available at all hours of the day. Sure, most of what we talk about has nothing to do with writing, but I wouldn't trade it for the world! Jenni, thank you, thank you for talking me through the beta changes for this book. Seriously.

Thank you to all of my beta readers: Staci Brillhart, Stacey Lynn, and Brittainy Cherry! Your feedback was wonderful and truly, truly appreciated! Thank you for putting up with my changes and talking me through this book. You all helped bring this book to life.

Thank you to my amazing editor over at Taylor K.'s Editing Services.

Thank you to my awesome proofreaders at Grammar Inspection Task Force.

GIANT thank you to my street team!!!! R.S. Grey's

Girls is such fun group to be a part of. You all know how to make an author feel special!

Jennifer Flory-Van Wyk, I cannot thank you enough. Every day you help spread the word about my books and it completely astounds me. Your generosity knows no bounds and I am ETERNALLY grateful!!

Patricia Lee, you are a constant supporter and such a good friend to have in this writing community! Thank you so much for everything you do.

Jamie Taliaferro & Gabbs Warner – I love you both so much!! Thank you for the amazing support!

Thank you to all of my fellow indie authors (within Author Support 101 & Write Club). I don't think I'd have the energy to write without the help from all of you ladies. Thank you for providing support and a sense of community within a crazy world!

Thank you to everyone who accepted an ARC edition of this book and hanging with me for all the tweaks and changes!

If you're still reading these acknowledgements then you deserve a thank you as well, haha!

Other Books by R.S. Grey:

Scoring Wilder
USA TODAY BEST-SELLER
New Adult Sports Romance

What started out as a joke-- seduce Coach Wilder--soon became a goal she had to score.

With Olympic tryouts on the horizon, the last thing nineteen-year-old Kinsley Bryant needs to add to her plate is Liam Wilder. He's a professional soccer player, America's favorite bad-boy, and has all the qualities of a skilled panty-dropper.

* A face that makes girls weep - check.

* Abs that can shred Parmesan cheese (the expensive kind) - check.

* Enough confidence to shift the earth's gravitational pull - double check.

Not to mention Liam is strictly off limits. Forbidden. Her coaches have made that perfectly clear. (i.e. "Score with Coach Wilder anywhere other than the field and you'll be cut from the team faster than you can count his tattoos.") But that just makes him all the more enticing...Besides, Kinsley's already counted the visible ones, and she is not one to leave a project unfinished.

Kinsley tries to play the game her way as they navigate through forbidden territory, but Liam is determined to teach her a whole new definition for the term "team bonding."

Recommended for ages 17+ due to language and sexual situations.

Available on: AMAZON

With This Heart
New Adult Romance

If someone had told me a year ago that I was about to fall in love, go on an epic road trip, ride a Triceratops, sing on a bar, and lose my virginity, I would have assumed they were on drugs.

Well, that is, until I met Beckham.

Beck was mostly to blame for my recklessness. Gorgeous, clever, undeniably charming Beck barreled into my life as if it were his mission to make sure I never took living for granted. He showed me that there were no boundaries, rules were for the spineless, and a kiss was supposed to happen when I least expected.

Beck was the plot twist that took me by surprise. Two months before I met him, death was knocking at my door. I'd all but given up my last scrap of hope when suddenly I was given a second chance at life. This time around, I wasn't going to let it slip through my fingers.

We set out on a road trip with nothing to lose and no guarantees of tomorrow.

Our road trip was about young, reckless love. The kind of love that burns bright.

The kind of love that no road-map could bring me back from.

Recommended for ages 17+ due to language and sexual situations.

Available on: AMAZON

Behind His Lens
Adult Romance

Twenty-three year old model Charley Whitlock built a quiet life for herself after disaster struck four years ago. She hides beneath her beautiful mask, never revealing her true self to the world... until she comes face-to-face with her new photographer — sexy, possessive Jude Anderson. It's clear from the first time she meets him that she's playing by his rules. He says jump, she asks how high. He tells her to unzip her cream Dior gown, she knows she has to comply. But what if she wants him to take charge outside of the studio as well?

Jude Anderson has a strict "no model" dating policy. But everything about Charley sets his body on fire.

When a tropical photo shoot in Hawaii forces the stubborn pair into sexually charged situations, their chemistry can no longer be ignored. They'll have to decide if they're willing to break their rules and leave the past behind or if they'll stay consumed by their demons forever. Will Jude persuade Charley to give in to her deepest desires?

Recommended for ages 17+ due to language and sexual situations.

Available on: AMAZON